"Excuse my naivete, but what makes a woman worth bedding?"

Cavan cracked a brief smile. "You are shrewder than I thought."

"Have you an answer?"

"Do you truly wish for me to answer?"

"However will I learn to please you if I do not know?"

"You *wish* to please me?" he asked, reaching out to take her hand and slowly drawing her closer to him in front of the hearth.

How could his nearness cause Honora to feel thrilled and intimidated all at the same time? "It is my obligation."

He nodded slowly, then lowered his cheek to press lightly against her inflamed one. He began with a whisper in her ear. "The scent of a woman."

He brought his forehead to rest against hers as his finger stroked ever so lightly along her jaw line, down across her neck, to finally trace circles around her breasts as he murmured, "The feel of a woman."

He nibbled at her lips until they pulsated, moved to her neck to send the flesh quivering and traveled across her shoulder. "The taste of a woman."

He laughed softly in her ear. "The sounds of a woman as she reaches pleasure."

Books by
Donna Fletcher

Return of the Rogue

DONNA FLETCHER

AVON

An Imprint of HarperCollinsPublishers

This is a work of fiction. Names, characters, places, and incidents are products of the author's imagination or are used fictitiously and are not to be construed as real. Any resemblance to actual events, locales, organizations, or persons, living or dead, is entirely coincidental.

AVON BOOKS
An Imprint of HarperCollins*Publishers*
10 East 53rd Street
New York, New York 10022-5299

Copyright © 2008 by Donna Fletcher
ISBN: 978-0-06-137543-9
www.avonromance.com

First Avon Books paperback printing: March 2008

Avon Trademark Reg. U.S. Pat. Off. and in Other Countries, Marca Registrada, Hecho en U.S.A.
HarperCollins® is a registered trademark of HarperCollins Publishers.

Printed in the U.S.A.

10 9 8 7 6 5 4 3 2

Return of the Rogue

Chapter 1

Northern Scotland, late 1500s

*S*he twirled in circles, her skinny little arms stretched out from her sides and a broad smile on her thin face. She would twirl and twirl and when she stopped, her head still spinning, the barren moor would magically dance in front of her eyes.

She laughed with glee and clapped her small hands until the dancing stopped, then went in search of wildflowers. The yellow ones were nice, but the violet ones were her favorite. The pretty color matched her eyes, or so her mum told her when they picked flowers together.

A frown suddenly captured her face. She wished her mum were with her today but she had too much work to do. Though her stepfather, Calum Tannach, expected her to help her mum, her mum would often chase her off to have fun, joining her now and again when she was certain Calum wouldn't learn of it.

Today her mum had shooed her off, telling her to have a day of fun since it was a special day. It was her birthday. She was eight years old today.

A smile quickly reclaimed her thin face. Her mum wouldn't want her to waste her birthday feeling sad. She would be waiting to hear of her fun day.

She rushed around picking flowers. They would make her mum smile. Her mum didn't smile very often. She wished she would but she didn't, but the flowers never failed to bring a smile, even a small one.

She stopped, tilting her head to the sky. Was that thunder? It was cloudy and gray. Then she heard the distant rumble again, only this time the ground quaked beneath her small feet. She stumbled backward; clutching the few flowers, she cast a glance across the moor.

She squinted at the black specks in the distance then rubbed her eyes, but the black specks remained, growing larger by the second.

Warriors! her mind screamed, and fearing they could be from a marauding clan, she did what she had been taught—she ran.

She clutched her flowers tighter as her skinny legs pumped faster and faster, the quaking growing stronger beneath her pounding feet. She told herself to keep going, don't look back, but fear forced a quick glance over her shoulder and the shock of the riders bearing down on her caused her to stumble.

She landed hard on her backside and instinct had her crawling backward away from the riders as fast as she could.

The ground shook and the thunderous roar of horses' hooves vibrated the air and tears filled her violet eyes as she struggled to avoid the rush of horses.

With a sudden yank, she was snatched off the ground, swung up in the air and planted with a thud in the lap of a large warrior. He reined in his horse sharply, holding her tight, and then slowed the animal to a trot.

She sat in shocked silence, too frightened to move or speak, though not to stare at him. Her first glance had her thinking he was the devil himself, his dark eyes matching his dark attire, his look grim and his mouth angry.

"Look," he ordered, his hand grabbing her chin and forcibly turning her head.

She began to tremble. The horse stood at the edge of a cliff that she knew dropped off sharply to the North Sea.

"That's where you were going."

She shivered at the thought, tears pooling in her eyes until they spilled one by one down her thin cheeks. She would have died if not for the warrior, never to see her mum again. She stared at him, unable to speak and not knowing if she should, since she recognized him. He was Cavan Sinclare, eldest son of Laird Tavish Sinclare of the Earldom of Caithness, a fierce warrior.

He hoisted her up and off the horse, depositing her on the ground. He leaned his face close to hers, so close that his warm breath tickled her nose when he spoke.

"Watch what you're doing, lass. Next time someone may not be there to save you."

Honora woke with his words resonating in her head. It was always that way with the recurring dream, near twelve years now. She stretched her arms above her head, sighed and let the dream fade. She need not be thinking of the past today. Today she began her future. Today was her wedding day.

She snuggled under the wool coverlet, the sun yet to rise, and wondered for the hundredth time if this was right for her. But then, what did it matter? The choice wasn't hers. Her stepfather had arranged the marriage; she had little to say about it.

She had never imagined marrying a Sinclare. Actually, two years ago she *feared* marrying one; the one Sinclare she had prayed she would never set eyes on again. Her stepfather, Calum Tannach, had other ideas. He approached laird Tavish Sinclare, to offer her as wife to his son Cavan. Calum had touted her virtues and how she would serve the future laird well, being an obedient and dutiful wife. He had used a strong hand in raising her, he said, and guaranteed that she would not flinch if her husband saw fit to do the same.

He had been right about that. Calum Tannach had not only forced his stepdaughter to take his name when he wed her mother, but used a forceful hand on her more often than Honora cared to remember.

She would never have been able to defy her stepfather and refuse to wed Cavan, and so she was relieved to receive the news that Cavan had no interest in wedding her. He claimed she lacked strength and courage, and he wanted both in a wife. Her stepfather had been furious and, of course, taken his disappointment out on her.

Not enough strength and courage? She certainly had it that night when her stepfather delivered a good beating on her for not being good enough for Cavan Sinclare. He called her worthless and said it was a good thing her dear mother had passed five years before and was not there to witness the shame she had brought the family.

Honora had hoped to find a love that would help her escape her stepfather. But Calum Tannach had plans for her to wed a man of his choice, and he ordered her to keep herself pure or else. She did as she was told; not that it was difficult, since no man showed interest in her. Meanwhile, she hoped, even prayed, to find herself wed to a good man.

Her prayers had been answered, and oddly enough, she would wed a Sinclare. A year ago during a battle with a northern barbarian tribe, Cavan Sinclare and the youngest Sinclare brother Ronan were taken captive. Artair and Lachlan, the two remaining brothers, could not find them. It was known that Cavan and Ronan had been wounded, and many believed them dead, though Artair and Lachlan refused to accept that. They intended to find their brothers and bring them home.

Taking advantage of the situation, Calum Tannach approached Tavish Sinclare about a union between Honora and Artair, next in line to lead the clan Sinclare. This time her stepfather wasn't turned down, though Artair made a stipulation. He would meet with Honora and then decide. Her stepfather warned her not to ruin this opportunity for him or indeed she would be sorry.

Honora had trembled when meeting Artair, not knowing what to expect from him, and not having any experience in dealing with men. He towered over her five feet five inches, and while lean in body, his strength was obvious in his sinewy arm muscles and bulging veins. And to say he was handsome was not doing the man justice. His brother

Lachlan claimed always to be the most handsome brother and the favorite of the women. But everyone knew—though none would say, especially in front of Lachlan—that Artair was the handsomest of all the brothers.

Dark brown eyes dominated his striking features, and his long hair matched their color, though the bright sunlight sparked red strands. He was firm in voice and confident in stance, Honora detected fairness in his eyes and her trembling faded as he spoke with her.

He had asked her if she was agreeable with the arrangement, and after she nodded, fearing her voice would fail her, he explained what he expected from his wife.

"Honor our vows, respect my word, give me sons and daughters, and I will do the same for you and always see you safe from harm."

That had sealed it for Honora. She would no longer need to fear her stepfather. She would be free of him and wed to a man who would always keep her safe. It was more than she had hoped for, and it with a smile she accepted his terms.

Over the months that followed, she learned more about her future husband and realized that he was a man of his word, dependable and practical, as well as gentle with her. He was not loud, nor did he boast or drink himself drunk. He took his duty to the clan seriously, though he smiled and laughed often enough. He would make a good husband, she hoped, and now she was relieved that her wedding day was finally here.

A knock sounded at the door before it opened, and Addie Sinclare, Artair's mother, entered the room with an anxious flourish.

"The sun is up," she said, "the feast is being prepared, the great hall is being decked in splendor, and now it is time for the bride to prepare."

Honora sat up, ready to jump out of bed, Addie Sinclare having intimidated her since they first met. Not that the woman was harsh or mean. She was simply beautiful, confident and generous, and Honora envied her strong nature.

"No. No. Stay where you are," Addie insisted, tucking the cover around her. "Part of preparing is relaxing for the big day ahead of you."

Honora smiled at the startlingly beautiful woman. Her red hair showed traces of gray yet curled softly around her narrow face, which bore few lines for a woman two years from fifty. She was slim in shape and stood almost four inches over her. She was a remarkable woman, and Honora wished she had just a fraction of her strength.

"An hour or so in bed and then it's a nice leisurely bath, hair preparation, and finally time to dress and be ready to take your vows . . . and then," she said with an exhausted sigh, "it's time to celebrate, and a wonderful celebration it will be."

"I am lucky," Honora said.

Addie laughed. "It is my son who is lucky to be getting such a beautiful and gentle bride."

No one had ever told her she was beautiful or gentle. Plain and frightened was how she had thought of herself and how she believed others thought of her.

Honora noticed how the woman's dark green wool tunic sparked her green eyes, and how she had rolled up the sleeves to the pale green linen shift beneath, ready to tackle whatever chore was necessary. How she wished she could be that confident and determined to face anything that came her way.

The hours rolled by, and Honora found herself pampered as she never before. She had been relieved when Addie insisted that she spend the night before her wedding day at the Sinclare keep, and her stepfather had not protested, especially when a room was provided for him as well.

Honora knew Calum would not raise his hand to her in front of anyone. He always delivered her punishment when they were alone, though now, from this day on, she would not have to worry about his heavy hand any longer.

Her husband would protect her.

It was with a sense of peace and strong resolve that she prepared to take her vows, though apprehension poked at her now and again. What could go wrong now? she asked herself. She was to wed the next laird of the Clan Sinclare. The marriage documents had been signed and the Sinclare seal affixed. Today she would become a Sinclare.

Several hours later, with a tear in her eye, Addie said to her, "You are a rare beauty."

Honora, for the first time in her life, felt beautiful. Her rich purple velvet dress flowed from beneath her full breasts to her feet in a magnificent swirl, inserts of silk violet catching the eye. The same silk violet threaded along the dipping bodice and into the long sleeves. Her long black hair parted in the middle and fell straight down the middle of her back, while a green wreath laden with violet wildflowers rested on her head. Her cheeks were tinged a deep pink from the excitement of it all, and her narrow lips glistened like a flagrant, dew-kissed rose.

She took a deep breath and followed her future mother-in-law out the door. Addie had changed into a dark red velvet dress that hugged her shapely body, and when they came upon laird Tavish Sinclare, she could see how the two fit each other so perfectly and how much love there was between them. She could only hope she would find the same in her own marriage.

The great hall was aglow with candles and a roaring fire. Greenery was decked with berries and trimmed the mantel, tables, and dais. Tables were laden with pitchers of ale and wine, and platters of sweet breads and fruits; succulent meats, stews, and pies would soon join them. And clansmen dominated the room, so many there were not enough seats for everyone.

Her glance finally settled on Artair, and he smiled and walked toward her. He was so very handsome, and wore his plaid of dark green and black with honor. His hair shined as if recently washed, and the sleeves of his dark green linen shirt were rolled up to his elbows, exposing the lean muscles of his forearms.

He reached his hand out to her, and she took it with some hesitation. She had to get used to holding hands and being kissed, and refused to even think about the intimacy she would share with him.

"I am a lucky man," Artair said, squeezing her hand.

"I said the same myself to her this morning," Addie said with a pat to their joined hands.

"Honora is the lucky one," Calum Tannach said, joining them.

Honora stepped closer to Artair, away from her stepfather, and was grateful when Artair slipped his arm around her. Calum might have cleaned himself up, even washing his shoulder length gray hair and garbing himself in the Sinclare plaid, but he would always be a nasty and mean man.

"And it's a grateful and obedient wife she'll be to you, Artair, I can guarantee that," Calum boasted. "I raised her right."

"I have no doubt you did, Calum," Artair said. "But shortly she'll be my wife and she will concern you no more."

"Yes, well—but—"

"Time to start the ceremony," Tavish interrupted, and they followed him to the front of the dais.

Honora could feel her stepfather's angry eyes digging into her back. She knew he thought this marriage would lighten his lot in life. And while a goodly amount had been settled on him, she was aware he expected more. He expected to reap the rewards of his daughter's match and somehow gain influence and power.

Lachlan joined them, giving Honora an exuberant kiss. "You come to me, little sister, if he"—he jabbed Artair in the chest—"gives you any trouble."

Honora nodded with a smile. She didn't know Lachlan well. He was always off somewhere and it usually involved a woman. She had to admit, there was something about his dark eyes that immediately drew a woman's attention and interest. Even she found herself drawn in, which was why she avoided contact with him as much as possible.

"Find your own wife," Artair said laughingly. "Wait a minute, you don't want a wife, or is it that no one will have you?"

It took getting used to the way the brothers teased each other, but she was learning, and smiled now, along with others, at the good-natured teasing.

"*Too many* want me." Lachlan grinned and stepped aside.

Everyone took their positions and the solemn cleric stepped forward and began the ceremony. It went faster than Honora expected, or perhaps she was anxious about becoming Artair's wife. She only knew that her stomach turned over repeatedly, and she doubted she would be eating a morsel of the delicious feast tonight.

She held her breath and waited for the final words announcing that they were wed, and when they were spoken, she was about to let out a gentle sigh when a large crash resonated throughout the hall, causing everyone to turn with a start.

The door had swung open, a sharp wind ripping it out of the hand of the stranger who entered with a mass of swirling autumn debris. His identity was impossible to determine since he wore a long black cloak whose hood concealed his face.

He paused while the relentless wind extinguished several candles and one of the warriors rushed over and fought the door shut.

No one moved. No one spoke. It was almost as if everyone feared the hooded stranger, his identity concealed from all onlookers.

Tavish Sinclare stepped forward, flanked by his two sons. "You have business here, stranger?"

The hood-covered head nodded, and he walked slowly toward the laird Sinclare.

Artair and Lachlan were quick to place their hands on the hilts of the swords that hung at their sides. But Tavish never made a move for his own sword. He stood tall and proud and without fear.

Honora held her breath. Something was wrong, very wrong. She could feel it as she had the day her mother died. She had known running home from the moor that day that her life was about to change forever.

The stranger threw his hood back just before he stopped in front of Tavish Sinclare. "I finally made it home, Father."

Chapter 2

Honora stepped back away from the chaos. Tavish Sinclare immediately embraced his son Cavan, though not for long since his wife Addie pushed through to reach her eldest son and hug him as only a loving mother could.

The brothers shared less emotional embraces, and Honora noticed that they all smiled except for Cavan. His expression remained stoic, as if he was unmoved or unsure of those around him. But then, it had been a year since his capture, and surely things had changed for him. His appearance certainly had. She remembered him lean, but no longer. He was a mass of hard muscle, his chest broad beneath a tan linen shirt and his arms thick. He wore deer-hide leggings and fur-trimmed boots. His dark brown hair fell past his shoulders and looked in need of a good washing, as did his dirt-stained face, though the grime could not hide the thin red scar that ran from the corner of his right eye down to his chin bone.

Her eyes caught his for a second and she shivered and quickly turned her head. She wasn't sure what she had seen in the dark depths, and she didn't want to know.

"Has Ronan returned?" Cavan asked.

Tavish placed a consoling hand on his son's shoulder. "We've had no success in finding him."

Cavan shook his head slowly. "We were separated once captured. He was injured—"

His father squeezed his shoulder. "We'll discuss it later. You are in need of rest and nourishment."

"Of which we have plenty," Lachlan teased, stretching his arms out at the laden tables.

Honora had a feeling Tavish spoke of far different nourishment. She could see the ache of concern for his son in the older man's narrowed eyes.

"What do you celebrate?" Cavan asked.

"My wedding," Artair boasted.

"Not so," someone shouted, and Honora's flesh prickled when her stepfather stepped forward to approach Tavish Sinclare.

The feeling of dread caught Honora strong and hard this time, twisting her stomach until she wanted to scream for her stepfather to stop. Whatever Calum was about to say did not bode well for her at all.

"We have a problem here," Calum said, his arms crossed firmly over his chest as he spoke directly to Tavish. "Our agreement and the signed and seal-affixed documents state that my daughter was to wed the next laird of the Clan Sinclare, who at the time was believed to be Artair. With Cavan's return, it means that Honora is wed to Cavan, not Artair."

"What nonsense is this?" Artair demanded.

Calum remained firm in his claim. "Our agreement is binding and I will see you held to it, Tavish Sinclare."

The hall remained quiet, except for the whispers that began to sound like buzzing bees. All waited to see how their laird would settle the dispute.

"Let the feast begin while this matter is discussed in private," Tavish announced, and then walked away, a signal for his family and Calum to follow.

Honora hurried along with them; after all, this was her future they would discuss.

"You wait here." Calum's bark had her jumping back, and she bumped against what felt like a solid tree trunk.

Her eyes widened when she glanced over her shoulder to see that she leaned against Cavan. She stumbled over her own feet to get away from him. Or was she trying to get away from the possibility of him becoming her husband? she wondered. He was quick to grab her arm and help secure her footing.

"She comes with us," Cavan said, giving no further explanation and dragging Honora along with him.

She wasn't surprised that her stepfather didn't object. The look in Cavan's dark eyes challenged anyone to defy him. In fact, it appeared that he'd welcome the defiance, and pity the poor fool who obliged him.

Cavan didn't release her until they entered his father's solar. Though there were chairs aplenty, no one took a seat. Artair joined his brother Lachlan, who stood beside their father. Cavan stood close to the blazing hearth, his cloak discarded over a chair. Addie stood with Honora to the side.

Calum stood in the center of the gathering, stiff in posture and resolve, and with a shout ordered his daughter to his side. "Honora, here, now!"

She obeyed without question, as she had for as long as she could remember. For a moment she feared he might raise his hand to her, but then realized he would not do so in front of the Sinclares. He but demonstrated his authority over her for all to see and know that his daughter was loyal to him and would do as told.

Calum spoke directly to Tavish. "You will recall how adamant I was when the documents were drawn up that it be stated that my daughter would wed the next laird of the Sinclare clan."

Tavish nodded. "I do recall that, but she has wed Artair."

"Not so," Calum said. "Artair was never mentioned in the agreement. The vows were between the next laird and Honora. Artair simply represented the next laird of the Sinclare clan, who with his return is Cavan."

"I agreed to no such arrangement," Cavan said.

"That makes no difference," Calum protested. "Your father agreed and with him being laird of the clan, his decision is final."

Honora listened, her heart beating madly. This couldn't be happening. She couldn't be wed to Cavan Sinclare. He didn't want her when once she had been offered to him, and he still didn't want her, and she didn't want him.

"I will not wed the frightened little mouse," Cavan said defiantly.

Calum smiled smugly. "You are already wed to her. Ask the cleric, he'll confirm the truth of it."

Was that how he saw her, as a frightened little mouse? Scurrying about, running and hiding while all the time attempting to survive. Sadly, wasn't that how she lived her life?

"I want no wife, Artair does," Cavan said. "She is his wife, not mine."

"I did agree to take Honora as a wife," Artair said. "And I will honor that agreement."

Her husband had finally spoken up, but his words were not what she had expected. It seemed that Artair had no feelings for her. He had simply agreed to an arranged marriage, no more. She was nothing but chattel to these men, a brood mare who would bear sons so the Sinclare line would continue.

"That wasn't the agreement," Calum said, pointing an accusing finger at Tavish. "The arrangement was clear, and you know it. Honora wed to the next laird of the Sinclare clan." He swung his accusing finger at Cavan. "And that would be him, Cavan Sinclare, husband to my daughter Honora."

"This is ridiculous," Lachlan said. "The cleric just claimed Artair and Honora wed."

"No. I say again, he sanctioned the vows of the next laird of the Sinclare clan husband to Honora," Calum said haughtily, settling his arms across his chest in satisfaction. "Ask the cleric yourself. He will confirm my claim."

"Addie, will you please bring the cleric here?" Tavish asked his wife, who turned with a nod and left the solar.

"I only ask the agreement be honored as written," Calum said confidently.

"Why?" Cavan asked, walking over to him, to stand in similar fashion, arms across his chest. "Want to rid yourself of the little mouse?"

Honora glared at him, wishing she had the courage to defend herself.

"So, the mouse rears her head," Cavan said.

Calum snatched Honora's wrist and twisted it. "I'll brook no disobedience from you, daughter."

Honora leaned into her stepfather to ease the pressure of the pain.

"Let her go." Cavan ordered.

The angry growl was more animal than human, and her stepfather eased his hold, though he did not release her.

Honora saw that Cavan had stepped closer, as had Artair and Lachlan. They stood beside their brother, ready to follow his lead.

"Do you claim my daughter as wife?" Calum challenged. "If you do, then you have a right to dictate to her. If not? My daughter obeys me."

Cavan made a move to step forward, his dark eyes burning into Calum, and to Honora's surprise, she felt her stepfather tremble.

The door opened before Cavan took another step, and Addie hurried in, followed by a frantic cleric.

The short, skinny man, his face full of wrinkles,

shook his head. "What madness is this? I claimed this pair man and wife."

Tavish stepped forward and detailed the problem for the cleric. The man listened intently, nodding now and again.

Calum added his opinion. "You do recall our talk before the ceremony? I expressly made it known how the vows were to be spoken and confirmed."

"That you did," the cleric said. "And you provided the signed marriage papers as proof of the arrangement."

Honora didn't like the sound of what she was hearing. She couldn't be Cavan's wife. She didn't want to be his wife. She wished she had never set eyes on any of the Sinclare men.

"Then my claim is valid," Calum said. "Honora is wife to Cavan."

"She is wife to Artair," Cavan protested.

The cleric shook his head. "Calum Tannach is right. The documents state Honora was to wed the next laird of Clan Sinclare, therefore, Artair proved to be proxy for his brother Cavan, since Cavan has returned, and appropriately enough on his wedding day.

"This is nonsense," Cavan argued.

The cleric appeared mortified, his thin face turning bright red. "How dare you question my authority. The documents are binding. You are husband to Honora."

Cavan pointed to Artair. "She is my brother's wife."

The cleric shook his head. "Calum Tannach is correct. As the marriage papers state, Artair was but proxy for you, and I will not debate the matter. It is settled, and there is a union to celebrate and vows to be consummated. Do your duty as the next laird of Clan Sinclare and as a husband."

The cleric stomped out of the room, his abrupt departure announcing that the matter was at an end.

Honora felt her senses spinning out of control. She couldn't be wife to Cavan. She didn't want to be wife to Cavan. Presently, she didn't want to be wife to anyone; she simply wished to be free.

Cavan turned to Artair. "Do you love her?" he asked.

"I barely know her."

His words hurt her heart, though they were the truth. There was no love between them. She had hoped perhaps there could be in time, but Artair was nothing more than an acquaintance, and Cavan even less than that to her.

"None of that matters," Calum demanded. "You heard the cleric. It is settled. Cavan and Honora are wed."

Tavish stepped forward, his sons moving aside in respect not only to their father, but also to their laird.

"Leave us, Calum," Tavish ordered firmly.

Calum bristled. "I have a right to protect my daughter's rights."

"No longer," Tavish said calmly. "Honora is now a Sinclare, wife to Cavan. You no longer have say over her. Now leave and join the celebration."

Calum nodded with a smug smile and walked out the door.

Once it shut behind him, Tavish turned to Cavan. "I am sorry you are forced into a union you do not want, but it is done, and as my heir I ask that you honor the marriage arrangement and do your duty."

"Not the homecoming I expected," Cavan said.

"Unfortunate, but you are home with family, and that means more to me than you could possibly know, and a wife for you is necessary to the future of this clan. Honora may not be the wife of your choice, but I have come to know her, and she is a good person and I believe she will be a good wife to you."

Tavish reached out and took Honora's hand, then held his hand out to Cavan.

Honora hoped and prayed silently for Cavan not to take her hand, to deny her as his wife, but she knew better. Like all Sinclares, Cavan would do his duty and serve and protect his clan under any circumstances.

Indeed, Cavan did not hesitate. He stretched his hand out to his father, and Tavish placed Honora's hand in his son's. "To the future of the Sinclare clan," the laird said.

The brothers shouted out a cheer, and then Lachlan suggested they join the celebration, to celebrate not only the wedding, but also Cavan's safe return.

Honora attempted to slip her hand out of her husband's grasp but he held tight. He wasn't about to let go of her, and she wondered why.

"Go and I will join you soon enough," Cavan said. "I wish to wash up and wear the clan colors proudly."

Addie stepped forward. "I will see that a bath is prepared for you."

"Thank you, Mother, but it will be my wife who tends me."

Chapter 3

Cavan climbed the stone staircase to his bedchamber on the third floor, close to the battlements he had often walked on sleepless nights. Tonight, he felt, would be one of those nights, where sleep eluded him and thoughts plagued him, even more so now that he had acquired an unexpected and most unwanted wife.

She followed dutifully behind him on the staircase, quiet as a mouse. He sensed her worry and need to flee, but also sensed her fear to do either. She was not made of strong stuff, and he had wanted, actually expected, to have a courageous wife; no other would do for the next laird of the Clan Sinclare.

Fate had dealt him a cruel blow, returning home only to discover he was married to a weak woman. Would she give him the sons he hoped for, he wondered, or stand strong on her own while he was off to war?

Worst of all were his concerns about how she would deal with him now, after he'd been held captive for a year at the hands of barbarians. He was different, and most uncomfortable with who he had been forced to become.

Cavan stood at the open door, waiting for Honora to enter before him, and when the door shut with a slam, she jumped, her hand rushing to press against her chest, and there she remained.

He was disgusted that she should just stand there and do nothing, not take the initiative and see to the preparation of his bath. He did not want a wife who needed instructions. She didn't even look at him; she kept her head bowed and her eyes focused on the floor.

"Do you know how to tend a husband's bath?" he snapped, irritated with her and the situation.

Her head came up but she avoided his eyes. "I will see to it."

She made a wide berth around him when she approached the door, but his reflexes had sharpened considerably while captive and his hand snatched her wrist and yanked her to him so quickly that she swiftly braced as if he meant to strike her.

He softened his grasp but held her against him for a moment, allowing her sweet scent to drift around him, to gratefully fill his nostrils and remove the everlasting stench of blood, sweat, and fear that had clung to him for this past year. God, but she smelled so good, so sweet, so pure, and he simply wanted to bury his face in her and get lost in her alluring scent.

Instead he snapped more harshly than intended, "I will not hurt you."

Her eyes rounded like full moons in the dark

night sky, only they were violet, the color of the wild-flowers that grow on the moors, the color that had always managed to capture his attention, as it did now. Only it was not the flower he gazed upon but his wife's eyes, and he found them beyond lovely, he found them profoundly innocent.

He shoved her away. "See to my bath now."

She ran from the room, leaving the door to shut behind her.

Cavan growled low beneath his breath. He did not need this extra burden upon his return. He had hoped Ronan had found his way home, but now he planned on finding him no matter how long it took. He would not leave his brother in the hands of such cruel men. He and Ronan had fought side by side and were captured together and then separated, though not before he had sworn to his brother that he would find him. He had to keep that promise. He had to.

Cavan rubbed the stubbles at his chin and knew he must look a sight. He had walked endlessly, and when in safer territory begged farmers on their way to market for a ride in their carts. He had bartered a day's service on a farm for fresh garments, having been dirt-ridden and threadbare, not that the ones he wore had been as fresh as promised, but they were far better than what he had and fair enough to wear for his arrival home.

Now home, he wanted nothing more than a hot bath and his own fresh clothes. He quickly searched the room for his trunk and sighed with relief when he spotted it under the window. He felt a tug at his gut realizing that his mother had kept his bed-chamber the same; she had expected his return. The confidence she had in his strength gave him more of it, and made him feel all the more pleased to be home with family and—

Cavan didn't want to think about his wife again. He still couldn't believe himself married, and to the woman he had once rejected, and for good reasons. However, none of that mattered now; she was his wife, though he felt like no husband.

The door creaked open slowly and Honora gave a quick peek around.

"What are you waiting for?"

She hurried in without saying a word, followed by several servants lugging a wooden tub and pails of water. The tub was filled and Cavan disrobed, wanting to get into the heated water before it cooled. It wasn't until he was settled in the steaming water, hair soaked wet, that he noticed his wife stiff as a statue standing at the end of the bed a few feet away, staring at him.

"Don't tell me you've never seen a naked man before?"

The two remaining servant girls giggled and his wife's cheeks grew bright red.

"Shall I see to washing you, my lord? After all, we wouldn't want to get the bride's dress all wet," one of servant girls asked with a smile.

Cavan glanced at his wife, waiting for her to advise the servant that it wouldn't be necessary, that she would see to her husband, but once again she remained silent.

He kept his eyes on her as he answered the lass. "No, my wife will see to me."

The two girls bowed respectfully and closed the door behind them.

"You haven't got the slightest idea what is expected of you, do you?" The absurdity of it had his mind reeling, for he couldn't fathom what would happen if he attempted to make love with her.

She had to clear her throat before she could finally speak. "I wasn't expecting *you*."

"Nor was I expecting *you*," he countered, and began scrubbing his hair with the bar of soap the servant girl had left on the small stool beside the tub along with towels.

"I know you don't want me—"

"Want you or not, I'm stuck with you," Cavan said before dunking his head to rinse out the soap and to finally start scrubbing the grime off his body. He gave himself a rough scrub, to rid himself of every morsel and stench of the barbarians.

"I will be a dutiful wife."

Cavan stopped scrubbing for a moment. "Are you trying to convince me or yourself?"

"I will grow used to you."

He shook his head. "Again it sounds more like you're trying to convince yourself rather than me." He held up the soap. "Start now. Scrub my back."

She surprised him when she didn't hesitate; she pushed up her sleeves, walked over to him, took the soap and went behind him to do as he asked. When he heard her gasp, he realized she possessed little strength and he grew angry.

"Scars from the whippings I took at the hands of the barbarians. If you cannot stomach touching them, I will have a servant see to my back."

He felt the soap against his back and thought that as long as she didn't have to lay her hands on his scars she was all right; therefore, he was stunned when he felt her hands lather the soap across his back, and was even more stunned when he felt himself grow hard at her gentle touch.

He remained still and silent, enjoying the feel of her hands tenderly massaging across his shoulders, down the center of his back, and along his sides, though she never once went past the water to more intimate territory.

He grew hotter not from the steaming water but in response to her innocent touch. He throbbed like a man ready to explode, and at that moment his only thought was to get out of the tub, throw her on the bed, hike up her dress, and drive into her until he satisfied his raging need.

A barbaric thought for sure and one that made him angry, angry that he could even think like a barbarian much less act like one. Honora was his wife and an innocent, she didn't deserve his wrath or to be the instrument that quenched his need.

"Get out!" he bellowed, and he heard her stumble and fall. "Now!"

He heard the door slam shut and groaned. It had been long, too long since he'd had a woman, and his hunger was too much for an innocent one to suffer. He could take one of the willing servants, as he had many times before, but it was his wedding night and he would disgrace his wife if he did.

He groaned and knew he would need to relieve himself if he was ever to get through this night, and when he was finally done, dressed, and walking down the staircase, he realized that his new wife and her gentle touch had never once left his thoughts.

Chapter 4

Honora knew when her husband entered the hall. All the women's eyes shifted and the servant girls smiled while some cheeks blossomed red. The men cheered, and she had no choice but to look his way.

He was a laird in every sense of the word, tall, broad-shouldered, proud, defiant, and much more handsome devoid of grime. But then, she already knew that, having gotten a full view of him in their bedchamber. If he ever thought to strike her, she would surely suffer pain. Her stepfather had raised his hand to her for years. Was it only a matter of time before Cavan did too? He had told her he wouldn't hurt her, but her stepfather had promised the same. How would she protect herself against a man the size and strength of Cavan?

And what would it be like to be intimate with him? In her mind's eye Honora saw her husband naked, and that frightened her. He was much too large and she too small for the likes of him. She was not completely ignorant of men and marriage, though she'd learned what she knew from listening to other women in the village.

She knew her duty, though not how she would carry it out. Cavan was more, much more, than she ever imagined. Oddly, the thought of intimacy with Artair had not disturbed her, but then he had been kind and gentle with her; not so Cavan.

"Where is my plate, wife?"

Honora jerked her head up to see Cavan towering over her on the dais. His dark eyes remained fixed on her, as if delving deep inside her soul, and she quickly reached for the empty pewter plate in front of her and began piling it with food from the platters spread on the table.

Cavan took the vacant seat between her and his brother Lachlan and tapped at his plate. "Whose plate do you prepare?"

"Yours of course," she answered, and swapped his empty plate with the full one in her hand.

"What of you?"

She couldn't eat a speck of food; she knew her stomach would not tolerate it.

He seemed to read her thoughts with his question. "Not hungry?"

She shook her head.

She thought he would force her, but he simply turned away to speak with his father, who sat on the other side of the table. Relieved that he would not torment her with demands to eat, Honora remained seated at the edge of her chair with a sharp eye on her husband's plate and his tankard, to make sure both remained full.

Her stepfather walked by and leaned down to reprimand her, "Tend your husband, daughter, or you'll feel my hand."

Honora froze, not believing her ears. She thought marriage would free her from her stepfather's brutality, but with a husband who didn't want her, would he care how her stepfather treated her?

"Honora."

She heard her name being called far in the distance but couldn't answer.

"Honora, what's wrong?'

She shook her head, realizing her husband was speaking to her, and quickly made an excuse. "Deep in thought."

"You often turn ghostly pale when deep in thought?"

Was that concern she heard in his query? She could not be certain since his scowl made it appear otherwise, and yet, she was almost certain he had sounded as if he actually cared. Perhaps it was simply wishful thinking on her part, to have a husband to worry over her.

"She pales for what she knows she must face tonight, brother," Lachlan said with a laugh and a slap on Cavan's back.

Honora was grateful for the distraction since she had no truthful answer for her husband.

"You have not changed, Lachlan," Cavan said.

Honora was surprised by Cavan's accusatory tone. His brother jested with him, while he appeared so serious.

"Why change when I am perfect the way I am?"

Lachlan laughed and gripped his brother's shoulder. "You're home now. There's nothing more to worry about."

"There's Ronan."

Lachlan took a deep breath. "We have searched endlessly for him as we have for you."

"Do you continue to search?" Cavan asked.

"Every day," his father answered. "Perhaps it is time for us to talk. That is, if your wife does not mind your absence."

Honora was not surprised when Cavan turned to her and said, "I will see you later in our bedchamber."

He stood, as did his brothers and father, and left her alone, though she was immediately joined by Addie, who scooted past the empty chairs to sit beside her.

"This must be difficult for you," her mother-in-law said, placing a gentle hand on Honora's arm.

"Cavan is a stranger to me. I at least had gotten to know something of Artair." Honora shook her head. "I know nothing about Cavan."

Addie sighed. "I would tell you of my son, but I do not know if the son I knew is the son who has returned home."

"He appears different to you?"

Addie nodded and leaned closer, keeping their discussion private. "I believe his capture has left him with scars."

Honora shivered.

Addie squeezed her arm, her eyes glazing over with unshed tears. "Visible scars can leave reminders of scars that cut far deeper than the flesh. Be patient with my son, he is a good man."

Honora simply nodded, not knowing how to voice her own concerns.

"I know this is not easy for you, Honora. You woke this morning ready to start a new life with Artair, and here you find yourself wed to Cavan. At least you and Artair held no feelings for each other. With time you will come to know Cavan and establish a good life with him."

"Do I have a choice?" As soon as she spoke, Honora gasped at her own audacity, then quickly apologized. "I am sorry."

"Nonsense, you have a right to question and doubt. I only attempt to advise that you give your marriage a chance. If from the start you fear, then you will never find happiness. And unfortunately, the truth is you do not have a choice. Cavan is your husband, you his wife, and that will not change. You will either make the most of it or suffer the arrangement."

"You speak the truth, and I appreciate that and will give your advice consideration."

"Then at least it will give you a chance at some happiness," Addie said with a smile.

"I never considered happiness."

"What did you consider?" her mother-in-law asked.

"Being safe," she whispered too low for anyone to hear.

* * *

Honora sat alone in Cavan's bedchamber, having snuck away from the festivities when no one was paying attention to her, but then, few did pay her heed. She had always remained obscured, in the background, too fearful or distrustful to stand up for herself. She had grown accustomed to not being seen or heard, and actually preferred it. Her stepfather never questioned her solitary walks on the moor or her retreat to her corner of their small cottage where she could be relatively safe and free in her own thoughts.

She would have that no more, not with a husband. She was answerable to him, and it appeared that her stepfather intended to see that she remained a dutiful wife. She would never be free, though she had hoped her marriage to Artair would have granted her some sense of freedom. He'd seemed willing enough to allow her it when they talked. He had not voiced any objection to her request for solitary time once wed and had encouraged her to pursue her interests; after, of course, she had attended to her duties.

Honora knew nothing of what Cavan expected of her, and she wasn't in a hurry to find out. She also wasn't in a hurry to consummate their vows, but that was another choice that wasn't hers. Her life had been filled with choices that weren't hers, and she'd managed to survive. She would survive this night and all the nights to follow.

She decided to prepare for bed and wait on her husband's return, as was expected of a dutiful wife.

She slipped into a pale blue night shift, the wool so soft that it felt as if it whispered against her skin. It fell to her ankles. The sleeves skimmed her wrists and the neckline scooped so low that it barely covered her breasts. She combed her long black hair, took some dried lavender leaves from the bowl on the stand near the bed and crushed them between her fingers, and after discarding the remnants, ran her fingers through her hair.

She would look presentable and smell sweet for her husband and hope for the best.

After several hours passed with no sign of Cavan, she crawled into bed on a yawn and snuggled beneath the green wool coverlet. Soon the bed linens took on her body heat and the steady warmth and comfort of the soft bedding lolled her off to sleep.

A strong pop and crackle of a log in the hearth woke her with a start. She sat up, realizing she was alone in the bed, and searched the room. Still, there was no sign of her husband. She wondered if she should see what kept him, but then, was it her place to question his absence from their bedchamber? And didn't she truly prefer him to remain as absent as long as possible?

She snuggled once again beneath the blanket, thinking Cavan would arrive any moment and she must be ready to receive him. Time passed without his arrival and sleep once again claimed her.

The next time she woke for no apparent reason at all, though perhaps something had alerted her to a change in the room. She knew she was not alone; she felt his presence. It was strong, overpowering, as if there wasn't room enough for anyone but him. She lay silent, trying not to tremble when his shadow loomed large, like a bird of prey, over the ceiling.

She shut her eyes tight, fearing he would swoop down and descend on her like a mighty bird on the hunt, and after several anxious moments passed and nothing happened, she slowly opened her eyes to have a peek.

No shadow hovered over her, and she briefly wondered if she had dreamed it all, until she once again felt his presence. He was in the room. What should she do? What was expected of her? Did she sit up, acknowledge him, welcome him?

Honora wanted to cry out in frustration, but instead remained silent and waited. When Cavan did not make himself known, she grew curious and inched herself up slowly in the bed. She stared with confusion at her husband, who she now could see was sleeping on the floor in front of the fire, a single blanket over him, his arm a pillow.

Relief rushed over her, though she quelled it fast enough when she realized their vows would not be sealed tonight, which meant their marriage was not valid. Why would he deny himself his husbandly rights? Did he not find her attractive? Did he think to somehow rid himself of her?

Honora lay back down and pulled the cover up to her chin. What would happen if her father found out? If anyone found out? Surely she would be to blame.

She shivered. Her wedding day had turned disastrous and her wedding night had become a nightmare she would have never imagined possible. She felt ashamed, as she knew her father would if he learned that her husband rejected her. She had no idea what she should do.

Perhaps the morning would offer new insights. She would rise early and see to her husband's breakfast and her duties. If he saw what a respectful wife she was, perhaps then he would want her.

A yawn interrupted her worries, and before she could dwell any longer on them, her eyes closed and she fell fast asleep.

She woke with a slow stretch and a smile for the sunshine that fell across her face, then jumped up, realizing it was well past sunrise. When she looked to the hearth, she gasped.

Her husband was gone.

Chapter 5

Cavan walked the moor alone, some areas so thick with heather that they cast a purple glow in the early morning light. He needed time to consolidate his thoughts and deal with his anger. He had thought his arrival home would heal his many wounds, but not so; he seemed to have worsened. He didn't feel fit to be with his family, let alone a wife.

He came to a spot on the moor where he had often come, a place of solitude and beauty for it had a view of the sea and the angry waves that continuously pounded the cliff as if demanding it get out of the way.

He empathized with the senseless battering for that was how he had felt while imprisoned. His anger would futilely clash with the barbarians and he'd be left like the pounding waves against the jagged cliff, getting nowhere, still imprisoned, still suffering, still longing to return home.

Now that he was home, he felt as if he no longer belonged, had no right to be here, especially since his brother Ronan was still among the barbarians.

The idea that Ronan continued to suffer while he was finally free angered him beyond words. He wanted his brother home with family; maybe then he himself would feel that he once again belonged.

Unfortunately, Artair and Lachlan objected to his plan to search for Ronan. They had informed him last night that search parties were continually sent out in hopes of finding their brother and that Artair or Lachlan, sometimes both of them, would go and investigate claims that Ronan was spotted in a particular area. All that could be done was being done and had been done for him and Ronan, they told Cavan, from the first day of capture.

Cavan had exchanged heated words with his brothers last night, and his father had spoken to him after sending his disgruntled brothers away. His father's tone was gentle yet firm, letting him know he understood that his capture at the hands of the barbarians could not have been easy, but he had survived and escaped, and if he had, then why not Ronan?

Tavish Sinclare had confidence in both his sons and expected that Ronan would also one day return home; of that he had no doubt. He said as much. He also said that did not mean the search would not continue, but told Cavan he had to understand that Artair and Lachlan were doing their best and felt just as strongly about Ronan's absence as they had about his own.

Tavish had cautioned his son to take time to know that everyone was relieved and pleased that he was once again home with them. He had also advised

Cavan to take his marriage seriously, treat his new wife well, and waste no time in producing a fine son to carry on the Sinclare name.

Cavan understood the wisdom of his father's words but found it difficult to take them into his heart and follow them, especially where his marriage was concerned.

He couldn't say he wasn't attracted to Honora. She was a beauty, which he only realized when he took the time to consider her. Her face was flawless and kissed by the sun, and her violet eyes were like none he had ever seen, with long lashes that matched stark black hair that fell straight to the middle of her back. Most women he had known possessed endless curls and waves, but Honora's silky locks held not a single curl or twist.

Then there was her body, which he did not want to think about because every time he did he grew hard with the want of her. While she appeared a meek mouse, she was generous in size and shape, her breasts full, her waist slim, and her hips substantial. She would certainly be able to take a hardy lovemaking without protest, and Lord how he wanted to mount her and enjoy the ride. But she was not simply a wench to ride; Honora was his wife.

She deserved more, and he wasn't certain he could give it to her.

Cavan stretched himself to a stand, wondering if he would ever again grow accustomed to a bed after spending a year sleeping on a hard, dirt-packed floor. He hadn't dared look at the bed where his wife slept soundly last night. He'd brought a blanket with him to the room and lay down in front of the hearth, relishing the fire's warmth. He had spent too many nights shivering himself to sleep from the cold and often dreamed of sleeping before a fire. Last night his dreams finally come true.

He thought of his father's words about fully returning home. He was home, and yet he wasn't, and he needed to do as his father suggested. He had to reconnect with family and friends and find a way to accept his wife, though that would take time. Or was it that he wondered if she could ever fully accept him and, even more so, possibly love him?

But then, could he ever possibly love her?

By the time Cavan returned to the keep, clouds were quickly gathering overhead and the sky had turned a dark gray. Clansmen called out greetings to him as they rushed to finish work before the rain started, and many invited him in for a tankard of ale, which he declined until another time.

He knew that having survived capture, they thought highly of him, admired and respected him. But he didn't feel worthy of their praise for there had been times during his capture that he'd wished that he had died, and no warrior could admire that.

"The moor is still your favorite haunt?"

Cavan nodded and slowed his pace so his brother Artair could join him. "The moor provides solitude."

"I thought you would have had enough of that by now."

"There are different kinds of solitude," Cavan said.

"Well, I for one hope to spend more time with you, for I have missed your ugly face."

Cavan grinned. "Isn't that Lachlan you're referring to?"

Artair laughed. "Lachlan does believe himself the most handsome brother."

"And the most foolish one."

"I heard that," Lachlan said, hurrying up alongside Cavan. "And let me remind you both that it is I who all the women favor."

"You mean it is you who chase after all the women," Artair corrected.

"Chase?" Lachlan asked with such profound surprise that he had Artair laughing and Cavan's smile growing broad. "I've never chased after a woman in my life and I never will."

"That's a challenge to the heavens, Lachlan, you better be careful," Artair warned with a tease.

"The heavens know the ladies love me. I'm sure they will send me a most beautiful angel when I am ready to settle down and wed."

Cavan had yet to join his brothers in laughter, though a silent chuckle tickled his throat.

"Ronan would agree with me," Lachlan boasted.

Cavan stopped dead and turned on Lachlan. "Then you should have found him and returned him home so he could side with your ridiculous notion."

He turned to leave and caught sight of Honora nearby. "Where have you been, wife? You neglect your duties."

Cavan did not see his father-in-law nearby

watching the exchange or the way the man glared at Honora, but it was not lost to Honora, and Cavan's action was not lost on the clansmen and women who mulled about. As a result, tongues started wagging.

"I'm hungry," Cavan said, snatching Honora's hand and pulling her along, meanwhile grumbling beneath his breath.

Ronan's capture tormented him. He could not forget that day, the battle, the capture and the look on his youngest brother's face when the barbarians dragged Ronan away. He wanted to pound his fists, cry out his rage, and he could do nothing but direct his anger at his innocent wife. He had never before held a woman responsible for feeding him. If he were hungry, he found food; he needed no one to serve him, so why demand it now from his wife?

Servants and warriors lingered around the great hall enjoying ale and conversation and avoiding the inevitable rainstorm, thunder now grumbling in the distance, and they called to Cavan to join them. At one time he would have gladly joined in talk and drink and the heat of the large fireplace. But now he simply wanted to escape from everyone, as he had escaped from the barbarians.

"I'll get your food for you and the men," Honora said.

Cavan stopped her with a tug. "I'll take my meal in our bedchamber." He grew more annoyed watching his wife pale and assume he wanted more than food in their bedchamber. He lowered his voice, though it was with a snarling growl he spoke. "I want food, not sex."

He released her, and ignoring the invitations from the warriors, left the hall and took the stone stairs two at a time. He was running and he knew it, but the need to seek seclusion was a wrenching twist to his gut. He slammed the door behind him and dropped back against it, his hands fisted at his sides.

He had imagined his return would set everything right, but it hadn't. Now what did he do? How did he manage to be the man he once was? Did that man even exist anymore?

A sudden chill descended over him, and he went to stand in front of the hearth, wanting nothing more than to let the fire's heat warm him and let the silence free his mind of endless worrisome thoughts.

"My lord? My lord?"

It took a moment before Cavan realized his wife was speaking to him. He had finally and gratefully gone to a quiet place in his mind where he had found solace, and had not wanted to leave it, but the intruding voice forced him from it.

"Cavan," he said sharply. "I am neither laird nor lord of this clan."

She dipped her head in a respectful nod. "I have brought your food."

"I'm not hungry."

"But you said—"

"Do I need to repeat myself?" he snapped, and she jumped back.

With an agitated sigh he rubbed at the back of his neck. He had not meant to bark at her.

"Have I offended you somehow?"

Her question surprised him since she was obviously uneasy around him, looking forever as if she wished to flee or slink into the shadows and hide. So where had she gotten a kernel of nerve to question him?

"Why do you ask?"

Her nerve faltered, delaying her response for a moment. "You seem angry with me."

Lord, but her violet eyes were beautiful and her rosy lips so plump and her skin looked so very soft. He raised his hand, and when he realized he was about to caress her face, snapped it back and shouted, "Get out!"

She stumbled over her own feet on the way to the door and slammed it behind her.

Cavan closed his eyes and rubbed his forehead. What was so wrong in finding his wife attractive? Wasn't that a blessing for an arranged marriage? But he wasn't ready to be married. He wasn't ready for anything at the moment, save one.

Battle.

Cavan was a warrior and proud of it. He could ride into battle right now and fight tirelessly forever. Nothing stopped him from entering a battle, and he wished for one now, a physical battle, not this inner battle he waged. With a shield and a sword, he knew how to defend and protect against an enemy.

The Sinclares were warriors protecting the farthest region of Scotland against marauding bands of barbarians from across the sea for king and country. It had been their duty for generations and would be for generations to come. But this time his enemy was himself, and how did you defend and protect against yourself? How did you win a battle with yourself?

He shook his head and charged from the room. The hell with solitude. He would seek the company of other warriors and drink, and soon his troubled thoughts would plague him no more.

Chapter 6

Honora did not know what to make of her husband. He was gone when she woke and had not made himself known until hours later, and now, for the past several hours, he sat and drank with the other warriors. He showed no sign of interest in her at all, and she feared gossip was already spreading. A couple of servant girls had whispered and giggled when she passed by.

Her concern was more for what her father would hear, think, and do to her if he felt she wasn't attending to her wifely duties. But how did she deal with a husband who intimidated her? She kept reminding herself to be patient, but with the day waning on and her husband ignoring her, she wondered if patience would work.

What else was there for her to do?

With no answer to her disturbing question, Honora, not the least bit hungry, she left the hall where all were gathering for the evening meal. She wished it wasn't raining for she would have walked the moor, breathed in the crisp autumn air and felt at peace. Instead she wandered up the stairs, but rather than go to her bedchamber, retreated to the small sewing room one floor down, knowing it would be empty at this hour and give her a modicum of the peace she found on the moor.

Scooping up an embroidery piece, a blouse, from the basket she had worked on the past week, Honora settled in the chair before the hearth. In minutes, with her mind concentrated on her stitching, she found the peace she sought.

"Honora! Honora!"

She jumped, her embroidery falling to the floor. She thought she had heard her stepfather's angry voice frantically summoning her. Thinking it must have been a dream, she wondered how long she'd dozed.

"Honora! Honora!"

She shivered down to the bone. It hadn't been a dream; her stepfather was indeed searching for her. She heard his quick footsteps grow heavy on the stairs. In no time he would descend on her, and more than likely with a heavy hand.

She hastily searched the room, and with his heavy footfalls fast approaching, hurried to the door and braced herself against the wall so that when the door opened, she'd be safely tucked behind it, hopefully.

In minutes the wooden door swung open, her father gave a quick glance around, and then left, slamming the door behind him. Honora didn't dare take a deep breath until she heard his footsteps fade down the stairs.

Why did he search for her? Was it later than she thought? Had her husband been looking for her? She returned her embroidery to the basket and quietly left the room, and just as quietly climbed the stairs, then crept along the hall to her bedchamber and closed the door ever so gently after she entered.

"Sneaking in at such a late hour? Whatever has my wife been up to?"

Honora gasped and stumbled back against the door, her hand pressed firm to her chest as if that might still her wildly beating heart. Her husband had scared the wits out of her.

"Forgive me," she said, offering a hasty apology. "I was not hungry and sought solace in the sewing room, only to have fallen asleep."

"You could not find solace in our bedchamber?"

Honora didn't answer; she stood staring at him. His face was bloody and bruised, and she went straight to his side. "What happened?"

"A disagreement with a warrior worth fighting."

She didn't hesitate; she reached out and gently probed the bruised and bleeding areas, his cheek, eye, and lip. "I'll tend them." Taking his hand, she led him to sit on the edge of the bed, then gathered water, cloth, and salve to mend him.

"I'm fine," he protested weakly.

"Nonsense, you need care," she insisted. "Please remove your shirt so I may soak the blood from it before the stain sets."

She expected him to ignore her request, but surprisingly, he did as she suggested and slipped off his shirt. While she had seen him fully naked before, she couldn't say why his half nakedness now disturbed her. Perhaps it was the breadth and width of him, the muscles so taut that the veins in his arms bugled with the strength that ran through him.

She placed a ceramic basin of warm water on the small bench she had moved near the bed and dropped cloths and the salve on the bed beside him. She wet and rinsed a cloth and began cleaning his wounds with tender strokes.

As she'd suspected after first examining them, they were not bad, and she let him know. "Mere surface abrasions. You'll suffer no scars."

"It makes no difference. What's one more scar to the many I've already suffered?"

She dabbed gently at his bloody lip and wished to offer him sympathy but somehow knew he would not take kindly to it. She worked diligently on him and noticed how his hard, angry glint turned soft with time and touch.

He reminded her of a wounded animal who at first refuses help, until the one who helps him has proven trustworthy. Did she need to prove trustful to him? But then, wasn't she looking for the same from him? Didn't she hope that instead of fearing him, she could count on him to protect and care for her?

She lingered, applying soothing salve over the wounds, enjoying the feel of his warm skin, and the strength of his defined bones and the scent of him haunted her, sweeping around her, permeating deep inside her. She had thought he would smell of nothing but ale, but that odor merely tinged the nostrils while a more potent scent emerged. She couldn't quite define it, but then how could she, since it belonged strictly to him and no other? Earth and fire came to mind and suited him well, and while she wished she could remain lingering in his pleasing scent, she knew it wasn't a wise idea and backed away from him.

"Finished," she announced, and reached for the cloths and the jar of salve on the bed beside him.

He grabbed her hand and placed it flat against his chest. She near gasped but contained herself, though not for long since the heat of his flesh rushed up along her arm and raced through her entire body, setting her toes to tingle and the spot between her legs to dampen with a strange ache.

"Thank you."

Honora was struck by the sincerity in his eyes and voice, but it didn't last. He sprung off the bed and moved her aside as if discarding her, as if she meant nothing, and strode out of the room.

She stood there staring after the closed door. For a brief moment she had gotten a glimpse, she believed, of the man Cavan had once been, and she liked what she had seen. He seemed kind, thoughtful and appreciative.

Could she dare hope to possibly have such a husband? Perhaps the patience Addie advised her of would actually work given time, and she had more than enough time.

She was Cavan's wife until death parted them.

She sighed and shook her head. She wasn't officially his wife, since their marriage had yet to be consummated, and she wondered if others knew. Could they tell? Did they wonder? And if tongues began wagging, would her stepfather hear and question her? Berate her? Strike her?

A shiver ran through her. While at first she had preferred that her husband keep his distance, now she wished he would seal their vows properly so she need not worry about the consequences of her stepfather finding out.

She wished she had the courage to discuss the matter with Cavan, but knew she didn't. She could never bring herself to approach him with her worries. He would probably laugh at her, remind her that he'd never wanted her as a wife.

Would he ever want her?

Tears welled in her eyes, but she didn't cry; she rarely cried. She had learned a long time ago that tears never helped, and usually made matters worse. The last time she'd cried was when her mother died, and afterward she never cried again, not even when her stepfather beat her or lashed out at her with hurtful words. And she would not cry now.

Her only option was to make the most of her circumstances. Somehow she would need to learn to get along with her husband. They had been wed for no more than a day, and if she asked herself what she'd learned about him in that brief time, she would say perhaps that he kept his distance from people; not only his wife, but his family as well.

Was he a man who preferred solitude?

That certainly would be an asset, since she enjoyed the same herself.

A gentle knock at the door had her opening it without fear it would be her stepfather. He would never knock so gently.

Addie entered the room with a concerned smile. "Is everything all right?"

Honora responded with her own question after shutting the door. "Why do you ask?"

"It is only your second night as husband and wife, and my son is in the hall drinking alone at a late hour and you are here alone in the bedchamber."

Honora shook her head slowly as if any answer wouldn't be the correct one. "Cavan does as he wishes."

"True enough, but his dark eyes tell me a different story. Something disturbs him, something he refuses to speak of to anyone." Addie took Honora's hand. "My son is a good man."

Honora slipped her hand free of Addie's anxious grasp. "Good, bad, or indifferent, he remains my husband. But I don't know what to do for him."

A tear glistened at the corner of Addie's eye. "Be his wife."

Chapter 7

By week's end Honora didn't know what to do. Cavan completely ignored her, continuing to sleep in front of the hearth on the floor, wake before she did. Then he would disappear, on foot or on horse, for half the day, only to return and continue to keep his distance from her.

She'd heard Artair and Lachlan mumble about how much their brother had changed. Meanwhile Addie scolded both sons, insisting that Cavan needed time, and Tavish Sinclare urged them to give Cavan the respect due him.

Everyone seemed willing enough to oblige the clan laird; after all, he was their leader and had earned the trust and respect of the clan time and time again. So between Addie and Tavish Sinclare, Honora felt compelled to do as requested and be a good wife.

She still hadn't been able to wake before Cavan in the mornings, but she did make certain to see that his favorite foods were readily available, and she worked diligently on stitching new shirts for him. And always, she kept herself well groomed and freshly scented in hopes that he would find her attractive and consummate their vows.

So far nothing had worked, but she intended to keep trying, especially since she knew her stepfather was keeping a watchful eye on her. It weighed heavily on her mind that her marriage vows were not properly sealed and that if her stepfather ever found out he'd make her pay dearly.

Now, Honora entered the hall to raised voices and chilling commands. A nearby clan under the Sinclare protection was being attacked by a horde of barbarians. Warriors were already gathering for battle. Cavan wanted to lead them, and his father thought otherwise.

"Artair will lead the warriors," Tavish said, nearly shouting to be heard over the tumult. "Lachlan will join him. You are to remain at the keep."

"I am the eldest son. It is my duty," Cavan argued.

"You have only returned," Tavish said.

"What does that matter? Do you fear me incapable of leading the men?" Cavan accused harshly. "Or do you think perhaps that my loyalty now lies elsewhere?"

Tavish pounded the table. "How dare you speak that way to me!"

"Then prove me false—let me lead the men," Cavan challenged.

"Let Cavan lead the men, Father," Artair said, stepping forward. "He is a much braver warrior than I."

Cavan appeared surprised by his brother's confidence, or was that doubt she saw register on her husband's face? Could he think his brother issued a challenge of his own?

"Go," Tavish commanded. "And make certain that you all return home safe."

Honora saw the way her husband clenched his hands in tight fists at his sides, and when he turned and spotted her, he strode toward her, his strength trembling the rushes on the floor.

She wanted to cringe, brace herself for a strike, and shut her eyes tightly against the vision of him descending down upon her. But somehow she found the strength to stand as she was, straight and tall, though not without a tremble.

He halted abruptly barely inches from her face. "Don't dare leave the keep today."

Honora hadn't walked the moor in days and was aching for the peace it brought her, and that ache gave her the courage to say, "I intended to walk the moor—"

"No!" he shouted, and grasped her arms, his fingers digging into her flesh. "I forbid you to leave the keep until I return."

"She'll do as told."

Her stepfather's familiar voice caused her tremble to turn to a rippling shiver.

"See that she does," Cavan said, shoving his wife toward her stepfather. "I hold you responsible for her protection."

Honora would have laughed if she didn't find it so pitiful—her husband leaving her protection in the hands of the man she needed protection from.

"I've always protected her," Calum snapped, and reached out for her.

Honora instinctively backed away, her hands searching behind her for her husband, but he was already gone, a chill wind blowing in from the door he left open behind him.

Her stepfather whispered a harsh warning in her ear. "You'll be wise to watch your step, lass, and do as you're told."

There was no need for him to caution her, since he demonstrated by grabbing her wrist, and while to all who saw, it may have looked like a comforting gesture, he twisted the flesh until her eyes misted in pain.

"I have chores to tend to," she said, keeping the tremble of pain out of her voice.

"Then tend to them." He pushed her away and strutted with importance over to Tavish.

Honora wanted to get as far away from him as possible, and as she fled the hall she heard her stepfather say, "She'll do as told."

Not this time.

The thought brought a smile to her face. She had often fled to the moor against Calum's wishes, and he'd never learned of her disobedience. It had taken practice in slipping past him, though no practice in convincing him that she had been busy with chores that he never paid mind to. Her secret excursions helped keep her sane and allowed her a modicum of independence, something she had longed for yet knew all too well was far out of her reach.

She had promised herself that once she was wed

she would continue to keep her secret excursions. It kept a spark of courage alive in her and allowed her to hope.

Honora needed to get to the stables. She'd hidden a few garments there, a shawl, a cloak, so she could retrieve them without anyone knowing and be on her way for the day. Unfortunately, the warriors nearly surrounded the stable area at the moment, so she would need to be extremely careful and remain hidden until the time was right.

Honora snuck out, though she needn't had since everyone's attention was focused on the warriors, making sure they were prepared for battle. She hid in the shadows of the trees, the gray overcast sky making the shadows darker and concealment easier. She watched her husband mount his stallion. He was a true warrior in every way. His claymore was strapped to his back, a dirk tucked in a sheath at his waist, a battle-axe hanging from his saddle. His long, deep brown hair was thickly braided at the sides to keep it out of his face, a face stern and uncompromising; ready to battle to the death if necessary, and the thought chilled her.

Her husband obviously feared nothing, while she seemed to fear everything. How would she ever be the wife he expected?

The warriors were far down the road when she came out of hiding and hurried into the stable to retrieve her cloak to guard against the chill autumn air. A shadow descended over her just as she was about to turn and leave, and she hoped the sky hadn't grown darker or the rain started.

She turned and froze with a gasp.

Her husband stood a short distance away, feet apart, hands braced on hips as he glared at her with a fire in his dark eyes.

"What do you think you're doing?"

Honora was too stunned to answer, though she voiced her thought aloud. "You rode off with your men."

He approached her with a caustic laugh. "You underestimate my skill, wife."

She shook her head as she slowly asked, "How?"

He stopped in front of her, leaned his face down to rub his cheek against hers, and inhaled deeply. "Your scent is undeniable."

She would have melted against him if his lips hadn't grazed hers before he whispered, "Disobey me again and you'll be sorry."

Honora stumbled back, her arm instinctively shooting up to shield herself.

Cavan grabbed it just above her elbow, though with surprising gentleness, tenderly ran his hand down to her reddened wrist and cupped it kindly in his hand. "What happened?"

She stumbled over an explanation. Did she confide the truth to her husband? Would he believe her? Did she dare take the chance or would he defend her stepfather's actions? With no answer to satisfy her doubts and fears, she lied. "A kitchen mishap."

He seemed satisfied, though hesitated in releasing her. "I remind you again to stay in the keep."

"Why?"

His biting laugh had her wishing she had held her tongue. "You question me?"

"No, my lord—"

"Cavan!"

She jumped at his sharpness. "Cavan, I'm sorry, no, I do not question you, but I enjoy walking the moor and had hoped—"

"Not today," he interrupted, and surprised her when he explained, "The barbarian tribe that strikes our friends to the south could have other bands roaming the land. I will not take the chance of you being captured. You will remain in the keep until my return."

"I understand." And she did. It was his duty to look out for the clan.

"And you will do as I ask?"

He asked, not demanded, and his consideration surprised her. "Yes, Cavan, I will do as you ask."

"Good, then I will not worry over you."

He turned to leave, stopped and remained still for a moment before turning around and glaring at her as if he struggled with a thought.

She stepped over to him and instinctively offered concern and comfort with a gentle hand to his chest. "Are you all right?"

She thought she heard him growl deep down in his chest before he pressed his cheek to hers and whispered, "I like the scent of you."

Then he left abruptly, with such haste that he stirred the hay that littered the stable floor. As if through a hazy cloud she watched him disappear. It took her a few moments to regain her composure, though her flesh continued to tingle and shock wiped her smile away.

She pressed hesitant fingers to her lips. Where had the smile come from? Her fingers drifted to her cheek and she closed her eyes to linger in the heat that tingled her fingertips. Was the heat from her or from him?

I like the scent of you.

She thought he hadn't noticed, and had begun to wonder if she was wasting time scenting herself. But he had noticed, and he liked it.

Her shock didn't chase the smile, which lingered. It came from too deep inside her to dismiss easily, and had been a long time in coming. She couldn't recall when she had smiled with such pleasure before.

"What are you doing here? You were ordered to remain in the keep."

The familiar harsh voice chased her smile away in an instant, and sent fear racing through her. But she was quick with an explanation, keeping her distance as she walked past her stepfather. "I wished to bid my husband a safe and successful battle," she told him.

"Finally you do something right," Calum said, though it sounded more like an accusation.

"I must see to my chores," Honora said, hurrying her steps to get away from Calum before he could say or ask anything more, or before he found a reason to raise his hand to her.

"See that you do," he shouted as she left the stable.

Normally, she would worry over her stepfather's accusations or actions, but today was different. Today she thought about her husband, especially in the early afternoon when the rain began to fall gently and she sat in the sewing room stitching a shirt for him.

It was then his words grew strong in her head.

Good, then I will not worry over you.

Her husband worried over her. Her mother had been the last person to truly worry over her, and she'd forgotten what it felt like to have someone care. Her husband might only have worried over her because she was his wife, of course, and that was his duty, but he did worry, and that made her feel cared for and, in a way, loved.

Not that she was foolish enough to believe Cavan loved her. She did not. But she knew that he was an honorable man who did the honorable thing, which was to care for his wife whether he chose her or not.

And for that alone she cared for him.

Chapter 8

❦

Cavan dragged a wounded Lachlan off the battlefield and secured him behind the protection of a large boulder.

"Move and so help me God, I will finish you off myself."

His brother snickered. "Not likely."

Cavan shoved a protesting Lachlan back against the boulder. "Your leg took a severe blow."

"I can still fight."

"The hell you can." Cavan grabbed Lachlan's sword and stood. "Fair warning, brother, move, and I promise you, you will be sorry."

"My big brother warning me?" Lachlan laughed with a grimace.

"Your big brother promising you." Cavan squeezed his shoulder.

Lachlan laughed. "Go win the battle; I'll be waiting for you."

Cavan reentered the battle with an eye on Artair. His father had warned them all to return safely, and with him leading the battle, it was his responsibility to do as his father commanded.

He had lost one brother, he would not lose another.

Cavan fought like a man enraged, and when the battle was done, stood on the battlefield gripping his blood-soaked sword, his warriors staring wide-eyed at him. He had taken down more barbarians than all his warriors combined, and it wasn't admiration he saw in their faces, but pure fear.

"Cavan!"

He turned to look at his brother Artair.

"Lachlan needs help."

Cavan carried Lachlan into the keep, Artair following behind. Addie came running, Tavish preceding her, and servants hurried to assist. Lachlan was laid on a table before the hearth, his garments dampened by the rain that had turned heavy just as they entered the keep.

Lachlan was barely conscious. Family hovered around him, Addie examining the wound and shaking her head.

"It is deep."

Cavan spewed oaths beneath his breath. He should have protected Lachlan, he told himself. He should have been there to deflect the sword. It was his responsibility; he was the oldest brother.

"This wound is bad, very bad," Addie said, brushing her tears away. "It is deep and I do not know if stitches will hold it together." Her eyes sprung wide.

"What is it, Mother?" Cavan asked anxiously.

"Your wife, Honora. She is very good with a needle."

"Where is she?" Cavan asked.

"The sewing room," his mother said.

Cavan took the stairs two at a time and shoved the sewing room door open with such force that it crashed into the wall.

Honora jumped out of her seat, her stitching falling to the floor, and stared at him.

"I have need of you," Cavan said.

"Need?" she barely whispered.

"Lachlan has been injured and needs stitches. Mother says you are good with a needle." He grabbed her hand.

"I have only stitched garments, never people," she objected.

"There is a first time for everything."

Honora hurried alongside him, then stopped abruptly. "My needle and threads, I will need them."

"Hurry," he urged, and released her hand.

Cavan waited with little patience, and when she reappeared, snatched her by the hand and rushed her down the stairs and into the hall.

"Stitch him," he ordered when they stopped at the table where Lachlan lay sprawled.

Cavan feared she would protest and run in fright from the sight of the blood, but surprisingly, she remained calm, examining his brother's wounded leg while people talked around her.

"I think it will take many stitches to hold the flesh," Addie said.

Cavan watched as his wife reached out, placed a comforting hand on his mother's bloody one and calmed her with reassuring words.

"We can do this. We can mend his leg."

In no time the two women worked together, mostly in silence, his mother following his wife's instructions without hesitation. Cavan watched in amazement as Honora's fingers deftly stitched Lachlan's leg as if it were a delicate piece of embroidery. Her stitches were precise and evenly woven, and he was glad that Lachlan had remained unconscious since it took many stitches to close the wound.

"The stitches must be kept dry and the bandages clean," Honora said with a glance at Addie. "I recall my mother stitching a wound for a neighbor's lad and she was insistent about both. And Lachlan must remain in bed for a few days so the wound can begin to heal and the stitches can take hold."

"He'll stay put," Cavan and Artair said in unison, bringing a smile to all in the hall.

"Fever could set in," Addie said as they bandaged Lachlan's leg.

"No need to worry about that unless it happens," Honora cautioned. "We can only do what we can at this moment."

Cavan admired the way his wife handled his mother's concerns, forcing her to concentrate on the moment and not worry too far ahead. He had learned the wisdom of paying heed to the moment at hand while captured. If he'd thought in the future even only an hour or two, he would have lived in anticipation of the beatings he knew would come and linger in the thought of never seeing his homeland or family again. Instead he had lived for each moment, each day growing strong in mind and purpose, and was thus ready when the opportunity came to claim his freedom.

He and Artair carried Lachlan to their father's solar, where a bed had been prepared for him. It would make it easier for the women to tend him, since it was closer to the kitchen and the herbs and brews he would need to help in his recovery.

Lachlan finally regained consciousness after he was settled, though only for a moment, and after his mother fed him a special brew, he slipped into a comfortable slumber.

Cavan had no intention of leaving his brother's side, though he was exhausted from battle, and his wife seemed to understand his concern.

"I have had the servants prepare a bath for you," Honora said, her voice low in consideration for the sleeping Lachlan. "Go bathe, then sleep, and after you are rested you can come relieve your mother and me, for your brother will need looking after throughout the night."

Cavan leaned down and pressed his cool cheek next to her flushed one. The heat seared him like a branding iron, though he didn't mind being marked by her. "Thank you."

Honora nodded and quickly returned to Lachlan's side.

Cavan didn't return until dawn, exhaustion having claimed his battle-weary body. He rushed to the solar, Artair joining him along the way.

"Sleep imprisoned us both," Artair said with a sense of guilt.

"At least we are well rested and can relieve my wife and our mother so they may rest," Cavan said, reassuringly grasping his brother's shoulder just before entering the solar.

They both froze as they watched their mother and Honora frantically working over their brother, blood everywhere and Lachlan moaning.

"He ripped his stitches after fighting us while in the throes of a dream," Addie explained.

"Damn," Artair mumbled. "I should have remembered that Lachlan always relives the battle in his dreams from that day."

"Since when?" Cavan asked.

"Since you and Ronan had gone missing."

"That matters little at the moment," their mother insisted. "It is what must be done now that matters, and we could use your help in restraining him."

Cavan and Artair positioned themselves at the shoulders and feet of their brother as Honora once again stitched the wound.

When she was finally done, she would have toppled over if not for the quick reaction of her husband. He caught her arm and secured her in the crook of his shoulder.

"Honora is exhausted," Addie said. "She has not slept a wink, insisting that I take time to rest while she continued to care for Lachlan alone. If it wasn't for her calming voice and actions . . . " Addie shook her head. " . . . Lachlan would have continued to fight us."

"You will rest now," Cavan demanded, tilting his wife's chin up and seeing how the exhaustion consumed her lovely violet eyes.

"I would like that," she said with a yawn.

Cavan was about to swing his wife up into his arms when Lachlan suddenly attempted to bolt off the bed. He would have been successful if not for Artair's firm hold on his shoulders. Cavan helped him keep Lachlan stable, but the injured brother didn't settle completely until Honora rested her hand to his chest and spoke softly in his ear.

When Lachlan finally woke from his disturbed sleep, Cavan was able to order his wife to go rest. He wished he could join her, be alone with her and express his gratitude for what she'd done for his brother, but he was still needed at Lachlan's side.

He watched Honora, saw that fatigue had claimed her body, and he worried that she wouldn't have the strength to climb the stairs to their bedchamber.

"Tell me of the battle, Cavan," Lachlan said, his teeth gritted against the pain.

"Yes," Honora encouraged. "Tell your brother of the victory."

"It was a worthy win," Artair boasted, and soon the brothers were comparing their prowess with a sword.

Cavan slipped out of the solar a couple of hours later to check on his wife. He found her sound asleep in their bed, snuggled deep amidst the bedding, with a strong fire keeping a chill from the room, and he wished he was keeping her warm with his body.

The thought didn't startle him as he walked over to the fireplace and braced his hand against the mantel to stare down at the flames. Honora had been on his mind much too often and in ways that would probably shock and offend her innocence.

He had been pleased to realize she wasn't a complete little mouse, afraid of everything, but then again, that sudden knowledge made him all the more curious to learn how she would react to making love.

She had a gentle touch and a sincere kindness to her, and right now he wasn't prepared to deal with a tender woman. He needed one with strength and hunger for her husband, for his need for a woman bordered more on ferocious rather than tender.

He rubbed at the back of his neck, a steady pain pinching at the base. He growled low in his throat, and it reminded him of the animal he had been forced to become in order to survive. He hadn't been able to shed that beast inside him, for fear that it might be of use one day, but he worried that he would not always be able to control the beast.

The growl surfaced again when he recalled the trouble Lachlan had with disturbing dreams after battle, another fault he took to heart and considered his own. If he had been victorious against the barbarians, then Ronan would still be with them and Lachlan would not suffer as he did.

He was not the leader he should have been that day, and that was why he kept the beast alive and well inside him. Never would he allow one of his to be taken from him, never would he not protect his people and his land, and the beast remained to make sure of it.

Cavan walked over to the bed and bent down on his haunches to gently run his finger along his wife's cheek. "I will keep you safe, even from me."

Chapter 9

A few days later, after a brief bout with fever, Lachlan incessantly complained about being confined to his bed until Addie could no longer bear to listen and freed him, though not before issuing strict warnings as to what he could and could not do.

Honora kept her laughter to herself as she listened to Addie's commands, knowing full well that Lachlan would adhere to none of them. But satisfied that his leg seemed to be healing nicely, she didn't worry over it.

"And do you have anything to add?" Lachlan asked, drawing Honora out of her musing.

She smiled. "Keep the bandage clean and the stitches dry and you should fair well."

"I like her list better than yours, Mother," Lachlan said with a laugh.

"Then make certain you adhere to it," Addie cautioned and shook her finger at her son. "Or else."

Lachlan laughed louder. "Or else what?"

"Or you answer to me," Cavan said without an ounce of laughter or a pinch of a smile.

Lachlan's laughter turned to a grin. "A challenge you are certain to lose."

"I doubt it, but you are welcome to try." Cavan walked over to Honora and held out his hand. "Come, wife, I have need of you."

After briefly hesitating, Honora placed her hand in his. She wanted to ask him what need he spoke of, but another part of her didn't want to hear the answer. She thought to inform him that she had duties to tend to, but duty to her husband usurped all other matters. In truth, she knew she had no choice but to tend to his need, whatever it might be. His warm fingers closed strongly around her cool ones as if he didn't intend to let her go.

She was surprised when they stopped in the great hall and he retrieved her green wool cloak that sat on the end of one of the tables and handed it to her without explanation. Honora slipped it on, assuming he intended for them to go outdoors, but instead he directed her to the staircase and they climbed the stairs to the battlements.

He preceded her along the walkway and stopped to glance out over the land that stretched far out before them, Honora halting beside him to enjoy the view.

"I had hoped to take you for a walk across the moors today, in appreciation for all you have done for my brother," Cavan said, and pointed to a cloud-infested sky. "But the impending weather prohibits such an excursion."

"That is very thoughtful, thank you."

He turned to look at her, and she was caught by the gentleness in his handsome features. Gone was the harshness in his dark eyes and the squint of doubt lines that always fanned them. His mouth was visibly relaxed as if he could actually smile if he tried, and his strong chin, while still strong, didn't jut out as if prepared to suffer a blow. This tender soul, she could get to know.

Unfortunately, he disappeared in a flash, and she wondering if perhaps it was wishful thinking that had her believing she saw kindness in him.

"You served me well, wife."

"It is my duty," she said, and looked out across the barren moors that surrounded the keep.

"Vast emptiness," he said, his own glance following hers.

"Vast peacefulness," she corrected. "There is nothing there to obscure its beauty or hide from you. It leaves itself open, vulnerable, and invites you to do the same."

"It is not good to be vulnerable," he snapped.

"We are all vulnerable one way or another."

"Only if we allow it," he said. "You have a choice to be strong or weak."

"Strength comes in different ways," Honora argued gently, for she felt as if she defended herself. She knew he thought her meek, unable and perhaps unwilling to defend herself, but she had managed to protect herself since she was young with the only weapon she had—her wits. And while it wasn't as lethal as a sword, it had allowed her to survive.

Cavan nodded slowly. "You're right about that."

He turned silent and stared out over the land, and she wondered over his thoughts. He barely spoke with her. This outing had surprised her; even the few words he'd spoken to her were unexpected. Before, it seemed he had meant to ignore her and keep his distance, and recalling as much, she told herself that his behavior now must reflect merely gratitude, nothing more.

A strong chilled wind whipped around them and she shivered, hugging the wool cloak to her, while he stood unperturbed and in only his plaid, his shirt, and his sandals.

"You are cold," he said, and hugged her against him, snuggling her in the crook of his shoulder so she rested alongside the length of him.

His heat instantly assaulted her, slipping beneath her blue blouse and brown skirt until it settled into her flesh, and she almost sighed with the pleasure of it. It ran along every inch and depth of her, setting her skin to tingle and spark and ignite a heat of her own.

Thunder rumbled overhead, but she paid it no heed, simply settled her face to his chest and drank in the scent of him. She didn't know what it was about the smell of him, earth and pine and male, that attracted her; she only knew that she relished his distinct aroma.

She rubbed her cheek against his shirt and inhaled.

Abruptly, she was jerked away from him and held at arm's length while his dark eyes glared accusingly at her. She had no idea what she might have done to upset him, but he was clearly upset. His jaw jutted out, his lips locked tight, and his dark eyes were unforgiving.

"I'm sorry," she said quickly, hoping to correct whatever mistake she had made.

"For what?" he asked in a growl-like rumble that frightened her.

She stuttered, not knowing how to answer, for she could make no sense of his sudden anger.

Her hesitation seemed to further agitate him. "Can you not speak up for yourself?"

Honora closed her eyes for a moment, envisioned the kindness she had seen in his eyes and held the vision firm, for she could speak easily to that man. After a moment she opened them again. "I did not know I needed to defend myself. I had simply felt safe in your arms."

His expression softened for such a brief moment that Honora wondered if it was her imagination.

Cavan shoved her away from him. "Don't!"

She took another step back and stared at him, bewildered.

He spewed a frustrated grunt and ran anxious fingers through his hair. "Don't feel safe with me," he explained.

She shook her head. "But you are my husband."

He lunged at her and she hurriedly backed away, though not quick enough, for he grabbed her by the shoulders and yanked her to him. "I warned you once many years ago to watch where you stepped, and still you have not learned."

Honora turned her head and saw that she would have fallen off the battlement to certain death had he not saved her, though in her defense, she whispered, "You charged at me."

"There is no excuse for not watching where you step."

He was right. She had foolishly thought herself safe with him, and simply because for a single moment she thought she'd seen kindness in him. She thought she could trust him. In truth, she could trust no one. She had been alone in this world since her mother's death and had to accept it and continue to protect herself with her wits, as she'd been doing for so very long now.

With a breath of strength that rose up from deep inside her, she said, "This time, I will remember. May I be dismissed?"

"No," he snapped. "I brought you here so you could escape the confines of the keep and your duties. I will leave and you will stay."

She licked her lips, her mouth having gone dry, as it always did when she attempted to defend herself. "What if I—"

"Stop!"

Honora's eyes widened at his stern command. What had she done now?

"Don't lick your lips."

She offered an explanation. "They are dry."

He offered his own. "You invite when you do that."

"Invite?"

"A kiss."

She gasped. "I never meant—"

"Your innocence invited." He released her and stepped away.

Honora thought to turn and run, but she had a duty to this man and her vows, and her vows had yet to be sealed. Whether she favored the thought or not, their marriage had to be consummated.

She gathered the courage to say it and hopefully invite his response. "You are my husband."

"A husband who doesn't want you," he yelled, his words magnified by the howling wind that suddenly surrounded them.

His words struck like a finely aimed arrow, and they hurt her badly. She understood this marriage was forced upon them both, but what was done was done, and neither of them could change that. They could only make the most of the situation. Obviously, he did not feel the same way.

She did not know what to do, and feared her stepfather's response if he should learn of this. She wanted to run and hide, but where? She had no place to go. No real home. No one who truly wanted her, loved her.

Honora caught sight of the moors, which stretched out endlessly beyond the keep, and the small patch of trees where she and her mother would forage for plants and laugh together. Her mother's unconditional love stabbed at her heart, and she didn't pause to think, not even when the first raindrop struck her cheek. She turned and ran from her husband, down the stairs, ignoring his shouted command for her to stop, ignoring the curious eyes of all she passed as she bolted out of the keep and headed along the moors to what seemed to her a small spot of love.

Cavan pursued her while spewing a string of oaths that kept everyone out of his way. He knew his rage made him appear a man bent on reprisal and that tongues would certainly wag about the way he chased after his wife like a madman, or more appropriately, like a barbarian, but he could not help himself.

Honora was faster than he had expected. She flew across the moors like a winged beauty. Her cloak flared out, her long dark hair blew wildly in the wind, and the rain did not hinder her rapid pace.

He saw where she was headed, the small cropping of woods that many would not enter, fearing tales of fairies and gnomes that were none too inviting. His wife was either foolish or courageous, but then, didn't it take a fool to be courageous in the first place?

Cavan halted abruptly upon entering the woods. The place was dense with trees, bushes, and boulders, perfect hiding places for the wee people, and it was the heavy clouds and dense foliage in the woods that made it appear to be dusk. Rain trickled in a gentle rhythm over the leaves and rocks.

"Honora!" he called out, and his voice returned to him in an eerie echo.

There was no thought to leaving her there on her own to fend for herself against the creatures who inhabited the place. She was his wife, and it was his duty to protect her. Besides, it had been his callous words that caused her to flee.

He had not meant to hurt her. He merely wanted her to keep her distance from him, for his desire for her was growing stronger by the day. He could just take her and be done with it, but then, each time he looked into her eyes he saw her innocence, her need for a loving husband, not a barbarian who needed to assuage his own animalistic need.

He didn't want to leave her with scars, as had been done to him. She was his wife and deserved more; whether he could ever give her that, he wasn't sure. It was too early to tell.

Cavan made his way carefully past trees gnarled with age, branches that bowed in the wind to him, and whispers that had to be the wind whistling through the trees. Or was it a voice traveling upon the wind?

He decided to follow the voice and see where it led, and he wasn't surprised when it took him straight to his wife. She sat on a smooth rock as if talking with someone, and he paused in the shadows to see if he could catch sight of anyone or anything. When he saw no one about, he listened to what she was saying.

"I don't know what to do with him. He is my husband and I have a duty, but he does not like me. I think sometimes he hates me."

Her words pierced his chest like a sharp sword. He could never hate her. She was too good, too honorable, too pure.

Honora sighed. "He thinks me—"

She stopped and abruptly stood, looking frantically around her.

It seemed that she had somehow sensed him, or had something alerted her to his presence? He wished that she had finished what she was saying, wanting to know what she thought he thought of her.

"Watch where you step," she called out.

"Why?" he asked, taking cautious steps.

Honora turned toward the sound of his voice. "The vines can trap your feet."

Cavan heeded her warning and proceeded carefully, eventually entering the secluded clearing where she stood. He didn't want her to know he'd been listening, and so, though curious, didn't ask who she had been speaking with.

"These woods are not safe," he said.

She looked affronted. "These woods are safer than anyplace I know."

Her words slapped him hard. On the battlements she'd told him that she felt safe in his arms, and now she let him know it was here she felt the safest. But then, why should he expect otherwise after what he'd said to her? And why did her words disturb him?

He stepped closer to her and was caught by the beauty of her violet eyes. But it wasn't only beauty that shined in them. There was also a loving, peaceful tenderness he longed to taste. "You should not have run away from me and made me give chase."

"You need not have chased me."

He reached up to brush a strand of hair away from her mouth and his thumb brushed her lips. "I must see you safe. You are my wife."

He ran his thumb across her moist full lips over and over until he felt his loins grow hard and ache. Then a growl rumbled deep inside him and surfaced slowly until it burst forth and he grabbed Honora around the waist and yanked her hard against him to claim a kiss.

Chapter 10

The first taste of her told him he was in trouble and to stop, to go no further, to end it now, while he was still capable of sound reason. He ignored the silent warnings. How couldn't he? Honora did not deny him; she responded with innocence and gentleness, which only served to excite him more.

He silently warned himself not to draw her close to him, not to let their bodies touch; just enjoy the kiss, the pure taste of her. How she wound up in his arms, flush against him, he wasn't certain, nor did he care. His only thought was their lingering kiss and not the rush of passion to his loins, though he did acknowledge the strange feeling of utter contentment that snuck over him and laid claim.

Her slim tongue mated more easily with his as she relaxed in his arms, and his own pace slowed until their kiss turned to savoring each other, like fine food or wine one wished the palate to appreciate.

It took a forceful rush of wind to nearly rip them apart. Cavan wrapped his arms firmly around his wife as she buried her face in his chest and her long dark hair wiped at his face. He felt her shiver and wondered over its cause, the wind or his kiss?

When the wind died down, she glanced up at him, and he saw desire in her lovely eyes. He could take her here and now on the hard, cold ground, just as he'd seen the barbarians do to their women without thought or caring, just plain lust, plain fornication.

He shook the vivid images from his head and silently cursed himself. He had yet to shed the filth the barbarians had imprinted on him and he wondered if he would ever feel worthy enough to be the husband his wife deserved or the honorable clan leader his people expected.

Cavan gently set her away from him. "We must return to the keep before the weather worsens."

Honora stood speechless, staring at him.

She was obviously trying to make sense of their recent exchange, and while he could offer an explanation and set her mind at ease, he found himself unable or perhaps unwilling to confide in her. How could he expect her, an innocent, to understand his fear, when he himself was struggling to understand it?

"I am your wife," she said, as if the reminder might help him.

"You need not remind me." He didn't mean to sound caustic, though perhaps it was best for them both. She would keep her distance, and he would need to keep his until he felt ready, certain that he could be a good husband to her.

He held out his hand. "Let us return to the keep."

"I need no help," she said, and made her way past him.

"But I do," he whispered, and followed.

Honora fell into an easy routine, taking breakfast early and alone before anyone in the keep woke for the day. Weather permitting, she would then walk the moor or retire to the sewing chamber and tend to her stitching.

It had been a couple of weeks since her husband kissed her, and the kiss had lingered long in her memory. Surprisingly, she'd enjoyed it more than she had expected. He was strong yet gentle with her, and she felt unfamiliar stirrings she wished to explore.

Her husband, however, had not kissed her again since that day, purposely avoided her, and worst of all, continued to sleep on the hard floor in front of the fireplace. She didn't know what to do or even who to speak with about it. She had thought to confide in Addie, but then, she was Cavan's mother and would advise patience, as she had before.

Honora wished her mother were alive. She would have then discussed the matter with her, and her mother would have suggested and advised her, and offered her comfort. But there was no one to offer her comfort; she was alone.

"I have come to seek the company of my little sister."

Honora jumped at the sound of Lachlan's voice and turned to see him close the sewing room door behind him.

She greeted him with a smile as he sat in the chair to her right and stretched his long legs out in front of the hearth.

Lachlan was a ruggedly handsome man, like most of the Sinclare men, but possessed considerable charm that made him appear all the more handsome. Honora often thought it was the twinkle in his brown eyes and the sinfully playful smile he constantly wore that made him so appealing to women.

"Is my brother a good husband?"

His direct and unexpected query startled her.

Lachlan shrugged. "You two don't spend much time together, and soon tongues will begin to wag, and you know what happens when gossip gets started."

She did; truth somehow got distorted when gossip reigned. She chose her words carefully for she did not feel comfortable discussing her husband with his brother. "Cavan is busy with plans to find Ronan."

"You mean his obsession to find Ronan."

Honora was quick to defend her husband. "He knows what your brother suffers far better than you. How can you not expect him to be obsessed with finding Ronan?"

Lachlan nodded. "True enough. I sought you out in hopes of gaining some insight to my own brother. He is not who he once was. Cavan often laughed and joked and trusted Artair and myself, and would talk often with our father. He now seeks solitude, as do you, and I wish to understand why."

Honora knew he was truly concerned; his playful smile had faded away. But she was at a loss as to how to help, especially since she wished to understand herself.

She shrugged and spoke the truth. "I don't know."

"That's what I thought. He ignores you as much as he does us." He shook his head. "And he angers so easily. That was something Cavan never did. He always remained calm and in control, even when others shouted and threatened. Now anger possesses him and he snaps and shouts most of the time."

"He has suffered—"

"All warriors suffer one time or another," Lachlan said as if affronted. "Cavan knows this and was prepared to do whatever it took to survive and escape."

"I know nothing of being a warrior."

"I beg to differ."

Honora looked at Lachlan as if he were crazy. "I am no warrior."

His smile returned. "I've watched the way your stepfather speaks to you and treats you. You have to be a warrior to deal with that man, and if my brother wasn't wallowing so much in his own self-pity he'd see it for himself and know what a gem of a wife he has gotten."

She was speechless.

Lachlan stood. "You're a good woman, Honora. any man would be proud to have you as his wife. Hopefully someday my foolish brother will realize it." He gave her a kiss on the cheek. "I'm proud to call you sister."

Honora sat stunned. She had never considered herself a warrior or would have known that Lachlan gave any thought to her, other than being his brother's wife. He had been grateful for her help in healing him and they had shared a few interesting conversations when she tended him, but she did not realize that she'd made any impression on him.

She felt a twinge of guilt for seeking continued solitude. It was a way of protecting herself against her stepfather; if he didn't see her, he couldn't hurt her. She supposed she thought the same of her situation with Cavan. If she kept out of his sight, she need not concern herself with their marriage.

However, she was no longer a child who could run and hide. She was a grown woman who needed to be mindful of her duties. And what of gossip? It was sure to start if Cavan and she remained distant from one another. What then?

She shivered with the thought of her father finding out. She'd have far more to fear from him than from anyone else. While she didn't consider or believe herself a warrior, she did possess survival instincts. She needed Cavan to be a husband to her, and the only way she could achieve that was by being a wife to him.

No matter how daunting the task seemed or how much she preferred to seek the comfort of solitude, she had to make sure she survived, and the only way to be certain of that was to make sure her marriage was secure.

Honora placed her sewing in the basket beside her chair, stood, smoothed the wrinkles from her green wool skirt, adjusted the ties on her blouse, ran her fingers through her long dark hair, and then went in search of her husband.

Cavan pounded the table with his fist. The sturdy wood didn't creak or budge, nor did his father, who sat opposite him. He had always admired his father's ability to remain calm and unwavering in confrontations, though today was different. Today he wanted his father to capitulate and allow him free reign in the search for Ronan.

It was only he and his father in the solar, and he wanted it that way. He didn't need his brothers' interference or their opinions. None of them understood, none of them knew or could imagine the horrors Ronan was probably suffering, and if his brother had succumbed to his injuries and torture, then he wanted his body brought home for a proper burial.

"With enough men and my leadership, I can attack Mordrac and seize his land—"

His father interrupted with a firm "No."

"Afraid," Cavan said accusingly, and instantly regretted it. His father was an honorable man who taught his sons that fear was not to be feared, but to be embraced and used as a weapon against the enemy.

His father reflected the barb with a knowing nod and a reasonable explanation. "An attack on Mordrac would take sizable troops and time and leave our land and people vulnerable. It is not a wise choice, though a difficult one since I too want Ronan home."

"It can be done—"

"But not without significant consequences that I am not willing to take," his father said.

Cavan wanted to strike out at someone or anything, his hurt was so great. How could he have returned safely home without Ronan? He was his youngest brother and he should have looked out for him, protected him, kept him safe.

"Cavan," his father said calmly, and motioned for his son to sit.

With a slump of defeat, Cavan sank into one of the two chairs in front of the table. He knew his father was right, but it didn't make it any easier for him and his efforts to find his brother.

"Your brothers and I have never stopped searching for Ronan and we never will, but as clan leader I must do what is best for the clan, not only for my immediate family. You must understand this, for one day you will lead the clan and need to make decisions you don't always favor. Besides, we discovered there is a chance that Mordrac may have sold Ronan."

"When . . . how . . . where was he taken?"

His father held up a hand. "We only discovered the news this morning."

Cavan shook his head. "And if I had given you a chance to speak when I burst into your solar, you would have told me."

His father leaned forward, bracing his arms on

the table. "I can understand your need to find your brother. You above any of us know what Ronan suffers. But then you also know how important it is for us to be wise in our response. There is more at stake here than just Ronan's life."

Cavan didn't want to listen to what his father told him, but understood it completely. Their enemy could very well be using Ronan as a weapon against them, expecting the Sinclares to charge recklessly into battle, especially now with his own return home. If plans weren't carefully followed, endless lives could be lost, not to mention land holdings.

"Artair has men out now verifying the news and seeing if we can discover where Ronan was taken," his father said. "His men are good. Give them time and they will have an answer soon enough."

"It is hard to sit and do nothing," Cavan admitted.

"Take time to heal and be with your wife. When the time comes—and it will—to rescue Ronan, you will ride with your brothers and free him. Now go and see your mother, and look happy before she drives me crazy with worry over you."

Cavan laughed. "You are the leader. Order her to stop—"

His father laughed even louder. "Order your mother?"

Cavan winced. "I should know better. I will go speak with her and ease her concerns."

"And what of your wife?"

Cavan's smile vanished and his body grew visibly rigid.

"Cavan!" his father snapped.

He reluctantly met his father's eyes.

"Tell me you have sealed your marriage vows."

Cavan remained silent and continued to hold his father's questioning stare.

His father stood with a start. "You are the next laird of the Clan Sinclare. You have a responsibility, and that includes producing an heir. I know you did not choose Honora for a wife, and for that I am sorry, but she is your wife and you have a duty. I expect you to honor it."

"Is there anything I have a choice in since my return?" Cavan asked.

"You will lead this clan, and as I've cautioned, make difficult choices. That is all there is to it."

Cavan laughed caustically. "That simple?"

His father folded his arms over his chest, looking like the formidable clan leader. "It is never simple, and never think it is, and do not make the mistake of not making a friend of your wife, for she will be there when no one else is. She will hold your hand when needed, listen to your complaints, speak truthfully about your faults but only to you, and stand by your side when others feel you wrong. She is your partner and will always be there for you."

Cavan shook his head. "You speak of love. There is no love between Honora and me."

"You have not given it a chance."

"And now I have no choice."

"Yes, you do," his father said.

Cavan shook his head. "No, I don't have a choice. I have an obligation, a duty to my clan."

"There still remains a choice, and when you realize that, then you will be ready to lead this clan."

"A riddle for me to solve, Father?"

"An easy decision for a wise leader."

Cavan walked to the door and swung it open before turning back around to his father. "Perhaps," he said, "I'm not a wise leader."

Chapter 11

Honora watched her husband stomp through the great hall swearing, people moving out of his way, the women quick to huddle in gossip. She'd been so busy keeping to herself that she had not paid attention to the wagging tongues and the damage they were sure to cause.

She adjusted her blue shawl on her shoulders and made her way to the kitchen, alert now to the whispers around her while appearing lost in her thoughts. Her husband had left the hall, leaving the door open behind him, men rushing to close it against the cold wind or perhaps against Cavan. From the grumbling she overheard, it appeared the clan was concerned with Cavan's strange behavior since his return. She even heard one woman refer to him as a barbarian, and another made mention of Cavan constantly arguing with his father. She knew that since everyone in the clan respected their laird, a son who disagreed or failed to show him respect would always be the subject of much gossip.

Honora berated herself as she exited the kitchen, the servants glaring at her and whispering as she went past. They lay the blame on her, as Cavan's wife. She had a duty to her husband, and it was obvious that she had been neglecting him.

She could only imagine what her stepfather must be thinking. She had to make things right or no doubt he would show her the error of her ways.

She returned to the kitchen and spoke with the cook, giving her directions for the evening meal she wanted served to her and Cavan in their bedchamber. The cook's sour expression didn't change, though she nodded forcefully, as if letting her know it was about time she tended to her duties.

Honora rushed through the great hall and up the stairs to her bedchamber. She wanted to gather the last of the heather on the moor and needed her cloak, since the day had turned blustery. As she ran back down the stairs, she recalled Lachlan's words about her being a warrior and smiled. Perhaps she did have a little bit of a warrior in her.

"Honora."

Addie's sharp call caused her to stop abruptly and wrap her cloak around her like a protective shield.

"I haven't seen much of you—or my son—lately."

Honora stumbled over her words, not knowing how to respond and not wanting to offer an explanation. It was enough trying to cope with a husband who kissed her yet didn't want her, much less express her own misgivings about the situation.

"I—I've be-been—"

"Staying to yourself," Addie accused.

Honora lowered her head, feeling guilty.

"I'm sorry," Addie said.

Honora raised her head, her eyes wide.

"My son, who always talked with me, ignores me . . . and my new daughter, whom I admire, seeks solitude rather than speak with me. I merely wish to help, to be a shoulder for you to lean on when necessary. It is not easy marrying a stranger, and even harder marrying a stranger who never approved of the union."

"I must admit, it has been confusing," Honora said.

"Then we should talk."

Still, she was hesitant to ask Addie to join her. She had only shared the moors with her mother. But then, in a sense Addie was now her mother and had only been kind to her. "I was just about to gather heather from the moor. Would you like to join me?"

Addie smiled. "I would love to."

"Mother."

Both women jumped and turned to see Cavan making his way to them.

"I wish to speak with you," he said.

All eyes turned as his strong voice boomed off the walls of the great hall and remained fixed on him. He was a sight to behold, his stance proud and confident, his demeanor commanding, the scar on his ruggedly handsome face reminding all of his bravery and also of his time spent with the barbarians.

"Another time?" Addie said to her. "My son needs me."

Honora nodded and acknowledged her husband

with another nod as she passed him, eager to retreat to a place she felt safe and hoping that one day she would feel that way about her husband.

His hand shot out and grabbed hold of her arm. "Where are you going?"

"To gather heather."

"Be careful where you step," he cautioned, and released her arm to take hold of his mother's hand.

Honora hurried away, annoyed with herself. However was she going to grow at ease with her husband when he so often intimidated her?

Honora lost track of time and her worries while picking the last of the heather before winter turned it dormant. There were several uses for the fragrant flower, but at the moment she intended to scent her bedchamber with it. She was trying everything she could to get her husband to accept her as his wife in every sense of the word.

Her basket was full when she entered the village, though it grew lighter after she shared a few sprigs with the women she stopped to speak with along the way. She was nearing the keep when she heard her name shouted, and she cringed before daring to turn and face her stepfather. He approached her with rapid strides, his face splotched red, a sure sign of his anger.

He grabbed her arm so tightly she winced.

"You embarrass me," he said in a harsh whisper, and dragged her around to the side of the keep where no one could see them. "People are saying you are no wife to Cavan."

"I am doing my best." She knew nothing she might say would please him, not when gossip told him otherwise.

He shook her. "It isn't good enough."

"I will try harder," she said, only to appease him so he would leave her be and she would suffer no more than a sore arm.

"Try harder?" he said, enraged, spittle spraying her cheek. "You should have done your duty from the start. I warned you, and you foolishly ignored me."

"I did not, I did my best," she said, trying to free herself from his vicious grip.

"Liar!" He yanked her arm hard and she stumbled, which dislodged his grip.

She staggered away from him, but not far enough. He delivered a stinging blow to her face that sent her sprawling to the ground, her basket of heather spilling out around her. Then grabbing her arm, he yanked her up before she had a chance to catch her breath. Instinctively she braced herself for another blow.

"Tend to your husband, daughter, or you will know real pain," he said roughly, and shoved her to the ground once again.

She remained there watching him march off, still feeling the sting to her cheek and the ache to her heart. She had never understood why her stepfather hated her so very much.

Her father had died when she was a baby and all she knew of him had been from the stories her mother had told her. He had smiled often, her mother told her, and walked the moors with her. She thought her new father might do the same, and at first when her mother married Calum, she was happy. But it hadn't taken long for Calum to show his true nature, by then it was too late. He made her and her mother suffer for too many years, and Honora often wondered if her mother had simply given up and died, being unable to withstand his brutality any longer.

Now, in the keep, when Calum disappeared from sight, Honora stood up, brushed the dirt from her garments, and picked up the scattered heather. She had not seen Calum of late and assumed he was busy enjoying the honor and privileges her marriage had afforded him. Why had he suddenly come after her? He had to have been aware of the gossip, and yet hadn't approached her until now.

She adjusted her cloak, hooked the basket on her arm and, before turning the corner of the keep, placed her cool hand to her cheek. The heat near stung her palm, and she realized that her cheek must be bright red. Would people assume her husband had struck her? And what would Cavan do when he saw her flaming cheek?

A bit of time and the heat would fade and no one would be the wiser, she told herself. She just needed to get to her bedchamber before anyone noticed. She bowed her head and draped her long black hair around her face. People would think she was busy watching her step or deep in thought and leave her be. Or so she hoped. Keeping her head bent, she hurried away.

* * *

Cavan sat at the table in front of the fireplace talking with his mother. His father was right—he'd ignored his mother since his return. But then, his father usually was right. It was what made him a great leader, though he credited his wife's wisdom and guidance for his leadership qualities, and Cavan could understand why. His mother listened more than she spoke, and when she did speak, you heard more than you realized.

He reached out, took her hand, and noticed that though she had aged since his absence, it was not with lines and wrinkles, but wisdom.

"I am glad to be home."

She squeezed his hand tightly. "I am so relieved to have you home. I have missed our talks."

He could not help but ask, "Do you miss Ronan?"

Her smile faded and she nodded slowly. "As much as I missed you." Her smile returned. "He will return as you did, I am certain of it."

"You do not believe we will find him?" Cavan asked anxiously, for he wanted nothing more than to find his brother and return him home safely.

"No, I believe Ronan will return home without any help from his family. I believe it is his destiny."

"To suffer?" Cavan shook his head. "That makes no sense."

"You see your brother as someone you must protect."

"He is my youngest brother, and have you forgotten how many times I have protected him?"

Addie laughed and clapped her hands together. "How could I? You were forever carrying him home wounded or frightened from nasty tricks your brothers played on him. But he is a young lad no more; he is a man."

Cavan wanted badly to tell his mother of the last time he saw Ronan, how his brother cried out to him for help and how he had failed Ronan, but he knew it would only break her heart.

Addie patted his hand reassuringly. "Ronan will return home."

"I pray you are right, Mother." He prayed all the time for Ronan, and prayed he would forgive him for not having saved him.

Cavan caught a rush of someone entering the great hall from the corner of his eye and turned to see his wife, her steps hasty and her head down, her long dark hair obscuring her face. He had seen her many times walking while deep in thought, noticing no one around her, but never had she appeared to be hiding.

But what did she hide?

He stood and called out, "Honora."

She acknowledged him with a wave and kept going.

"Honora," he shouted again, and his mother quietly took her leave.

Cavan was surprised and annoyed when she simply ignored him. It wasn't like her; she had been a dutiful wife even though he'd paid her little heed, especially since he had kissed her. It had affected him more than he was willing to acknowledge. He didn't want to remember how much he'd enjoyed it. The memory always managed to stir his loins.

She had reached the staircase when Cavan caught up with her, grabbed her by the arm turned her about. Her long dark hair swung around her face as she hastily faced him, and when the silky strands settled, he saw what she'd been hiding.

He reached out and gently touched the red welt on her cheek, unmistakably made by a rough hand. Fury mounted inside him, that anyone would dare touch his wife. "Who did this?"

She placed her hand over his on her cheek. Her touch was tender, her flesh cool, and the combination ran a shiver through him.

"It is nothing."

He touched her other cheek, cupping her face, and leaned down until his nose almost touched hers. "You are my wife," he declared, his voice rumbling with anger. "No one—*no one*—touches you, but me."

Her violet eyes, which always managed to stir his soul, pleaded with him to let it be, but that was not possible.

"Answer me, Honora." He was surprised how calmly he spoke, for within him he boiled with anger.

She hesitated several times before she finally answered. "I angered my stepfather."

Cavan felt his gut tighten. "Go to our bedchamber and wait for me."

She grabbed hold of his arm as he turned to leave. "It was not his fault."

Cavan cupped her injured cheek. "It does not matter. He raised his hand to you, and that I will not tolerate."

She gripped his arm tighter. "But I was at fault."

"Then he should have come to me with his grievance. He dishonors me by raising his hand against you. Now do as I say. Wait for me in our bedchamber."

He turned and left the keep, and with each step, his fury mounted.

Cavan found his prey not far from the keep. Calum looked to be sweet-talking a young woman, plying her, most likely, with falsehoods of his importance. Cavan hadn't liked the man from the very first time Tannach approached him years ago about a union with Honora. It seemed he wished to sell his only child, and he only spoke about how obedient she was and would be to a husband. Cavan hadn't wanted strict obedience in a wife; he wanted a woman who would stand by his side equal in strength and intelligence.

His thoughts fueled his already raging temper, and by the time he reached Calum, he descended upon him with fury. Grabbing him by the scruff of the neck, he tossed him to the ground and planted his foot firmly against Calum's throat.

The man wiggled beneath his heel like a squealing pig, his hands frantically trying to push Cavan's foot off while he gasped for breath.

"You dare strike my wife?"

Calum's eyes bugged wide and he choked, trying to speak.

"Do not bother to try to offer an explanation, for there is none. You had no right. Honora belongs to me."

Calum nodded as best he could while his hands clutched Cavan's ankle, still trying to break free.

"Strike her again and I will kill you."

Calum gagged on what little breath he had left when Cavan freed him, and he crawled off choking and coughing, no one daring to help him.

Cavan returned to the keep, gossip already spreading about how he protected his wife, and the people taking it as a good sign. He went straight to his bedchamber, his wife jumping out of the chair she sat in near the hearth.

"How often has your stepfather raised his hand to you?" Cavan asked, unable to keep the annoyance out of his voice. "And don't hesitate or make excuses. I want the truth."

"As often as pleased him."

"Since you were young?" he asked.

"From the day my mother married him," she confirmed.

This knowledge brought him a bit more understanding of his wife, and while he sympathized with her plight, he also grew annoyed with her. What if he wasn't around to protect her? Would she shrink and wail in fear? And if she couldn't protect herself, what of their children? Who would protect them when necessary?

"You never attempted to protect yourself?"

"Submitting was my only protection," she confessed.

"Not anymore."

She looked relieved, and he knew she thought that he meant he would now protect her. While he indeed would let no harm befall her, he was wise enough to realize that he might not always be there when she needed protecting. "Thank you," she said softly.

"Don't thank me yet."

She shook her head, showing her confusion.

He thumped his chest. "I'm going to teach you how to defend yourself."

Chapter 12

Honora stood staring at her husband. She had heard him, though she couldn't quite make sense of what he'd said, and his words had also hurt. She was aware that he thought of her as weak, and now he added coward to how he felt about her.

It had taken all her strength to outfox Calum, and she'd learned by trail and error until she was finally able to protect herself the only way she could—by outwitting him. She never thought of herself as a coward or a warrior; her only thought was survival, as was it now.

"If that is what you wish," she said.

"Do you always comply so easily?"

She heard his annoyance and did not intend to suffer over it. "You've made yourself clear. Why argue?"

"Always the obedient wife."

"I do my duty," she said, not meaning to sound as if she accused, but he believed otherwise.

"Perhaps if I had a wife worth bedding . . . "

He may not have raised his hand to her but she felt the sting just as sharply, and for a moment she thought she caught him wince as if he suffered the blow along with her. Had he regretted his harsh words?

With her astuteness having served her well in the past, she decided to continue to rely on it and said, "Excuse my naiveté, but what makes a woman worth bedding?"

She almost smiled at his stunned expression, and felt as if she had just delivered a sharp blow and without raising a hand.

He cracked a brief smile. "You are shrewder than I thought."

She bowed her head respectfully. "I but ask a question." She raised her head, her chin up a bit more than was necessary. "Have you an answer?"

"Do you truly wish for me to answer?"

His distinct challenge caused her innards to tremble, while she surprisingly presented a calm and innocent exterior. "However will I learn to please you if I do not know?"

"You *wish* to please me?" he asked, reaching out to take her hand and slowly drawing her closer to him in front of the hearth.

How could his nearness cause her to feel thrilled and intimidated all at the same time? "It is my obligation."

He nodded slowly, as if affirming the truth of it, then lowered his cheek to press lightly against her inflamed one. She thought she heard the sizzle of hot meeting cold, and she definitely heard him inhale deeply after nestling his nose in her hair.

He began with a whisper in her ear. "The scent of a woman."

She barely heard him; she had become lost in the array of feelings that were waging war within her. She wanted to put distance between them and yet ached to move closer. It made no sense.

He brought his forehead to rest against hers as his finger stroked ever so lightly along her jawline, down across her neck, to finally trace circles around her breasts as he murmured, "The feel of a woman."

Then he nibbled at her lips until they pulsated, moved to her neck to send the flesh quivering, and traveled across her shoulder until she shockingly ached for him to taste her breasts.

"The taste of a woman," he murmured, and nuzzled her neck with a combination of his lips and teeth until, to her surprise, she moaned from the pleasure he brought her.

He laughed softly in her ear. "And last but by far from the least the sounds of a woman as she reaches pleasure."

Honora gasped sharply and skittered away from him.

His hand shot out and nabbed her wrist, yanking her to him. "First rule in protecting yourself—never trust your opponent to play fair. Second rule, keep a fair distance or . . . "

She followed his glance down between them and gasped again. He held his dirk to her stomach.

"You didn't even know I drew my weapon."

"I didn't think you would draw a weapon against me."

"Never assume anything and be prepared for everything," Cavan said, returning his dirk to the sheath hooked to his kilt.

It had been a lesson, nothing more. The scent, feel, taste, and sound of her had not aroused him as he had aroused her. He had not in any way found her appealing, and she felt appalled that he had tweaked her passion.

"I will instruct you in defending yourself against all types of foes."

She nodded, though it wasn't in approval, but rather because he had already done just that.

"You will learn how to use weapons and . . . " He scratched his head. "Tell me you know how to ride a horse."

"Of course I do . . ."

He looked relieved, though his expression changed when she finished.

" . . . it is just that I haven't had much occasion to do so."

"That will change immediately, and I will show you how to sneak about without being noticed."

In truth, she had mastered that many years ago, when she learned it was best that Calum didn't notice her, for then it was less likely that he would find an excuse to hit her.

"And I will teach you how to survive off the woods."

She didn't bother to tell him that she could

probably teach him more than he her, for she and her mother often had to survive off the forest. It got to where she favored the plants and flowers more than the food slaughtered for the daily meals.

A knock sounded at the door, and Honora opened it to a servant who carried a tray, She remembered then that she had ordered the evening meal be brought to their room. Time had gotten away from her and she hadn't realized it had grown so late. She'd hoped to speak with Cavan before the meal was brought to the bedchamber.

She stepped aside for the servant to enter. "I asked for our meal to be served in our bedchamber this—"

"Nonsense," he snapped, and ordered the young woman gone with a wave.

Honora didn't let him see her cringe as she shut the door behind the woman. His rejection of her was certain to fuel gossip.

"You will not hide away in shame. I made certain your stepfather understood you belong to me now and that he is never to raise his hand to you again."

Clearly, he'd misunderstood her intentions—that she'd planned an intimate supper for them. But then, she reminded herself, he wasn't attracted to her. So why had it seemed that way when he'd kissed her? She wanted to shake her head in confusion but did not, fearing it would only confuse him as well.

"We will sup together with family," Cavan said.

So all could gossip over her plight, she thought, but acquiesced with a nod.

"We start tomorrow after the morning meal." He held his arm out to her when he reached the door, where she stood. "All will know you are protected now."

And all would know her husband rejected her.

Honora was quiet throughout the meal. Addie attempted to converse with her, but after several failed attempts she simply patted her hand and advised in a whisper that everything would be all right.

Honora did not believe her. How could anything be all right when her husband openly rejected her? And she worried when she didn't see her stepfather in the great hall for the evening meal. Calum was a boastful man and delighted in the fact that he was the father-in-law of the future clan chieftain. His absence told her that he was off somewhere brooding, and no good came of Calum's brooding. She would need to be on guard, for her stepfather was a devious man and one who certainly couldn't be trusted.

Normally, she waited for her husband to announce that they would take their leave. However, she could not bare another moment of sly glances and whispers. She wanted to be gone; off to hide, as most would assume, and wallow in pity. However, she simply wanted peace of mind and heart for the remainder of the night.

She placed a gentle hand on her husband's arm where he sat beside her. "Cavan."

He turned, not to stare at her, but rather at her

hand where it lay lightly on his forearm. After several seconds passed he finally looked at her.

"I am not feeling well—"

"What is wrong?" he asked anxiously, and took her hand.

His dark eyes filled with concern, and she thought perhaps it was a trick of light from the flames in the fireplace, and so she held his gaze. His concern didn't vanish, but appeared to grow with worry.

"Honora?" he questioned nervously.

She lowered her head with a barely detectable shake. What was he doing to her? One minute it appeared as if he could care less for her, and the next he looked as if he was worried to death over her.

"I shall fetch the healer," he said, and would have stood if not for her hand stopping him with a light tug.

"I ache for sleep, that is all," she said, not wanting to upset him.

"You tired yourself on the moors today," he insisted.

She didn't want to tell him that she'd walked the moors too many years to ever tire herself out walking them, but it was easier letting him think what he wished.

Leaning close to him, she whispered, "May I take my leave?"

She near shivered when she saw passion ignite in his eyes, though she chastised herself for even thinking such a ridiculous notion. How then did she explain that glint, the fire that flamed in his dark orbs?

He placed his cheek next to hers so he could murmur in her ear. "Do you wish me to carry you?"

His hot breath fanned her neck, and if she didn't hold herself stiff she would have collapsed against him. Was he inviting an interlude or he simply being a good husband? If she accepted, would he reject her once they entered the room? Would she once again appear the fool?

Honora did not have the stamina for further rejection this evening. She responded softly, with some regret, "No, I will be fine on my own."

He moved away from her and with dark eyes that now accused and said, "As you wish."

She hesitated a moment, for it wasn't what she wished. She wished for her husband to claim his husbandly rights and seal their wedding vows. He was the one who had made it clear he didn't want her and rejected her. What did he expect from her?

"Change your mind?" he challenged.

His grin annoyed her. "Have you?" she snipped, and with a huff turned and left the hall.

She thought he might follow, annoyed with her, but heard no heavy footfalls behind her, and Cavan was too large and solidly built for her not to hear him, though he'd informed her earlier how he would teach her to sneak about undetected.

The thought caused her to pause anxiously on the staircase and wait. After several silent minutes passed without hearing anything or without anyone approaching, she continued up the stairs.

She shed her garments, quickly slipping into the comfort of her pale blue, soft wool night shift, and crawled into bed beneath the safety of the coverlet. Why she felt safe in the bed, she didn't know, although it could be because Cavan had never once attempted to share the bed with her. Since that first day nearly a month ago, he'd slept on the floor.

She had tried to make sense of his preference, and did not want to think that he preferred the floor to sharing a bed with her, though what other explanation would make sense, she could not say.

Yawns attacked her, and her eyes grew heavy. She was grateful that sleep would soon claim her and she would no longer dwell on her worries. For a time, at least, she would be free, she thought, and snuggled contentedly under the cover.

When she woke, it was as if someone had nagged her out of sleep. She lay still for a moment, expecting someone to nudge her further awake. Then she heard the sound, a groaning or mewling of sorts; she was not quite sure how to define it, though there was no doubt that someone suffered.

Surely no animal had crawled in the room, so that meant . . .

She turned on her side and peered over the edge of the bed. Her husband lay as he did night after night in front of the hearth; only tonight his sleep appeared disturbed. His body jerked and the strange sounds continued in depth and strength.

He was in the throes of a nightmare. He had tossed his covers off and looked to be shivering. The room did feel chilled, and she noticed that the fire had dwindled more than usual. Had Cavan forgotten to add a log before he fell asleep? He always made sure to stoke the fire before bedding down for the night. Had his mind been so overwrought that he paid no heed to the fire? And if so, what was on his mind?

She wished they could talk. She had not had a trusted friend since her mother died. Calum chased away any lad who showed interest in her, and frightened away any young girls who had attempted to befriend her. He had been successful in keeping her isolated.

Now she longed for a friend, a good friend, a trusted friend, and thought how wonderful it would be for that friend to be her husband.

His sorrowful groan caused her to bolt up in bed, and she saw that his shivers had turned to a constant tremble. Quitely, she eased out of bed and slowly made her way over to her husband. She picked up the wool blanket crumbled at Cavan's feet and gently placed it over her husband, covering him from his bare feet to his bare shoulders, his kilt covering what lay in between.

His shivers eased though didn't entirely dissipate, and she crept around him and as quietly as possible added a couple of logs to the fire. She jumped back when one popped and cracked loudly, not wanting Cavan to see her if he should wake, but the sounds did not disturb him.

She hunched down a fair distance from him, as he had warned her to do earlier when facing a foe. And at the moment she wasn't sure if he was friend or foe, so if he should wake, she didn't want to be in arm's reach of him. His eyelids fluttered and his mouth twitched, and though he'd stopped trembling and grown silent, his sleep still appeared disturbed.

The scar on his face appeared red and sore from the fire's light, and she cringed thinking what he must have suffered. He never spoke of his capture by the barbarians. She assumed he shared the details with his father or brothers, though she'd noticed that he hadn't spent much time with any of them since his return. He seemed to isolate himself, as she herself had.

While the scar on his face attested to his suffering, she wondered if it was the scars no one saw that caused the most damage. She knew all too well about invisible scars, for she had suffered with them for years.

She edged a hand out to softly brush stray strands of hair off his cheek, and wished she could touch him and help ease his ache, just as she wished for someone to ease hers. He didn't wake, and she daringly stroked his hair. It wasn't soft or coarse, but thick and strong, like him.

His heavy sigh had her retreating into the dark a few inches away. She waited, barely breathing so he would not know she was there, but he didn't wake. She saw that his sleep had turned content and hoped she had helped him achieve the peaceful slumber.

She wished this man would be a husband to her and that they could have a good life together, otherwise he and she would always be alone and lonely. But how did she get him to see reason, the wisdom in such a match?

He stirred again but remained asleep.

Honora struggled with what she felt were her inadequacies as a wife and as a woman, and with no one to turn to, she felt completely alone. She missed her mother at that moment, for she had always been there to guide and advise and to love her unconditionally.

Addie was good to her and often attempted to talk with her, but she felt there was only so much she could comfortably discuss with Addie. She was Cavan's mother, after all, and there was a strong protective bond between mother and son; as there had been between herself and her mother.

Honora's soft gaze fell over her husband and she smiled sadly before whispering, "We could be happy you and I, if only . . . "

Cavan didn't stir; he didn't hear her, and she hadn't meant him to, though perhaps she hoped somehow the words would settle over him, seep deep inside and touch his heart and soul.

She stood, stretched the kinks from her legs, and gave her husband one last glance before returning to her bed and slipping beneath the blanket. Then she peeked over the edge of the bed to take one last look at her husband.

Chapter 13

$\sim\!\!\infty\!\!\sim$

Cavan stretched himself awake, rolling his shoulders and arching his back, then suddenly jolted up. His glance went directly to the bed, and sure enough it was empty. How did Honora sneak out without him hearing her? He shook his head and coughed a laugh, recalling how he intended to teach her to move about unnoticed and that she apparently already possessed the skill.

He stood with a stretch, working the stiffness out of his back and legs, and stopped abruptly, glancing down at the blanket. He stared at the crumpled piece of wool and fought to remember.

It hit him like a punch to the gut, and he almost stumbled back from the blow. He had woken in the middle of the night, his blanket pulled up over his shoulders, the fire stoked, and thought he had seen his wife peeking at him over the edge of the bed.

Had she tucked the blanket over him?

He scooped up the blanket and rubbed the soft wool between his fingers. He recalled kicking it off him and shivering, the ambers dying in the hearth. He cursed himself for having forgotten to

stoke the fire last night. He'd drowned his sorrows
and his desire for his wife in too much drink. He
had given her a choice last night—why, he couldn't
say—and she'd rejected him and it hurt him more
than he wanted to admit, more than he wanted
to feel. He drank after that with his brothers and
father, arguing over the search for Ronan until, in
disgust, he had left them and stumbled to his room.
He collapsed before the hearth after stripping off
his shirt and discarding his sandals, and pulled the
blanket over him.

He remembered kicking the blanket off and the
dreams—no, the nightmares—of his capture. His
time with the barbarians haunted him mercilessly
and forever disturbed his sleep.

Why then had he woken with the blanket over
him and his wife peering over the edge of the bed at
him, and with the fire blazing?

He shook the hazy thoughts from his mind to
clear his head for a more vivid recall. His findings
startled him, actually had him thinking he was
crazy for believing what he remembered.

His wife had seen to his care. She had covered
him with the blanket and stoked the fire.

Why?

He had hardly been a good husband to her, and
yet she'd tended him.

Why?

He had ignored her, spoken carelessly to her, and
still she looked after him.

Why?

She was his wife and that was her duty.

He shook his head. He couldn't say he knew his wife well, but he felt as if he knew something about Honora—that she cared and had a good heart. She was a good, honest woman. Why then had *he* rejected her?

He growled, the rumble coming deep from his chest until it burst forth like an angry snarl. Why did he fight himself? Why deny his wife? Why deny having a good life?

Ronan.

He felt responsible for his brother's capture and could not escape the guilt. He should have protected Ronan. He should have saved him from the barbarians. He would never forget the look on his youngest brother's face as the barbarians dragged him away.

Ronan had been filled with pure fear.

Cavan shook his head, chasing away the painful memory.

He did not deserve to live, to have a good life, until he found his brother and set things right. He didn't deserve Honora and her kind nature, but she did deserve to be protected. And if he wasn't around to protect her, then he wanted to make certain she could take care of herself.

Today his wife would have her first lesson in defending herself.

He dressed, though did not hurry. He knew that Honora would not be far, and whether on the moor, in the kitchen, or in the sewing room, she would be alone. In a way, she was much like him of late, seeking solitude, putting herself at a distance from others.

They were a pair, the two of them, an unlikely pair but matching nonetheless. He almost chuckled at the thought. If he was honest with himself, he'd admit that Honora had brought a smile to his face on several occasions.

He quickly lost the smile. There was no time for frivolity. He had his search for Ronan to concentrate on, and to make certain his wife knew how to protect herself.

Artair was at the table in front of the hearth when he entered the great hall, which was near empty. The few who remained quickly took their leave when he joined his brother. It was obvious that Artair had purposely waited for him.

"Do I get to eat before you pounce on me?" Cavan asked, sitting across from him.

Artair grinned. "Now you sound like the brother I knew."

"He is no more," Cavan snapped.

"I disagree. My brother may battle foes unknown to me, but he is still my brother, and I would fight to the death beside him, whether asked or not."

"I can fight my own battles," Cavan argued.

"I recall fighting more often together than separate."

"What do you want of me?" Cavan asked irritably.

"I want my brother to return."

"I have," Cavan said curtly.

Artair shook his head. "No, you haven't. You keep to yourself and sulk—"

"I do not sulk—"

"You sulk like a spoiled child."

"I warn you, Artair, watch your words."

"Does the truth hurt?"

"What do you know of the truth?" Cavan snarled, his fisted knuckles turning white.

"Enlighten me," Artair challenged.

Cavan near snorted with anger. How dare his brother disrespect him? How dare he judge him? How dare he . . .

He released a deep breath, and with it went some of his anger, though not all, for that would take time. And then there was the beast inside him, which could very well reside there permanently. What he did know was that Artair didn't deserve his anger, that he sought an explanation. However, he wasn't certain yet if he could give Artair an adequate one, or if he was even ready to discuss it with him.

Artair had always been the sensible one. The brother who reasoned and found solutions on many occasions when others thought there were none. Cavan had counted on his pragmatic nature many times, and Artair had never failed him, had never failed anyone. How then would Artair understand that he thought himself a failure?

"You wouldn't understand," Cavan said, returning his attention to his brother.

"I have before. What makes you believe this time would be any different?"

"Because it is different."

"Why, because you say so? Share this burden that so obviously weighs on your shoulders with me so that I may help you carry it."

That was Artair, taking on everyone's problem and solving it, and damned if he didn't find solutions. But it wasn't always for him to solve. This burden was his and his alone, and only he could ease the weight.

"This time it is for me to do, brother."

"Hear what you say, *brother*. Brothers help each other. We may argue, even throw punches on occasion, and sometimes not like each other for one ridiculous reason or another, but brothers we are and that means always looking out for each other."

"Like I did for Ronan?"

"You did what you could and—"

"I should have done more," Cavan snapped.

"You are not Ronan's keeper."

Cavan laughed gruffly. "In one breath you tell me brothers always look out for each other and in another you say I am not my brother's keeper."

"You forget I said I would always stand by your side whether asked or not. I did not say I would stand in front of you or behind you, but *beside* you. You never stopped seeing Ronan as your youngest brother who needed protecting. Ronan is a warrior and he will do what he must to survive and return home, just as you have. So stop pitying yourself and be a brother once again."

Artair stood with a shake of his head and walked out of the great hall.

Cavan didn't follow his brother's departure; he turned instead to gaze aimlessly at the hearth. What did Artair know? He wasn't there to hear the crack of the whip and know in a second that the leather would split the flesh open. He didn't know of the filth and stench he had to endure, or what he'd been forced to eat to survive, or of the never ending cold that crept into your bones and caused your innards to shiver. And then there were the screams and pleading of the tortured ringing endlessly in your ears long after they had died, and wondering if one of them could be your brother, though praying it wasn't.

Cavan shook the memories out of his head. They always brought anger with them, and while one day he would use that anger to seek his revenge, he knew it did him no good now to dwell on it. It only caused him to feel alone, removed from family and friends, from everything around him. And for the first time since his return, he didn't want to feel removed. He wanted to find his wife and teach her to survive in case he could not be there for her, in case he failed her, as he had his brother.

Cavan found her in the stable with a litter of pups about five weeks old. She laughed as they scampered over her crossed legs and tumbled around in the hay. Their tiny tails wagged joyously and their brave barks were nothing more then a squeak.

Honora scooped up an all black pup, a plump one that she seemed to favor as the pup did her. She cuddled it in her lap, and it jumped up against her chest, licking her face, and she cuddled the dog to her breasts and planted kisses on his face.

Cavan waited in the shadow. When the pup scampered closer to him, his little backside raised in the air with tail wagging, small paws stretched out in front of him while he challenged Honora with a bark, Cavan scooped him up.

The little fellow was so shocked it took him a moment to attack Cavan's fingers with tiny teeth that could not break the skin. He squirmed and protested with barks, but his efforts were futile. He was captured.

"You're upsetting him," Honora said, hurrying to her feet, the other puppies sensing danger and running off to hide.

"Be still," he ordered the puppy harshly, and the animal froze with fright.

"You're frightening him," Honora accused, and rushed Cavan. "Let him go."

In a second Honora was captured as the pup had been. Cavan had his arm tight against her neck and another arm tight around her waist, her back plastered tight against his body. The pup was on the ground bravely trying to help Honora, nipping at Cavan's sandals and barking.

Cavan gave him a gentle shove with his foot and the little fellow cried and ran off.

Honora elbowed Cavan in the rib and hit her mark.

"Brave but stupid," he said in her ear. "Now you've angered your captor and he will retaliate by punishing you."

"You were going to hurt the pup," she accused.

"You cared nothing for your safety, you merely thought of the pup, and that was why I was able to capture you so easily. You didn't think it through. You simply charged forward in anger. First rule of battle, do not let anger rule. It is an unwise leader."

He felt her relax against him once she realized his actions were meant to teach.

He gripped her more tightly and she gasped, yanking at his arm at her throat. "Never let your defenses down when in the presence of your foe," he said, and released her abruptly.

She stumbled away, the black pup appearing at her side to bark at Cavan, though from beneath the safety of Honora's brown skirt.

"Quiet!" Cavan commanded, and the pup vanished beneath the skirt.

"When he grows, the pup will protect me," Honora said in the little dog's defense.

"Only if you teach him as I teach you."

Honora hesitated. "I would like that, to teach the pup."

"To make him yours?" Cavan asked with a ridiculous twinge of jealously. How could he be jealous of a pup?

"If that would be all right with you?"

He wished she was strong enough to claim the pup as hers no matter what he said, then realized that had been her intention all along. She merely wanted him to believe she sought his approval.

He smiled, realizing he knew his wife better than he'd thought. "You would do it anyway, wouldn't you?"

She reached down, scooped up the pup from

beneath her skirt and hugged him against her breast. The little fellow delighted in the attention and cuddled closer to her. "Yes, I would. He's irresistible."

"Teach him to protect you and he is yours," Cavan challenged.

"He will learn along with me," she said with confidence, though the kisses she rained over his face had Cavan doubting and that twinge of jealously nipping sharply at him once again.

"We start now. The pup is too young. Once weaned off his mother there will be time to start training him."

Honora nodded and smiled at the pup, which was too playful for her to continue to hold. She placed him on the ground and he scampered off to join the other pups in play. "My lesson for today?"

"Know that an enemy will use whatever means he can against you."

"You refer to my love for the pup."

"Correct. Once I saw how you cared, it was easy to use him to get to you," Cavan said, her violet eyes intent on his, which wasn't good since the strange color always stirred his senses.

"How do I free myself from the hold you had on me?"

He'd had a good hold of her. She had been so firm against him that he could feel her every breath, sense her fear, smell her womanly sweat, which instantly intoxicated him. It was all too familiar to him now, and all too appealing. That was why he'd released her abruptly; he couldn't chance keeping her that close, so near that he could almost taste or want to taste her.

"Does your silence tell me that the question challenges you?" She teased with a smile, and he liked it. It showed she had courage.

He grinned. "It is you who are challenged. How do you think you could extract yourself from such a situation? The man is larger, stronger than you. How do you escape his binding hold?"

She paced the stall for a moment then stopped. "Can we resume the positions of my capture?"

"Certainly," he said, and within seconds she was once again flat up against him, his arm not as tight to her neck or her waist, which he told himself was for his own sanity not her comfort.

She began to take deep breaths as if she struggled to breathe, her body heaving against him, her bottom flush to his groin and digging in with each heavy breath. She tried yanking at his arm, squirming, kicking, and with each thrust his groin hardened until finally . . .

In a second Cavan had her on her back on the hay strewn ground, him on top of her. Her eyes bulged in shock and her chest heaved as he remained spread over her, her wrists clamped tight in his one hand.

"Now I'll show you the results of your inept attempt to escape."

His hand shot down to pull her skirt up while his fingers crawled along the soft flesh between her legs, but with much difficulty he stopped himself from going any further.

"See what would be done to you," he said through labored breath.

Her breasts heaved against him, her cheeks flushed red, her breath turned rapid, and her violet eyes begged.

"Not the way to escape," he said through gritted teeth, fighting his passion, his need to take her there and then. She was his wife; he had every right, but no right to frighten her.

She nodded, her breathing labored, her fear palpable.

He groaned without realizing it and rested his forehead to hers. "I will kill anyone who dares lay a hand on you," he said. "You belong to me."

Chapter 14

Honora sat in the sewing room staring at the flames dancing wildly in the hearth, her arms wrapped around her, fighting a persistent chill. She didn't recall her walk from the stable to the keep, her mind too busy with thoughts of what had just happened between Cavan and her.

She had been shocked how fast she found herself on the ground and he on top of her. And if that hadn't stunned her enough, there was the way he had intimately touched her, but worse than that, the way she'd felt about it.

Another shiver claimed her, though she knew it was not from being cold, but from her surprising response to her husband's touch and the knowledge that she knew he would not hurt her or force her. She knew him to be a good man. She'd known as much before she even met him, for the villagers had often spoken of his courage with respect. He had proven that with his determination to find his brother Ronan, and in the many ways he'd protected her. He even followed her into the forest so many believed was haunted with magic.

She thought it brave of him to come to her rescue, while the village gossiped over his odd behavior since his return and that he could emerge from the strange forest unaffected.

Then there was the kiss that she could not forget. She ran gentle fingers over her moist lips recalling the taste of her husband. It had made her tingle inside and out and she hadn't wanted him to stop. She enjoyed it more than she ever imagined possible. Her hand drifted away, returning to hug herself against the continued cold.

She not only enjoyed his kiss, but now found pleasure in his touch. The thought alarmed and thrilled her and left her completely confused.

And his claim, *You belong to me and I will kill anyone who dares lay a hand on you*, fed a need in her. Finally, she belonged to someone who cared enough to protect her. She had not felt similar comfort since her mother died. She'd struggled alone to survive the brutality of her stepfather, and that would no longer be necessary. She had a husband to protect her and a family who seemed to care for her, even if it was out of duty.

This marriage was proving beneficial in so many different ways. She never thought she would be grateful to her stepfather for arranging it, but if viewing the situation with prudence, she realized her marriage was the best thing that had ever happened to her.

There was just the matter of getting her husband to see the wisdom of their union and, of course, of sealing their vows.

The door creaked opened and Honora turned to see the pudgy black pup nosing his way around inside with a peek. Spotting her, he charged as fast as his little legs would carry him.

Honora plopped cross-legged on the floor and the pup jumped, though actually tripped over her folded legs to stretch his paws up on her chest and lick at her chin, his tail wagging wildly.

"How did you ever—"

"The little fellow seemed miserable without you so I thought I'd bring him for a visit."

Honora was surprised to see Cavan at the open door, his arms crossed over his broad chest, leaning against the door frame.

"After all, he does belong to you now."

Her face lit with delight. "Truly? You do not mind?"

"I like the thought of someone else besides me protecting you, and someone I can trust unconditionally."

"You will help me teach him," she said, rather than asked, and watched the pup make a beeline for the basket of garments in need of stitching, jumping in, only to knock the basket and himself over.

Cavan walked into the room and scooped the pup from amid the strewn garments. "I think he'll need many lessons."

Honora smiled at the way the pup seemed to take to Cavan. He didn't appear as frightened as before, and Cavan even seemed different toward the animal, more friendly and loving.

"As will I," she said bravely. "I did not fair well with the first lesson."

Cavan dumped the pup gently in Honora's lap and lowered himself beside her on the floor, his knee raised and his arm braced over it. Her breath near caught, for the firelight captured the rugged angles and lines of his handsome face perfectly.

"What matters is that you tried," he insisted.

"I also learned a valuable lesson," she said softly, favoring the deep richness of his dark eyes. There was not only strength in the dark depths, but integrity, and dare she acknowledge a spark of passion?

"What lesson is that?"

"Think before I leap," she said with a gentle smile.

"A wise tactic for any warrior."

"Lachlan thinks me a warrior," she said, petting the pup, who had curled up contentedly in the hollow of her lap.

"Lachlan is perceptive, especially when it comes to women."

"He chases after them all," she said with a giggle.

"You noticed."

Honora rolled her eyes. "You would have to be blind not to see, though I think the women favor Artair, for he is very handsome."

"You think my brother handsome?" he asked tartly.

The sting of his accusation surprised her. "I voice what everyone believes and is obvious."

He grinned, though she believed grudgingly. "You are right. I suppose I am jealous."

He startled her, and she was quick to ask. "Whatever for?"

"You think Artair handsome. What of me?"

She smiled softly and lowered her glance. "I like the look of you."

He lifted her chin gently with his one finger. "Truly?"

"Yes. There is much your features tell me."

His finger drifted off her. "What do my features tell you?"

She bravely scooted closer to him and reached out to tenderly trace the fine lines at the corner of his eyes. "These faint lines tell me of the wisdom you put into your thoughts and decisions." Her finger traveled ever so lightly to his chin. "Your chin juts just enough to let me know you can be stubborn."

His eyes danced with merriment though he said nothing.

Her finger casually traced his lips. "The faint fan lines circling your mouth tell me that you have not spoken often in anger, but rather hold tight to your words and give thought before you speak." She returned to his eyes, her finger caressing beneath each one. "The color of your eyes brightens and darkens with your moods." She lowered her voice to a whisper. "And with your passion." She quickly ran her finger to his scar and with a feather-light touch traced the length of it. "This scar speaks of your strength and courage." She wanted to cringe, imagining the pain he must have suffered, but she would not ask, not remind him of such a horrifying experience. Her finger hurried to run down along his nose. "And this?" She tapped the tip. "Tells me nothing."

She laughed as she moved away from him, though her heart beat wildly in her chest and rippling heat replaced shivering chill. Lord, but she wanted to kiss him, taste him once again, though she hadn't when she first started touching him. She'd simply intended to answer his question. She had not thought her innocent demonstration would strike such passion in her.

Had it in him?

The thought spread her smile and she took a good look at him. He sat stock still, not moving an inch, simply staring at her, though his chest looked to heave a bit more heavily, unless her eyes played tricks. Or it was wishful thinking?

"Have I answered you satisfactorily?" she asked, breaking the awkward silence.

He nodded, and she thought he didn't intend to speak, but he did. "You examine me with more thought than I imagined."

"How else will I learn about my husband?"

"You wish to know more of me?" he asked.

"Why wouldn't I? You are my husband. We will share much together through the years. I would prefer to be friends rather than foes."

"You expect the same from me?"

Honora was relieved that he asked inquisitively, not accusingly, as if she had no right to expect that of him.

"I hoped . . . " She paused, wondering if it was right of her to express her hopes or whether she should simply accept the way things were. After all, her marriage had been arranged. She was expected to be a good wife and do her duty, but that didn't mean she and Cavan couldn't be friends. "I hoped you would want the same."

He appeared to weigh her words, almost wonder over them, as if he hadn't given their marriage the same thought and the idea required savoring.

Honora focused on the pup. They had befriended each other so easily, but then, there were no expectations between them, simply friendship.

"We are husband and wife," he said, as if that clarified it.

"That does not make us friends. You had not wished to wed me."

"But now you are my wife."

"So you have no choice but to be my friend?" she asked.

"We have no choice but to be husband and wife."

"But we have a choice to be friends." If nothing else, that choice could be a beginning for them both, a beginning of a good friendship, and if nothing else, at least they would have that between them.

"This is important to you?"

What chance did they have if he couldn't even bring himself to be her friend? Did he resent her that much? She could understand his reluctance and even his anger, returning home to find himself wed to a woman not of his choosing. And while he had no choice but to accept what had been done, he had a choice of how to live with it, with her.

"Is it not to you?"

"As I said, we are husband and wife, and will remain so. What does friendship matter?"

She thought to debate the issue with him, but what good would it do if he had no interest in being friends? It was enough to him that she was his wife; that status apparently covered it all.

Why did she bother to look for more from him? He would provide for her and protect her because it was his duty. Friendship she would need to find elsewhere.

Honora lifted and cradled the sleeping pup to her breast. "He will be my friend."

Cavan scowled to a stand. "I should return him to his mother so he can feed."

"I will take him."

"No," Cavan snapped. "Do your stitching, I will see to the pup."

"I would prefer to take him myself," she said, moving out of reach of his helping hand as she struggled to stand with the pup.

Cavan stepped forward, grabbed her around the waist and pulled her up. She stumbled against him and he held her firm, never disturbing the sleeping pup.

"The weather has turned cold—"

"A little cold will not bother me," she said, and moved away from him.

Why she debated the point with him, she couldn't say. She should simply let him take the pup to his mother to feed, and yet she argued, wanting to tend to the task herself. Or was it that she wanted to do as she pleased, not as she was told?

An odd thought since she had always without question done what she'd been told. This time, however, she felt protective of the pup and wished to look after him herself.

"Need I order you to remain here?" he asked sternly.

The pup woke and yawned, his tail wagging as soon as he looked at Honora.

"The pup is my responsibility," she insisted more firmly than intended.

"Not if I say otherwise."

"You go back on your word?" she challenged, her chin up, along with her temper.

He appeared so affronted by her accusation that she was surprised he hadn't stumbled from the blow.

"I do not renege on my word."

"Good, then I will see to *my* pup *myself.*"

"He is your pup but I will—"

"Leave his care to me," she finished, and headed for the door.

"Stop!"

Honora obeyed, though she swerved around to face him with a stern posture and sharp words. "Tell me, husband, do you wish me to give you children?"

"What kind of question is that? Of course I do."

"Will you expect me to protect and care for them?"

"What game do you play with me? Of course I expect you to be a good mother."

"But the question truly is, do you trust me to be

one? After all, you truly do not know me and we truly are not friends."

She walked out the door, stopped and returned to stand in the doorway, Cavan looking stunned.

"By the way, the pup's name is Champion, for he truly is my champion, since I have no doubt he will love me unconditionally, as I will him. He is my best friend."

She left, tears brimming in her eyes, hugging Champion to her breasts as he licked wildly at her chin.

"I will love you, always and always, Champion, have no doubt about that and I will protect you always. You, dear Champion, are my only friend."

Chapter 15

❧

Cavan played with Champion in the stable while waiting for his wife. The pup was rambunctious, not afraid but determined. He would serve Honora well. Cavan shook his head, still confused by what had transpired yesterday in the sewing room. He had seen a side of Honora that his wife had never revealed to him, and while her defiance stunned him, he'd also admired it. Beneath the mousy exterior she presented to everyone lurked the makings of a courageous woman.

It had even surprised him when she suggested they become friends. She all but admitted she wanted more from their marriage than just an arrangement. However, he worried whether he could give her what she wanted. A friend was always there for you, always reached out to help, to protect, and he had failed to do that with Ronan, his own brother.

How could he befriend his wife and then fail her? The disturbing thought nagged at him as badly as the memories of Ronan's capture.

"I brought food for us to enjoy after our lesson

is finished," Honora said, placing the basket high enough away from a sniffing, tail wagging pup and the other pups that suddenly appeared out of nowhere, chasing the scrumptious scent.

Cavan forced a smile aside. He would not have her seeing how pleased he was with her actions and her appearance. She wore a simple brown skirt and tan blouse, her cloak discarded along with the basket. Her long shiny black hair fell straight over her shoulders like a silky mantle framing her lovely features. She was a beauty, though not in the classic sense, since she was distinct, set apart from others, which made her beauty all the more potent.

She eagerly plopped on the hay-strewn ground to greet Champion, and the pup went wild. It was obvious that they had formed an attachment, and Cavan was hit with a twinge of envy. He silently admonished his foolishness and reached down to yank Honora to her feet.

The pup protested with a cry, and Honora scooped him up to comfort him with a hug and a kiss. "I will play with you when we are done, and I have a special treat for you and the other pups." She returned him to the ground, patted his rump, and gave him a little shove toward the pups in play.

"You will spoil him," Cavan snapped.

To his surprise, she simply laughed and nodded.

"Yes, I will spoil him, but then I love him and have the right to spoil him if I wish."

Damn, if her words didn't twist like a knife in his gut. She would rain love all over the animal with touches, kisses, and special treatment, and the pup would blossom and grow even more protective of her.

But then wouldn't she do the same for a husband she loved?

Another twist to the gut for him.

"What is my lesson today?"

He realized his lesson for the day, and it was a hard one to swallow, though a simple one to follow. *Love your wife and she will love you.*

He shook the thought from his head.

"Not sure?" she asked with a smile that struck like a well-aimed arrow.

"Extracting yourself from a binding hold."

"You mean a hold like you had me in yesterday?" she asked, her violet eyes sparkling with excitement. "I can actually break free from such a bind?"

"With courage and determination you can."

"You mean I can't be afraid to take the chance."

Cavan nodded. "Hesitation can cost dearly . . . "

He often wondered if it had cost Ronan's capture.

"I would claim I would not hesitate—" She shook her head. "—but I cannot for circumstances may be the deciding factor."

He stared at her as if she'd startled a realization in him and made him wonder if that was what happened with Ronan. Had his love for his brother caused him to react differently?

"You must know that yourself from all the battles you have fought," Honora said. "No battle, no decision, is ever truly the same. There must always be a deciding factor that precludes your decisions, even if it is at a moment's time."

"You would make a wise warrior."

"Really?" she asked, her smile wide.

"I speak truthfully."

"I am honored you should think that of me."

He reached out his hand. "Let's continue to shape you into a warrior."

She brushed his hand away. "No, you must grab me as you did before, so I feel that rush of fright and work through it, knowing it will try to interfere and I must not let it."

There she went, surprising him again, and he reached out with a ferocious growl that had the pups running for cover. He snatched and spun his wife around in his arms until her back was firmly planted against him.

"I can feel you tremble," he whispered in her ear.

"You frightened me as I requested."

"That fright is what will immobilize you, and your captor's most likely filthy breath against your face will add to your fear."

"Your breath is pleasant," she said softly.

"Think of it otherwise," he challenged, doing the same since her breath was sweet and her moist lips inviting.

He almost laughed as she scrunched her nose as if hit by a putrid odor. "What do I do to get away?" she asked anxiously.

"First try to remain out of arm's reach of any attacker. Second, if he grabs you, try to yank yourself free. Give a hard tug, for it will surprise him and give you time to escape, or at least put distance between you and him. If you find yourself in the position you are in now, your first attempt must be to break free and immobilize him."

She nodded, letting him know she understood.

"You bring your heel down on his foot as hard as possible; not merely his toes, but up high. At the same time, jab your elbow into his gut, which should set you free or loose enough to swerve around and slam him in the nose with the heel of your hand. You must do this quickly without thought, just motion and then run. Do not wait around to see the results of your assault. Victory can only be yours if you escape."

"I can do this," she assured him.

"Show me."

She turned her head, her lips grazing his cheek. "I will hurt you."

She already had, and much more than if she'd sent her elbow to his stomach. She had sparked his passion, and damn if he could contain it. "I will prevent each strike. I wish to see the force with which you deliver them."

"Promise you will not let me hurt you?"

He didn't want to offend her by telling her he'd have her on her back as fast as he had yesterday. That would have defeated the purpose of the lesson. He appeased her, and her sincere concern for him simply fueled his passion. "I promise."

She smiled and kissed his cheek before turning her face away from him. "Good, then I can be determined."

He barely had time to yank his foot away from her sharp attack, his cheek tingling and sending heat out to the rest of his body. He moved just in time to avoid her elbow and jolted his head back, quickly raising his hand to suffer the blow of her swing.

She stepped away from him with a huge smile. "How did I do?"

He grabbed her around the waist and dragged her up against him, his lips near touching hers. "You didn't run."

Too late he realized she didn't tremble, and by then the heel of her foot came down on his and he released her from the sheer shock of her unexpected attack. She was gone in a flash. Where? He hadn't seen.

He applauded her success while hobbling over to a bale of straw to sit. "Very good. You passed the lesson."

Honora bowed playfully after emerging from the shadows of a nearby stall. "Thank you."

She startled him when she hurried over and plopped down in front of him to examine his foot. "I am sorry, but I wanted to see if I could actually do it and—" She hesitated. "—make you proud of me." She tugged off the soft leather boot he wore and winced at the red mark. "I hurt you. My actions were foolish."

"They were those of a worthy warrior. I am proud of you."

"Truly?' she asked.

"Truly. And as for my foot? The little pain I suffer is worth it for I now know my wife will not hesitate in protecting herself."

"I am eager for you to teach me more," she said, examining his reddened flesh with a tender touch.

Her cool fingers felt good against the welt that emerged on his instep. He didn't want her to stop touching him. He closed his eyes as her cool hand settled over his foot and magically turned the heat to a tingle. The strange sensation crawled along his skin until it reached his groin, and he knew that was where he wished her hand had settled.

His eyes sprung open, startled, when he felt a tongue lick his toes, and he wasn't at all surprised to see it was Champion.

"We should eat," he said, grabbing his boot to put on after nudging the puppy off him.

"Then we will resume the lessons?" Honora asked, spreading her cloak on the ground and retrieving the basket.

"You are an eager pupil." Cavan took the basket from her and assisted her to sit, then plopped down opposite her while she spread out the food.

"I never imagined that I would enjoy combat."

"What I teach you is far from combat. Battle gives no time for thought or reason, or fear. One charges in and lashes out until nothing is left standing around you."

He recalled how he had stood that day on the battlefield surrounded by enemy, knowing he had lost the battle, and with a good chance of losing his life. It had been when he heard his brother Ronan screaming for help, and when he looked, his blood had turned cold. Ronan lay on the ground covered in blood and crying out in pain. Raising his sword, he attempted to cut a path to his brother's side. If they were to die they would die together. Then he was felled by a sword and landed inches from his brother. Their hands had reached out, their fingers barely touching when they were both dragged away, never to see each other again.

"You are right," Honora said, interrupting his thoughts. "I probably would not fare well in combat, but it is good to know I could protect myself if necessary."

Cavan grabbed hold of her chin. "Did your stepfather beat you daily?"

She paled and moved away from him, wrapping protective arms around her middle as the pup seemingly scurried to comfort her. Cavan had his answer without her speaking a word, and he cursed beneath his breath for the abuse and fear she'd had to endure.

She scooped the persistent pup up, nuzzled her face with his, his tiny pink tongue licking her with kisses, then she took a small sack and opened it, spreading the tiny bits of meat for the pup to enjoy. The other pups scampered over to get their fair share, stumbling over each other to get to the food.

He reached for a chunk of brown bread and waited patiently for an answer.

She handed him a hunk of cheese and sliced an apple, sharing the pieces with him before she spoke.

"He beat me often enough."

"You don't wish to speak of it?" he challenged.

"What is there to speak of? Calum has a heavy hand and that is the way of it."

"He need not hit you," Cavan argued.

"Right or wrong, it is the way of some men, and women can do no more than survive."

"I will not raise a hand to you."

"I know," she said, handing him another slice of apple.

He was surprised by her stanch reply. What was it that made her know, not doubt, that he would never raise a hand against her?

"How can you be so sure?" he asked.

"You are an honorable man."

Cavan dusted his hands roughly. "Don't be so sure."

"But I am," she insisted.

"You do not know me well enough to make such an assumption," he argued.

"It is not an assumption. It is fact."

"How so?" he asked, perplexed.

"You took my father to task for raising his hand to me. If you did not find his action objectionable, you would have ignored him."

"You forget you are my wife," he reminded.

"And as such I am afforded protection," she said. "Only an honorable man would react as you did."

A vision of Ronan, their fingers almost grasping, a look of sheer terror in his young eyes, pleading for his older brother to help him, to save him, assaulted Cavan like a slap in the face, and he quickly turned his head away. "I am not an honorable man."

"Do not deny the truth."

"You do not know what you say—" He raised his hand, warding off her response. "I will hear no more."

"Why do you refuse to listen and accept the truth?"

He pinned her with an angry glare. "Why do you speak when I order silence?"

She lowered her head. "Forgive me. I thought we had entered into a fair discussion."

Her accurate accusation caused him to relent with a partial grin. "We did."

She raised her head with a smile. "A fair answer then for a fair question?"

First he had to catch his breath. Her smile, the way her violet eyes lit with joy, her moist pink lips, and her chin thrust just enough in the air to appear victorious, all of it did him in. For a moment he got a peek at who she struggled to become, a woman strong enough to say what she thought without repercussions, and oddly enough, he had been the means that allowed her to take steps toward that strength. It made him feel good that he could give her that.

"Why do you refuse to believe yourself an honorable man?" she asked.

Did he confide in his wife? Did he tell her what haunted him? Did he confess his guilt? He had confided in no one the details of his and Ronan's capture. How he had failed to protect his brother, and how he would never forgive himself.

The confession came with a sense of relief. "I should have saved my brother."

"You tried."

He glared at her. "How do you know I did?"

"Because that is what an honorable man would do. I'm sure circumstances prevented you from saving him."

Cavan stretched his hand out and held it palm up, staring at his fingers. "I almost had him. He was in my grasp." He closed his hand.

"You were separated?" Honora asked.

Cavan nodded. "He was wounded. I don't know how badly but there was much blood. We were ripped away from each other and I tried to find out where he was taken." He shook his head. "It took months to discover that he was not in the same village as me, and I was never able to find out his location. It was as if he just disappeared, and I feared that he had died of his injuries until one day a slave whispered in my ear that my brother lived."

Cavan's hand fisted tightly. "I heard nothing more after that, and when escape became possible, I had no choice but to leave without any further information."

"You returned home; Ronan will as well," she assured him.

"I am a seasoned warrior; Ronan has little experience in battle."

"He can't be that inexperienced, having had three older brothers. You all must have taught him well. He most certainly will use what talents he has to survive and escape, just as you have. Do not underestimate your brother. He is, after all, a Sinclare, a man of honor and courage and strength."

She thought of his brother and what he was capable of, Cavan realized, while he had focused on how inadequate he'd felt for failing to keep Ronan safe. But then, she hadn't seen the look of terror in his young eyes.

"He needed my help," Cavan insisted.

"You gave what you could."

"It wasn't enough."

"Your guilt will do your brother no good," she said.

"You're wrong," he snapped. "My guilt sustains my hunger for revenge and my brother's recovery. I will find him and make those responsible pay dearly."

"How much will that revenge cost you?"

Cavan grabbed hold of her chin and captured her violet eyes with his dark ones. "I don't care. Whatever the price, I will pay it."

Chapter 16

Honora shielded her eyes against the bright sun that had burned the chill from the air by midday. Cavan had left the stable in a huff, and Champion curled up with the other pups to sleep contentedly after their special meal. Left to herself, she decided a walk on the moors would clear her head.

She was brought to an abrupt halt by the scene that confronted her when she turned the corner of the keep. Her husband was in an argument with Lachlan and it looked as if they would come to blows. She approached with caution and wasn't surprised to hear them squabbling over their missing brother.

A crowd had gathered, whispers circulated, heads shook, and Honora had no doubt that many took Lachlan's side. He was well liked and respected by the clan, and Cavan, since his return, hadn't endeared himself to clan members. He brooded and remained to himself and had only recently begun spending time with her, and that was because he insisted that she learn to protect herself; otherwise she doubted she would have seen much of him. He still continued to sleep on the floor in front of the fireplace. He mostly had remained to himself, showing no interest in the clan, and that caused people to wonder over the worthiness of their future laird.

However, Cavan was her husband, and wifely duty called for her to stand by him no matter her opinion. But after their recent discussion, she better understood what troubled him. He laid full blame on himself for failing to protect his brother, and nothing anyone said could change his mind. He would do anything to find Ronan, even if it meant arguing with his brothers.

In the keep, accusations and threats flew like weapons, each brother, hitting their mark and causing tempers to blaze, no doubt to soon rage out of control. She had to do something or before long fists would fly and gossipers would have fodder to feed their wagging tongues.

How to distract him?

A simple shout would probably be ignored, or Cavan would order her to be gone and she'd have to obey. What was she to do? A sudden thought struck her. Cavan immediately went after her father when he saw that Calum had injured her. What if he thought her ill? Would he come to her aid?

Do not hesitate.

His warning rang in her head. Too much time spent on a decision would cancel its effectiveness. She didn't hesitate. She screamed out to him while clutching her stomach.

"Cavan!"

He turned, his face full of rage.

"Help me," she cried, and letting her body go limp, dropped to the ground in a faint.

She kept her eyes closed as she lay there, and felt the ground tremble beneath her from rushing footfalls.

"Has she been sick?"

Lachlan's voice, not her husband's, though his followed anxiously.

"I don't believe so."

"Perhaps she's with child," Lachlan suggested.

"Perhaps," Cavan said.

His response didn't surprise her; after all, he couldn't very well tell his brother that it was impossible for her to be with child. She almost reacted to his tender touch when his fingers gently pushed her hair away from her face.

"Honora," he said, and she felt him probe her stomach lightly.

Whispers sounded like buzzing bees, and she could only imagine the crowd that had gathered. She had accomplished what she intended, for Cavan and Lachlan argued no more. She fluttered her eyelids and moaned softly.

Cavan urged her awake, repeatedly calling her name, and Honora felt her heart catch. His voice reverberated with sincere concern. He actually worried over her, as if he cared about her, truly cared.

She opened her eyes fully to gaze at her husband, and there for her to see, to confirm her suspicions, concern was written in the tight lines around his eyes, his narrowed brow and tight lips. His worry was real, so very real.

Guilt struck her hard. She wished it hadn't been necessary to make him suffer needlessly, and she cringed for the hurt she caused him.

"What's wrong? Are you in pain?"

"I am not feeling well."

He scooped her up in his arms and stood. He held her close, and she turned her face into his chest, breathing deeply, enticed by his scent, his strength, his concern.

"Get her to bed. I'll go find Mother," Lachlan said, and rushed off.

Cavan carried her without difficulty, as if she weighed no more than a small sack of grain. Crazy as it might seem, she could almost feel him wrap himself protectively around her, and an overwhelming sense of safety washed over her.

She wrapped her arm more tightly around his neck as they entered the keep.

He stopped and asked anxiously, "Are you all right?"

No, she wanted to scream. *I am not all right. I have feelings for you. Damn, I have feelings for you.*

Instead she simply nodded, not wanting to make the ruse worse.

He hurried his steps, and while Honora couldn't wait to get to her bedchamber, she also didn't wish to leave his arms. She felt safe and comfortable cradled in his embrace and could remain there indefinitely, and the thought troubled her.

She sighed when they entered the bedchamber, knowing her time in his arms was done and yearning to be alone so she could make sense of her yearnings.

Surprisingly, and to her relief, Cavan kept hold of her and sat in the chair near the hearth with her cradled in his lap.

"What bothers you?" he asked.

She shook her head, not trusting words for she feared she would blurt out how she was feeling.

"Are you in pain?"

She couldn't look at him for she feared he would see the truth, see her yearning for him. She kept her face buried against his shirt and was about to shake her head again when she realized she had to convince him that she was ill. She might not want to lie to him, but the truth would cause too much pain for them both. And she needed time to sort through her feelings before she let anyone even suspect that she was beginning to care for her husband.

She pressed at her stomach.

His hand followed, easing hers aside, and he gently rubbed where he assumed the source of her discomfort resided. "I would take your pain if I could."

He startled her; this man who earlier had claimed he would do anything to get revenge, who argued viciously with his brother, and who now was willing to suffer so she did not. Just when she thought she was beginning to understand him, he confused her.

"I would not let you have it," she said softly.

He kissed her forehead. "You would have no say in the matter."

"It is my pain," she insisted, and cringed with guilt.

"Rest," he urged, and slipped his hand beneath her waistband to stroke her stomach.

It didn't take long for her innards to tingle, her heart to pound, and her flesh to heat. She moved against his hand with a moan.

"You grow worse," he said.

She bit at her bottom lip, fearing she would spill the truth, not knowing what to do and not wanting to leave his arms. She almost groaned with relief when Addie burst into the room.

"What is wrong?" she asked, hurrying over to them.

"Her stomach," Cavan informed her.

"Put her on the bed," Addie ordered.

Honora saw the reluctance in his face, as if he didn't want to let her go, and she felt the same. She wanted to remain in his arms.

Addie placed a gentle hand on her son's shoulder. "I'll take good care of her."

It was as if Cavan emerged from a stupor. He shook his head then quickly changed it to a nod, stood and carried her to the bed, slowly placing her down. She clung to his neck until she realized she had to let him go and he had to let her go, but their fingers touched and neither one would break the bond.

"Go," Addie urged, giving her son a gentle nudge. "I will look after her."

Honora frowned when her husband broke contact with her, but he immediately returned to her side, taking her hand in his.

"She needs me. I will stay."

Though Honora wanted him to remain with her, she knew it wasn't a wise choice.

"Nonsense," she said, and swallowed hard the lie she was about to tell. "It is your mother I need now, not you."

"Listen to your wife," Addie said, her nudge turning to a gentle shove.

"I will wait outside the door—" Cavan halted a response from both women with an upheld hand. "That is the way it will be."

"As you wish," his mother said. "Now go so I may look after your wife."

"I'll be right outside the door," he reminded, his gaze on his wife, his finger pointing to the door.

Honora smiled that he cared enough to remain close by. "Thank you."

"Nonsense," he said sharply. "I am your husband." He turned and hurried out of the room.

"A husband unexpectedly falling in love with his wife," Addie said once he was gone.

"What did you say?" Honora asked, having heard her but not believing it.

"Let me help you out of your clothes and into your night shift," Addie said, fussing after her. "I've already ordered a brew prepared that will soothe your stomach pains." She paused a moment then added, "Your husband is falling in love with you."

Honora shook her head.

"Of course, he doesn't realize it yet, but I knew once he got to know you he couldn't help fall in love with you."

Honora shook her head again. Or had she ever stopped?

"Deny it if you must, but you will realize it yourself soon enough, as well as your own growing feelings for him."

She stopped shaking her head.

Addie laughed. "I knew it. I could see it in the way you look at my son. You are uncertain, of course, for it is so new to you, but in time you will see and feel it for yourself."

Honora groaned and threw herself back on the bed, but without her blouse, for Addie had slipped it off her.

"I better go see what's keeping that brew," Addie said, and headed to the door.

It was better that her mother-in-law assumed that an ailing stomach had caused the groan and did not know that her groan was due to the remark. It might confirm her own feelings, but to think that her husband could possibly be feeling the same way unnerved her, and yet excited her too.

"Help your wife into her night shift while I see about that brew, her stomach worsens," Honora heard Addie tell her son, and she nearly bolted off the bed. What was she to do? She lay half naked, and at the thought her face reddened and she quickly wrapped her arms over her breasts.

"I need no help changing into my night shift,"

she said as her husband entered the room and approached the bed after closing the door.

A grin spread slowly across his face. "You are making what you try to hide more appealing."

Honora looked down and near groaned, though caught herself. She didn't want Cavan to think her stomach had worsened, but then, he had her bulging breasts to focus on since the way she hugged them made them appear larger than they were.

He hunched down beside the bed and placed his hand on her arm. "I would be a sorry excuse for a husband if I ravaged an ailing wife."

"I know that, it is just that I . . . "

"Have never been naked in front of a man?"

Her eyes turned wide. "Never."

"That is good to hear."

She smiled, relieved that he understood.

"Now let me help you into your night shift," he said.

She sputtered in an attempt to respond.

He laughed softly. "Need I remind you that I am your husband?"

She tightened her arms around her breasts. "Not yet you're not."

He leaned in close and whispered in her ear. "Do you want me to remedy that right now?"

She recalled her earlier tactics, though instead of grabbing her stomach, she cringed. "Please, I need the brew your mother promised would soothe my aching stomach."

He immediately stood, his face flooded with concern. "Stay as you are, I'll be right back."

As soon as he left the room, she hurried to change into her night shift and slip beneath the covers with a sigh, feeling protected.

Cavan entered the room with his mother close on his heels, and shook his head when he saw her.

"You should have waited. I would have helped you," he said, assisting her to sit up and stuffing pillows behind her back.

"I was chilled," she said, pleased that it wasn't completely a lie. Her skin had chilled from lack of clothes and she'd felt herself shiver.

"I'll stoke the fire," Cavan said, tucking the covers up around her waist.

Addie handed her a tankard of steaming broth while Cavan went to tend the hearth.

"This will soothe the ache," Addie assured her.

If the broth was meant to soothe, it certainly couldn't hurt her stomach, so she sipped it without worry.

"It will make her sleep," Addie whispered to her son when he stood beside her, though not low enough that Honora didn't hear.

"I will stay with her," Cavan said.

"Nonsense," his mother argued. "Go and do what you must. I will remain with her."

"There is no pressing matter that needs my attention. I will stay with her."

Honora watched them as a mist settled around her, turning to a fog, and their voices seemed far off in the distance.

"You care for her," the woman said.

"She is my wife." The man sounded stern, possibly annoyed.

Her foggy mind made it difficult for Honora to follow the conversation, though the distinct male and female voices at least let her distinguish the two.

"Some men fall in love with the women they are forced to wed," the woman said.

"We are wed and that will not change. Isn't it better that I at least care for the wife I did not choose?" the man argued.

"It would be advisable." The woman sounded pleased.

"Let it be, Mother, this is between Honora and me."

"No, my son, it isn't. You will lead this clan one day and it would be better for you if you had a loving wife by your side, one you could count on in your darkest moments."

"You want for me what you and Father share," the man said.

"Yes, I want love for you and Honora."

Her name, she heard her name and the word love . . . someone loved her and watched over her, cared for her. That thought brought memories of her mother, and she suddenly felt the pain of her absence, a single tear trickling from the corner of her eye.

"She's crying," the man said, clearly upset.

Honora felt a tender touch on her cheek where the tear had traveled, and then a warm yet strong hand took hold of hers.

"I am here, Honora, I will let nothing happen to you. I will keep you safe always."

He squeezed her hand and kissed her cheek, kissing away her tear, and she shivered from his tenderness. She wanted to say something to him, to tell him how she felt, that she would be there for him as well. She would let nothing happen to him. She would keep him safe, and not out of duty but because he was a good man, a good husband. She would do it because she cared.

She wanted to tell him she cared for him and that one day perhaps soon she might discover she loved him. But her eyes were too heavy to open, she was unable to speak, she could barely move her lips, and the next thing she knew it turned dark and there was nothing.

Chapter 17

❧

Cavan watched his wife run around the moor with Champion nipping at her heels. Her cheeks were stung red from the cold wind that swept across the land since early morning and her long dark hair whipped around her smiling face. She looked so very happy and it brought joy to his heart.

He had been worried about her when she'd taken ill and insisted she remain abed a full day even though she claimed she was feeling fine. This morning he'd caught her before she could sneak past where he slept on the floor before the hearth. He didn't intend to let her go off on her own until he knew that she was fully recovered.

After they both ate a full breakfast, she had told him she was ready to resume her lessons, but he suggested a walk on the moor. She wanted to let Champion tag along. He intended that she rest for a day or two more, though Honora disagreed. Naturally, he got his way. Lessons wouldn't continue until tomorrow.

His own stomach wrenched when he recalled

how she called out to him in distress. He had been so enraged with his brother that his first thought was to dismiss her, but when he saw her clutching her stomach and watched her collapse to the ground, it felt as if his heart had stopped beating. It was even worse, though, when he wiped the tear off her cheek. He didn't know what caused her to cry, which disturbed him more than anything. Had she been in pain or was she unhappy being his wife? Did she fear him? Hate him? Not trust him? Did she feel alone even while surrounded by her new family?

Honora looked happy enough now, though she'd been quiet that morning while they ate and he'd wondered if she still didn't feel well, though her appetite was ravenous. At times they could converse so easily, as if they were old friends, and other times . . .

He shook his head. He didn't know what to make of his wife and wanted to learn more about her.

She stumbled toward him, Champion tripping her. Cavan caught her and was stunned when she kissed his cheek and laughed softly.

"That's twice you've saved me now," she said, holding onto his arms. "You truly are a hero."

He let her go and stepped away. "I'm no hero."

"You're my hero," she insisted, and Champion gave a yap, too young to produce a full-fledged bark. "The pup agrees."

He was no hero and he didn't want to be thought one. Heroes were remarkable men who performed remarkable feats. He had no such feats to his credit.

He was surprised when she took his arm and tugged him along until their steps evolved into a casual stroll, Champion happily bouncing along beside them.

"What else do you intend to teach me?" she asked.

He smiled. He couldn't help himself. She looked so lovely, with rosy red cheeks and her dark hair blowing wildly around her face, and she was smiling, and had been from her first step on the moor. She was a carefree lass, more herself there than anywhere else. But then, it had been her place to escape to, a place where she could be herself, let her guard down, feel safe as she did now.

She felt safe with him?

The thought jarred his heart, and he almost shook his head denying the notion. It was pure nonsense and he was a fool for even giving it thought. What did it matter if she felt safe with him or not? She was his wife and that was that.

Then why had the thought that she trusted him enough to feel safe with him nudge at his heart?

"You do intend to teach me more, don't you?" she asked hopefully.

He leaned closer to her. "What do you want to learn?"

"You mentioned riding, and I'd like to become proficient with weapons."

He coughed a laugh. "Weapons?"

She nodded vigorously.

"Any weapon in particular?"

"A dirk and perhaps a bow and arrow. I don't know about a sword."

Cavan laughed aloud. "And here I thought I had wed a mousy woman with not an ounce of courage. You do surprise me."

"I surprise myself," she admitted with a bit of reluctance. "You have shown me I am capable of more than I believed and I am grateful to you for that, and I look forward to learning more."

"Careful, I may teach you more than you want to know."

She shook her head. "I have tasted knowledge and wish to learn more, everything I can."

"Everything? That requires a very long time."

"We are husband and wife," she said. "We have our entire lives together."

It sounded as if she looked forward to a life with him, and he suddenly grew disturbed and walked a few feet away from her. He rubbed his chin, staring over the empty moor spreading out before him, and settled his glance on the keep resting high on the hill in the distance. He could not allow his wife, an actual stranger to him, to interfere with his plans. First and foremost he had to find his brother Ronan. He could not live, laugh, and enjoy life to the fullest until Ronan was safe. It was his duty, and he would not rest until he had seen it done.

"We should return," he said, swerving around to face her.

She was busy bouncing around happily with the yapping little pup, paying him no heed. He almost gave a second thought to depriving her of her joy, but then the image of his brother reaching out to him with fear in his eyes assaulted him and he walked over to Honora and grabbed her arm.

"Time to go," he said, dragging her along with him while the pup nipped at his heels.

"Is something wrong?" she asked, her steps finally matching his.

"There are things I need to attend to."

"I thought we might spend more time together."

"Tomorrow we will resume your lessons," he said, and scooped up the pup, shoving him into her arms. "Take him to our bedchamber and rest."

"I don't want to rest."

"Regardless, you will," he said sternly.

They didn't exchange another word on the remainder of their walk, and then, after ordering her once again to their bedchamber, Cavan left her side in search of his father.

Honora didn't understand what had happened. They were having a good time together, talking and playing with the pup. They had seemed a pair, two people who cared for each other. Especially after yesterday when he'd gotten so upset over her taking ill and remained with her even when his mother urged him to leave the care to her. And it hadn't been duty that held him there; it was something else, something she saw in his eyes and had seen on other occasions. It was that something that had made her regard him in a different light.

His own words had confirmed what she was beginning to realize—that her husband was a man with a good heart, who cared deeply for those he loved and would do anything for them, even giving his own life to save them.

Honora wandered over to the fireplace in the great hall. Champion curled up at her feet and was asleep in seconds. She poured herself a tankard of warm cider from the pitcher on the table and settled in with her thoughts.

Cavan believed himself responsible for everyone, and as future laird she supposed in a sense that was true. But his brothers had been trained for battle too, and all warriors accepted the possibility of capture or death when in combat. She recalled tales of Cavan's courage and his many victories, and she'd heard the gossip that the barbarians only captured him because he remained behind in search of his brother while ordering the others to retreat.

The only one who blamed Cavan for Ronan's capture was Cavan.

She wanted to help her husband; after all, she was stuck with him. She was his wife for the rest of their lives, and because he was a good man, she knew that somehow they could have a good marriage. He had made it known he wanted children, and children entailed intimacy.

Honora sipped at the cider. She would need to make certain they spent more time together. It was good that he was giving her lessons in protecting herself, and she would make sure that they shared meals together and took walks and talked. They needed to truly be husband and wife.

She couldn't have said as much yesterday. Her thinking had changed, and not just because of

Cavan's actions. Addie's remark had made an impression on her too. If Cavan's mother could detect a caring between them, then perhaps there really was a chance for them to have a loving marriage and not just an arranged one. That it was even a thought, a possibility, amazed her. She never imagined that she might care for Cavan. He had been rude and abrupt when they first met.

A giggle tickled her throat. She was young then. He had saved her, so in truth it wasn't twice he'd saved her but three times. Next time she would need to make certain that she saved herself, if only to show him that he'd taught her well, for since that day on the moors she had been careful where her steps took her.

"Are you feeling well?"

Honora looked up to see Addie holding a plate of honey cakes. She licked her lips. "Even if I wasn't I wouldn't turn down a honey cake."

"A daughter after my own heart," Addie said, placed the plate on the table and took a seat on the bench opposite her.

Addie had made her feel welcome from the first moment she was introduced to her. Addie had referred to her as her daughter, even before the wedding. She'd accepted her unconditionally, and Honora was grateful to once again have a loving mother.

"I thought to find Cavan with you," Addie said. "I saw that you headed out for the moors and thought to welcome you both back with a treat."

"Cavan searches for his father."

Addie frowned. "Is something wrong?"

Honora shrugged. "I don't believe so. We were having a joyous time when he suddenly insisted we return to the keep, where he went in search of his father."

Addie shook her head. "My son shoulders more responsibilities than is necessary."

"And blames himself needlessly."

Addie sighed with relief. "You understand."

"I believe I am beginning to. At first—"

"You thought you were stuck with a terrible husband."

"I—I—"

Addie laughed and patted her hand. "It's all right, dear, Cavan wasn't pleasant to you upon his return."

"He did have good reason, returning to find himself married to a woman he had once rejected."

"You defend him, that is good," Addie said with a smile. "A husband needs a wife who will stand by him."

A crash and loud, angry voices made both women jump to their feet, and the pup shook the sleep out of him and now looked alert.

The squabbling grew until it spilled into the great hall.

"If you do not have the courage to do it, I will," Cavan shouted at his father, who preceded him into the room.

Tavish Sinclare stopped abruptly and swerved to face his son. "How dare you disrespect me? I am the leader of this clan and you will show me the respect I not only deserve, but earned."

"Then prove it and allow me to take an army of warriors and attack the barbarians."

"No. I will not send my warriors on a senseless mission," Tavish argued.

"Is it senseless to rescue your son?" Cavan challenged.

Honora almost gasped. Addie did. Cavan had no right speaking to his father that way.

"Pride loses battles. Remember that when you become laird or you will jeopardize the safety of the clan and our lands. As for my son? Either I will find him or he will return home, for he is a warrior like his brother and will do the clan proud."

Tavish turned his back on his son and walked out of the keep. Addie followed him.

Cavan angrily descended on Honora. "I ordered you to rest."

The pup yapped at his irate approach.

"Quiet!" Cavan snapped harshly.

The pup ran for cover under Honora's skirt, but got in one last yap.

"Do not take your temper out on my friend," Honora said sharply.

"Then I will take it out on you. You were ordered to rest—"

"I am not tired."

"That makes no difference."

"It does to me," she said.

Cavan grabbed a tankard off the table and slammed it down hard, cider spilling over the sides. "You will do as I say or else."

"Or else what?" she asked bravely.

He stared at her, speechless.

Her heart beating wildly, Honora scooped up the pup, tossed her chin up, and stepped around her irate husband. "I have things to do," she said and walked away. She wanted to hurry her steps, to retreat from her husband as fast as she could, but kept her steps steady, knowing it would do her no good to show fear. If there was one thing Cavan had taught her, it was not to panic and allow your foe to sense your fear.

Honora paraded out of the great hall with a confidence she did not possess, but rather with legs that trembled so badly she thought surely she would crumble to the floor before she reached the door. When she did reach the door, she grabbed hold of the thick wood and steadied herself, took a breath and whispered to Champion, "We made it."

"Honora!"

She didn't bother to turn and respond to her husband's shout, but quickly vacated the hall and hurried as far from the keep as her wobbling legs would carry her.

She wound up behind the stable, tucked between two barrels. She wrapped her cloak around herself and the pup, grateful that she'd had enough sense to grab it as she left the hall. The pup settled contentedly in the niche her raised legs provided and took the opportunity to clean his paws.

But Honora remained alert, concerned that her husband would come in search of her and . . .

Or else.

The two little words stayed with her, and try as she might, she could not shed them. She wondered what he would do now that she'd refused to obey him. And what of her stepfather? Would he dare to confront her over her callous disregard for her husband?

It mattered little at the moment for the deed had been done. She had taken a stand and now must face the consequences. Addie had only just praised her about standing beside her husband. It proved to be short-lived praise. She had openly defied Cavan, and tongues were sure to spread the news.

Had she been mistaken? Had she been too hasty? Too angry?

This wifely duty was much too new to her, and particularly with Cavan. In contrast, she had been comfortable with Artair, mainly because he was honest with her.

Artair.

She scrambled to her feet and hurried to deposit the pup in the stable with the other pups. Then she went in search of Artair.

Chapter 18

H onora found him working in the blacksmith hut. He was shirtless, his bare chest shimmering with sweat while he hammered away at the red hot tip of a sword laid flat on an anvil. She couldn't help but compare him to her husband. Where Cavan was thick with muscle, Artair was lean and sinewy, defined and sculpted like a marble statue, though not cold and aloof like marble or like his brother could be at times. Artair was affable, his smile genuine, his nature pragmatic. He was a dependable and reasonable man, one easy to converse with. He had been honest about what he expected from her as a wife and made her feel as comfortable as possible with their forthcoming marriage arrangement.

When Artair saw her, he gave the sword one last hammer and then shoved the tip into the rain barrel, steam rising off the water before he deposited the weapon on a nearby worktable.

"Is something wrong?" he asked.

"Why do you ask?"

"Because we have barely exchanged more than salutations between us since you wed my brother."

"My fault," she admitted. "I cannot say it has been easy adjusting to the sudden change in my situation."

"I am sorry for that."

Honora smiled. "It wasn't your fault, though I felt I lost a good husband."

He laughed. "You're so sure of that?"

Honora nodded firmly. "You will make a woman a fine husband one day. She will be lucky to have you."

"And I will be lucky if she possesses half the good nature that you do. Actually, your pleasant temperament is what made the arrangement so appealing, but by now my brother must realize his good fortune in having you as a wife."

Honora shrugged. "I'm not sure how your brother feels. I thought perhaps you could help me to understand him better."

"I wish I could understand him better myself." Artair shook his head. "He is different since his return. He keeps himself removed from most everyone. We don't talk as much as we once did."

"It sounds as if you miss your brother."

"I do," he said.

"Have you tried speaking with him?"

"Obviously you came to me with concern for my brother, yet you are advising me on my concerns. You are a thoughtful woman, Honora." He winked playfully at her. "Perhaps I was foolish to let you go so easily."

"Perhaps you should respect the fact that she is your brother's wife."

Honora and Artair turned to see Cavan, his hands fisted at his sides.

"Artair was only teasing," Honora said.

"Let him find his own woman to tease," Cavan said, his dark eyes steady on his brother.

"I meant no disrespect," Artair apologized.

Honora was not well acquainted with men and their peculiarities, but she was certain that friction sizzled between the two. It seemed if she didn't separate them soon, an altercation would ensue.

"Make sure you don't," Cavan warned unnecessarily.

Artair made a civil attempt to lighten the atmosphere. "Remember that it's through my generosity that you have such a wonderful wife."

Cavan took a sharp step forward, and Honora, without thinking, stepped between the two men.

"I am feeling rather tired. Would you walk me back to the keep?"

Artair's glare remained locked with his brother's. "I'll be right here if you have anything else to say to me."

Honora slipped her arm around her husband's and gave a light tug. "Actually, I could use a hot brew. I'm feeling quite chilled." She forced a shiver to prove her point.

"We'll talk later," he said to his brother.

"I'd like that," Artair said, and turned to shove the sword he'd been working on into the fiery ambers.

Honora waited until they were a distance away

from the blacksmith hut to say, "Artair is a good man."

"Unfortunately, you're stuck with me as a husband, and you can thank your stepfather for that."

"You're right," she said, her head cast down as they walked along the pitted path to the keep.

Cavan's head snapped around to glare at her.

She raised her head and was quick to correct his misunderstanding. "You're right about my stepfather being at fault, not about me being stuck with you. I don't feel stuck with you. I am freer with you than with my stepfather. You don't confine me, and I appreciate that."

"False praise or gratitude will get you nowhere with me."

Honora was stunned by his caustic accusations and his assumption. "You think I lie?"

"Manipulate," he corrected.

"I do not," she said, halting their tracks.

His laugh was more a sneer. "All women do."

"I am not all women," she said, and stepped away from him, insulted.

His laughter was cut short by a shout that had him spinning around.

"You sonofabitch!" Lachlan yelled. "How dare you disrespect Father!"

Lachlan launched himself at Cavan, and fists flew and their bodies staggered before tumbling to the ground in an all out altercation. Honora stood staring speechless at the two warring brothers, then recovered enough to run to get help from Artair. Not that it did any good. Artair arrived to stand with arms crossed, watching his brothers battle it out. Her pleas to make them stop fighting were cut short when he informed her, "They need this. Let them be."

People gathered to cheer the brothers on. Blood began to spew from both combatants' mouths, and that was enough for Honora, who turned to leave.

Artair grabbed her arm. "You should remain and show support for your husband."

"I will not watch them battle each other senseless."

He laughed. "I suspect they will battle sense into each other."

"Then let them. I have no stomach for such idiocy." She stomped off and went straight to the sewing room, wanting nothing more than to forget the two fools fighting like children on the ground.

After discarding her cloak haphazardly on a chair, she paced in front of the fireplace. She didn't understand men and didn't know if she wanted to. She would much prefer to find a solitary spot in the woods, erect a cottage, and live there contentedly.

Her heartbeat quickened and she stopped pacing, but then wrung her hands together with nervous concern. The thought of being separated from her husband had jolted her. She unwittingly found herself attracted to him, caring about him, considering a good life with him. She wouldn't want to lose that. Perhaps that was why the fight disturbed her. She didn't want to see her husband hurt, in pain, or for a rift occur between brothers that could not be mended, and she felt helpless as to how she might prevent any of it.

She finally plopped into one of the chairs before the fireplace, too distraught to even consider her needlework. Being a wife was much more difficult than she'd imagined it would be. Or was it because she'd begun to have feelings for her husband? If she had simply regarded her marriage as an arranged one, with nothing to expect from it, she would not be disappointed. But she did expect things from her marriage, she thought, and should say as much to her husband.

Honora yawned and blamed the walk on the moors for her sudden tiredness, though her worries might have had something to do with her exhaustion. Either way, her eyes drifted shut and she was soon sound asleep.

Cavan and Lachlan supported each other as they stumbled into the great hall, Artair arriving before them to overflow their tankards with ale. Both brothers suffered similar minor bruises and cuts, nothing serious, but then, they were brothers. Never would they have badly hurt each other.

"To the Sinclare brothers," Artair toasted, his tankard raised.

Cavan and Lachlan cheered the toast and downed the ale.

Cavan reached for a fourth tankard, its brim overflowing, and Artair stopped him. "That's for Ronan. He is with us though he is not here . . . yet!"

Cavan refilled the tankards and this time it was he who made the toast. "To Ronan."

The brothers downed more ale and scrambled over the benches to sit at the table in front of the hearth.

"*We* will find Ronan," Lachlan said, taking his turn to refill the tankards.

"Just like we did when we were young," Artair reminded. "Ronan would get himself lost and—"

"One of us would find him," Lachlan finished with a slap to Cavan's back. "One of us, not only you. We each took our turn getting him out of someplace he shouldn't have been."

"That's what big brothers do," Cavan said.

His two brothers agreed with a nod and a snort.

"Food, my pretty lassie," Lachlan called out with a smile to a passing servant girl.

She giggled, nodded, and hurried off to do his bidding.

"One day you're going to come up against a woman who won't jump to your charming commands," Artair warned with a laugh.

"It will serve him right," Cavan said.

"That it will," Artair agreed, refilling empty tankards.

Out of the corner of his eye Cavan caught his father entering the hall along with his mother. Guilt punched him in the gut and he stood and called out, "Father, come join us."

His mother's relieved smile sent another guilty punch to his stomach, and he knew he owed his father an apology. He should never have spoken to him the way he had; his father didn't deserve it.

Artair and Lachlan remained silent, though both hid satisfied grins behind the tankards resting at their lips.

Cavan watched his mother kiss his father and hurry off with a smile. The genuine affection between his parents had been a constant in his life. It was a common sight to see the clan leader kiss his wife, hold her hand, laugh along with her, hug her. Cavan had wanted, hoped, ached, to share that binding love with a special woman one day. At first he had not thought that possible with the mousy Honora, but of late he'd come to admire the wife who was forced upon him by his father.

He watched his father approach, tall and powerfully built, a man of compassion and strength and honor; a leader to be proud of and a father he loved.

Cavan didn't wait for his father to reach him, he went to him. "Forgive me. I am a fool."

His father smiled and placed a strong hand on his son's shoulder. "You are much like me and do me proud."

Cavan shook his head. "I don't know how a foolish son can do you proud."

"It takes a foolish heart to be courageous."

He thought of a similar remark he had made to Honora. Perhaps he was like his father, thought like his father, and saw in people the courage they didn't see in themselves.

Cavan threw strong arms around his father and pounded his back, displaying his love the only way he knew how. "Come share in our toasts," he declared, and the father responded by joining his sons.

The men drank and ate away hours. They laughed, joked, argued, and renewed family bonds.

"What did my wife have to say to you?" Cavan asked Artair while Lachlan and Tavish were locked in a debate.

Artair laughed. "Ask your wife."

"You have a good wife," Lachlan said, raising his tankard. "She saved my life. She is a good woman. You are a lucky man."

Cavan didn't respond. He was too busy realizing his brothers admired and respected his wife, and he felt proud.

"I agree," his father said. "Honora is a good woman, a caring woman. She will make a good mother."

"It's been near two months and we've heard no news of a babe," Lachlan teased.

"Give them time," his father urged with a grin. "They are new to this."

Artair and Lachlan roared with laughter and Cavan cracked a smile. For the first time since his return home he felt he was part of his family, he felt he had finally come home.

"You need lessons, brother?" Lachlan laughed.

Cavan scratched his head. "Who was it who came to me when he didn't know what to do with a woman?"

"The hell you say," Lachlan said on a laugh.

"I remember that," Artair said, slapping Cavan's back.

Their father joined in the teasing. "You should have come to me, son."

"I needed no advice then or now. The women love me," Lachlan assured all.

The men joked and teased and drank the night away.

Cavan stumbled to his bedchamber well after dark to find it empty. It didn't take him long to realize where his wife was. He climbed the stairs to the sewing room to find her asleep before the hearth. He hunched down in front of Honora and gazed at her.

He had not thought much of her when years ago her stepfather approached Tavish concerning marriage. Honora had none of the qualities he'd wanted in a wife. He smiled, recalling how he hadn't liked her straight dark hair. What he hadn't known was how silky soft it was or how sweet smelling. He loved when lessons required closeness and he could rub his cheek against her hair and sniff its sweet scent.

He rose to brace his hands on the arms of the chair and leaned over his sleeping wife, burying his nose softly in her hair. He didn't want to wake her; he simply wanted to breathe in her familiar scent.

Its sweet richness was more intoxicating than all the tankards of ale he had drunk. He reluctantly moved away, but then returned to hunch down in front of her. He rarely got the opportunity to just drink in his wife's beauty, or perhaps he had finally discovered her beauty, or was it that she had simply crept into his heart before he could stop her?

He fought his attraction to her, didn't know where it came from and didn't care. He liked the tug he felt toward her. It seemed natural, as if they belonged together.

How could he feel so strongly about a woman he barely had kissed? Barely knew? Yet he felt as if he had known her forever.

Cavan ran a gentle hand over her dark hair and placed a tender kiss to her cheek, whispering, "I could fall in love with you."

His utterance disturbed him, though not unpleasantly, and he smiled. He wouldn't mind falling in love with his wife.

Honora yawned, stretched, and sighed mournfully before settling once again into the uncomfortable chair.

She belonged in his bed, and he thought to join her, but not yet; he wasn't ready, wasn't prepared to share such intimacy with her. He needed to know more, feel more, and understand more about her.

Leaning over her, Cavan brushed his lips over hers, pressed his cheek to hers, then lifted her gently into his arms. She stirred, snuggled against him and wrapped her arms around his neck.

He stood breathless. His wife instinctively felt safe without even opening her eyes, and from what he'd learned about her, he had been the only one to embrace her, hold her in his arms.

She knew he held her. She knew she was safe. She trusted him, and his heart soared with the thought. If she trusted him, then she could possibly love him.

Chapter 19

Honora woke with a start in the middle of the night. She was surprised to find herself in bed, her garments intact. She peeked over the edge and saw her husband sleeping as always on the floor in front of the hearth. He had to have been the one who placed her in bed.

Even in sleep she would have fought against a stranger touching her. But her husband? She would have responded willingly to him, therefore he had to have been the one to move her here, which meant he'd searched for her. He had never worried about her whereabouts. At first she'd thought he cared less about where she went and what she did. Obviously, she'd been wrong.

She rolled on her back to stare at the ceiling. She wondered how he had fared in the altercation with his brother and why he'd felt the need to find her. He had never worried about her whereabouts. At first she'd thought he cared less about where she went and what she did. Obviously, she'd been wrong.

She stilled, hearing a strange sound, heard nothing, but then it came again. It sounded as if someone was in pain, and she listened. There it was again. Hastily, she peered over the edge of the bed.

Cavan's body jerked and trembled. He looked again to be in the throes of a nightmare. Dare she help him, or should she leave him to fend for himself?

Honora pulled the blanket up under her chin like a protective shield, not certain how to proceed. Stay as she was, safe and sound in her bed? Or go to her husband in his hour of need?

She didn't need time to think it through; she slipped out of bed and padded barefoot across the room. Her husband wore only his plaid, which fit him loosely. His blanket had been pushed aside and yet he hugged his trembling body, though it was warmed by the heat of the hearth.

He looked vulnerable, his face grimaced as in pain, and her heart went out to him. He needed comfort and she didn't hesitate to give it to him. She scurried quietly back to the bed, snatched a blanket, and returned to him. She arranged his blanket over Cavan, added her own, then slipped beneath to join him, snuggling against him, burrowing herself to him until he instinctively wrapped his arms around her and settled comfortably into an easy embrace that chased his tremble away.

Her husband was warm, his heartbeat steady, and his scent all too familiar.

He belonged to her.

The thought quivered her soul. How could she think he belonged to her?

Simple. They were wed. He was her husband.

Could it be that simple? She didn't believe so. He could only belong to her if he wished to belong to her, just as she could only belong to him if she so chose. Otherwise it was an arrangement between families.

He shivered, and she hugged him to her, pressing her cheek to his and whispering soothing words. He quieted in no time, his arms tightening around her as he settled against her, burying his face in her hair.

She snuggled her face in his bare chest, her lips gracing his nipple. She thought to taste more of him but contained herself. He needed comfort, and so she placed her cheek to his chest and eased him with soothing words and promises to look after him and to be there for him whenever need be.

It felt so wonderful being there in his arms, snuggled beside him, comforting him, loving him. Did she dare love him? What if he didn't return that love? She felt confused and wished there was someone she could confide in, share her worries and doubts. There was Addie, but once again, she knew it would be awkward discussing the matter with her husband's mother. And she couldn't very well speak to her brothers-in-law about love.

She felt isolated, so very alone, though there were so many around her, and who truly was the one person she had confided in?

Her husband.

Since Cavan began teaching her to defend herself, they had spent more time together, which allowed for more conversations, getting to know each other better, and beginning to build trust between them. Cavan was quickly becoming her best friend, and she had quickly learned to relish the relationship, especially since such friendship had long been denied her.

Cavan even let her have a puppy of her own. He'd seen how much she cared for the pup, and instead of denying her the animal, encouraged their kinship. Her stepfather had not even allowed her that. He'd dictated every part of her life, all the while telling her it was for her own good so she would be an obedient wife who would never even think of defying her husband.

She was beginning to realize that all men did not expect extreme obedience from their wives. And seeing Addie's strong nature and how she spoke her mind, that all women needn't be compliant.

Cavan groaned again and hugged her tighter before loosening his grip on her, though he didn't release her, didn't push her away, didn't deny her. But then, he didn't know she was there. To him the feel of her was probably just a dream.

She settled once again comfortably against him and thought to remain with him for a while until she was certain his nightmares had passed before returning to her bed. He needn't know that she'd comforted him. It was enough for her to know it.

His warm body, his familiar scent, the heat from the hearth all served to relax and lull her to sleep.

Cavan woke with a tickle to his nose, and just as he was about to brush the annoying speck away, realized his arms were wrapped around a warm soft body. He almost released his wife with a start until common sense—or was it a spark of desire?—stilled him.

What was she doing in his arms?

Her cheek rested against his chest, her arm was draped across his waist, and one of her legs was tucked between his two, while his arms were wrapped protectively around her. His heart thudded madly and he grew hard in a flash.

"Damn," he mumbled.

She felt good in his arms, much too good, her breasts pressed against his chest, her knee resting just beneath his manhood, which sprouted in full-blown passion.

He wanted her, Lord how he wanted her.

He had been too long without a woman, and while he had every right—it was actually his duty—to join with his wife, he hesitated. He didn't want to ravish her out of need. He wanted to make love with her from his heart.

He was about to groan but managed to keep it silent, its ripple reverberating down his throat. How had he allowed his arranged marriage to become so complicated? He didn't like his own answer.

Stubbornness.

He had been stubborn about too many things since his return, only one deservingly so—his brother. His guilt would never be assuaged until he found Ronan.

He would never feel whole until then, and his wife didn't deserve only half of a man. She was entitled to a warrior, a true future chieftain.

She stirred in his arms, nestling closer, her body rubbing intimately against his.

He looked down to see that she still slept, her innocence obvious in her movements, as if she simply wanted to cuddle as closely as possible to him. He let her settle herself, though nearly swore aloud when her leg brushed his swelled manhood.

It would be so easy to have his way with her, and he had no doubt she would submit willingly, and their vows did need to be consummated. So many sound reasons to join with her, and yet one solid reason stopped him.

His wife deserved more.

"Are you all right?"

Her soft voice startled him, as did her sleepy violet eyes. She had barely woken, her eyes still droopy with sleep, her lashes fluttering, fighting to come fully awake.

"You had nightmares."

He had his answer as to why she was there with him, and it disturbed him. She had sought to comfort him; in a way, to protect him. He stilled suddenly.

She rubbed her cheek against his chest. "You are so very comfortable."

He groaned inwardly and knew that it was imperative that they separate soon or else he'd be in trouble. But damn she felt so good and so right in his arms. He'd hold her just a few more moments and then let her go. He had to let her go.

She sighed softly, then abruptly stilled.

He realized why. She had felt the swell of him, and no doubt it frightened her.

Surprisingly, she glanced up at him and with a smile said, "We are husband and wife."

She all but submitted to him. All he had to do was reach out, touch her, kiss her, love her. He had moved his mouth down, nearly covering hers, when the door burst open.

"We have word of Ronan," Artair said.

Cavan jumped to his feet. He scooped up his wife and deposited her in the bed, then grabbed his shirt and boots and was out the door with his brother.

"The bed isn't good enough for you," Artair said, grinning.

"Ronan?" Cavan asked sternly.

His brother's grin vanished. "A prisoner escaped from a barbarian raid to the east. It may be Ronan."

Cavan didn't want to hope, but he prayed. "We ride now," he ordered, though knew it was his father's choice.

"Father agrees."

Cavan almost roared with relief, though his relief was quickly replaced with the anticipation of who would lead the troop of warriors.

Artair settled it for him. "Father wants you to take charge of this mission."

Cavan halted, looked at his brother and knew. "You convinced him to give me this, didn't you?"

"I didn't have to convince him."

His words told Cavan much. His father trusted him, believed in him, and knew him capable and ready to do his duty.

He entered the great hall with Artair, the sun barely breaking the horizon, his father waiting along with Lachlan and his mother. The men were quick to huddle at the front table and plan decisive action. It was decided that Lachlan would accompany Cavan while Artair remained behind to keep Sinclare land secure.

He turned, reaching for his tankard of hot cider, and was surprised to see his wife at the next table with his mother. She had changed into a simple dark green skirt and yellow blouse. Her long hair was twisted and pinned to her head with a bone comb she favored and he knew had once belonged to her mother. She looked worried, though she smiled at him.

At the moment, he had no time to speak with her, but he would make time before he left. He needed and wanted to; after all, there was always a chance he wouldn't return.

Horses and warriors were busy preparing for the ride and battle if necessary, and it wasn't long before it was time for the warriors to leave.

Cavan approached his wife and with a gentle hand to her back guided her to a spot where they could speak alone.

"I do not know how long I will be gone," he said.

"I will be here praying for you and your brother's safe return," she said, though her voice trembled.

He took her into his arms. "You will continue to practice while I am gone, and there's Champion to train; you will be busy in my absence."

"I have much to occupy me," she confirmed, "though I will miss our lessons."

He smiled. "*Our* lessons?"

She placed a hand to his chest. "You cannot say you haven't learned something from our lessons?"

He covered her hand with his. "More than I expected."

"I am glad to hear that."

Her violet eyes entranced him. They held such truths. "Stay close to the keep while I am gone."

Honora smiled. "I know how to protect myself."

He pulled her close, wrapping his arms around her and hugging her waist. "I do not need to worry about you when I should be concerned with my mission."

"Worry not, I will do as you say," she said softly.

An empty ache hit him hard in the gut. He would miss his wife, miss her lovely violet eyes, the sweet scent of her hair, and—

She startled him with a gentle kiss, and stunned him even more when her arms eased around his neck and her body flattened against his. Her kiss was tentative, searching or beseeching him for more.

As much as he would have loved to oblige her, he was needed elsewhere. Kisses, passion, intimacy would have to wait.

He stepped away from her so quickly that she stumbled. He righted her with a firm hand, nodded, then turned and left, Lachlan following him out the door.

Honora felt her heart lurch, and she hurried outside along with Addie. While her mother-in-law went to her husband's side, Honora stood alone watching her husband mount his stallion. He was an impressive sight sitting tall and proud and anxious. She could see it in the tight lines in his face. This was what he had been waiting for, a chance to bring his brother home. She prayed he wouldn't be disappointed and that he would return safe.

She raised her hand to wave, but he wasn't looking at her. He was intent on his men and heading out, beginning the search or perhaps rescue of his brother. She dropped her hand and hugged herself around her middle, realizing she was chilled, the air cold, gray clouds hovering overhead.

Not a good day to send men off to battle. Some would declare a gray sky an omen, but she refused to accept it as a portent. She would think of it as a good beginning for them all, for didn't a rainstorm wash the earth clean and nourish the crops? And didn't the sun follow, heralding a new day?

Honora smiled and waved to her husband though he didn't look her way. It didn't matter and she didn't do it to be a dutiful wife; she did because she wanted to, because she would honestly miss him and worry over his safe return.

He might not have returned the kiss she'd given him so bravely and hastily, but she wasn't sorry she had kissed him. She liked kissing him. He tasted good, satisfying, and it made her skin tingle. And she intended to garnish as much courage as possible and kiss him again.

She continued to watch after her husband when he was long gone in the distance and everyone else had wandered off or returned inside the great hall. She stood there watching until the first raindrop splattered on her head and forced her inside.

Cavan had turned when one of his men hailed him, and while answering the man spied his wife in the distance waving. He knew it was her; he knew it in his heart. She never moved. She remained there becoming a mere speck until finally he could see her no more and she was gone.

The thought chilled and angered him. His only thought should be of the possible battle ahead and, hopefully, the return of his brother, and yet . . .

He could not get his wife out of his mind. Or was it the kiss he could not forget?

He had pulled away from her more reluctantly than he wanted to admit. If not for the need to find his brother, he would have scooped her up and . . .

He wanted to love her, and he didn't want to love her. He felt crazed with the thought of her, but hadn't his father warned him that love could do that to you—make you crazy?

He barely knew Honora, but what did falling in love have to do with time?

Cavan shook his head.

"Rejecting mental battle plans already?" Lachlan asked, riding up alongside him.

Cavan grunted.

Lachlan grinned. "Methinks you are waging a different battle in your head, perhaps concerning a wife?"

"Mind your business," Cavan snapped.

Lachlan rumbled with laughter. "Who would have thought it? Cavan Sinclare in love."

"I'm warning you, Lachlan—"

"Warn all you want. I intend to enjoy tormenting you."

Cavan turned a wicked grin on him. "Just remember your turn will come."

Lachlan laughed again. "Love will have nothing to do with my choice of a wife."

"So you say now."

"So I say. My wife will be a dutiful woman who obeys my every word and serves me well."

"And faithful?"

Lachlan flashed a sinful smile. "I will be faithful in my duty to her and treat her well."

"We shall see," Cavan said. "We shall see."

Chapter 20

Honora paced the floor in her bedchamber. It had been four days without a word from Cavan and she was worried senseless over him. What if he was hurt or, Lord forbid, captured again? She couldn't bear to think of such dire consequences.

She'd kept herself busy, though in an unorthodox manner, and had her husband to thank for it. With the few lessons he had given her, she gained courage and confidence that she could actually be capable of protecting herself if necessary, and she wanted to learn more. She wanted to become strong not just to impress her husband, but to claim her own self-worth. She'd made friends with John the bow maker and cajoled him into teaching her how to handle a bow. He balked at first, insisting he should get permission from her husband, but she insisted that she wanted to surprise him with her newly learned skill.

John had finally capitulated, though he made it clear he'd give her only one or two lessons. He changed his mind fast when she showed an aptitude for it. It was as if the weapon bowed to her command.

"You have a natural skill for it, lass." he told her, and continued to give her daily lessons with the bow.

She couldn't wait to show Cavan what she'd learned and wished he would return soon, though the fact that she missed him dearly was more of a reason for his return. She had gotten used to spending time with him, talking with him and taking walks with him. She wanted her husband home by her side so they could continue to grow close and finally seal their vows, making their marriage official.

Addie rushed into the room, causing Honora to jump with a start.

"Sorry to frighten you." Addie grinned. "But your husband returns."

Honora burst into a smile, hurrying over to her. "Is Ronan with them?"

"We don't know yet. They are a distance away and approach slow."

The two women hurried down the staircase and out of the keep, joining Tavish and Artair out front to wait for the approaching troop. Villagers gathered to welcome the returning warriors, and when word spread that they returned victorious, cheering shouts filled the crisp air.

However, Cavan's stone cold face warned Honora that the battle hadn't been victorious for her husband, which could only mean that Ronan had not been found.

Unlike many of the women who hurried to hug their mates, she didn't rush to greet her husband. His grim manner warned her that he would not appreciate it. Besides, his glance was fixed on his father, and Honora assumed he wished to speak with him first.

Lachlan followed Cavan to stand in front of their father.

"Ronan wasn't with the barbarians we attacked," Cavan said with obvious regret.

"Any word of him?" Tavish asked anxiously.

"Those men left with some breath in them did not say or would not say," Lachlan said.

"Let us discuss this in my solar," Tavish said, and turned to his wife. "Have a celebration feast prepared."

Honora stared after her husband, but he did not look her way, not a glance, not a slight turn of his head, not a peek from the corner of his eye. He ignored her and followed his father into the keep. She had spent every day worried over him, and he did not even acknowledge her presence. But then what had she expected? That he would miss her as much as she did him?

Foolish hopes and dreams. and hadn't her step-father dashed enough of her hopes and dreams through the years for her to learn never to count on anything or anyone?

She tapped her lips with a single finger and thought for a moment. Why hadn't she seen Calum of late? He usually lurked about during the day, not realizing she knew full well he spied on her. Since

Cavan had confronted Calum for raising his hand against her, he'd been less conspicuous, though he had remained vigilante in his spying attempts.

Yet this last week or more, she hadn't seen him, and while Calum was good at not being noticed when he didn't want to be, she had years to learn his tricks and knew when he was about without even seeing him.

"Come," Addie said. "We must see to the feast. The men will be looking forward to the celebration."

"Have you seen my stepfather lately?" she asked, keeping pace.

"I think I saw him near the stables the other day, though I can't be certain." Addie hurried her steps. "The tables must be kept heavy with food and drink for the men."

Honora nodded and kept pace, knowing it was her duty to help Addie, but she paused before entering the keep and cast a quick glance around the grounds. She knew exactly where to look, places Calum would go unnoticed so he could watch, but she saw nothing. He wasn't there.

She didn't know what frightened her more, that he watched her or that he didn't lurk in the shadows. Where could he be and what could he be doing?

But it was her husband who occupied most of her thoughts. While she helped Addie with the preparations for the celebration, she couldn't stop thinking about him. He had not only looked grim, but exhausted, and was covered with sweat, dirt, and dried blood.

She turned to Addie. "I'd like to have a bath waiting for my husband."

Addie smiled. "That is a good idea. I am sure he will appreciate it. As soon as the delicious smell of the food permeates the solar, the men will finish."

Honora chuckled and continued to help Addie until the scented meats, stews, and pies grew strong in the air, then she ordered a bath prepared in her bedchamber and Addie shooed her off before she could ask to take her leave.

Cavan climbed the stairs heavy in heart and tired in body. He had high hopes of finding his brother and bringing him home. He'd had no such luck and had not even discovered a single clue as to Ronan's whereabouts. Even killing a horde of barbarians didn't ease his disappointment. Finding his brother mattered more than revenge. He wanted Ronan home and safe.

He knew a celebration feast was prepared, but to him there was nothing to celebrate. He hadn't accomplished what he had set out to do, therefore this was not deserving of a celebration.

He wanted to find a way to drown his misery, to forget, to lose himself in—

He halted abruptly upon entering his bedchamber and stared at his wife standing in a pale yellow linen shift next to a steaming tub of water. The firelight outlined her naked body beneath, and her taut nipples poked sensually at the material. She waited with a smile to help him bathe.

"Get out!" he yelled at her, and stepped away from the door.

"I only meant—"

"Out!" His strong shout sent a tremble through his body.

Honora quickly grabbed her skirt and blouse off the bed and ran out of the room, her head down. He was grateful she hadn't glanced his way, for if he had seen even a speck of hurt in her violet eyes, he would have grabbed her and rained apologies and kisses all over her, which would have—

He shook his head and slammed the door shut, rushing to strip off his clothes. He would have taken her there and then, a quick act of sheer need, sheer desperation that would have hurt not only her but himself. He was in no mood to be gentle and kind. He was consumed with anger and contempt for himself for failing to find his brother. He didn't deserve kindness from his wife, or from anyone at the moment.

He dunked down in the water to soak his hair and came up sputtering, then grabbed the soap on top of the stack of towels and scrubbed, though he doubted he could rid himself of all the filth. He felt as if it had crept into his flesh and become part of him, and no matter how hard he tried, he'd never be fully clean.

In his year of capture he had been treated like an animal and made to live like one, and it had tormented his soul. He couldn't stand the thought that his brother continued to live such a degrading life.

He shook his head and dropped his face in his hands, and while he refused to weep, he felt as if his heart wept for him.

It took a couple of hours before he was ready to join the celebration, and with a clean shirt and fresh plaid and his hair shiny clean, he made his way to the great hall. It was a necessity for him to attend the feast, for if he did not, his absence would suggest that he didn't honor his warriors. They had fought bravely and he would show them the respect they deserved.

He took a seat at the table with his father and brothers, raising a tankard in toast to his men. He searched the room for Honora. Not finding her nor spotting his mother, he assumed they were busy seeing that the tables remained heavy with food and drink. It was better that he did not see her yet anyway, for he felt guilty over treating her so badly when she merely was being a dutiful wife.

Later he would apologize, but for now he'd get lost in the feast.

He ate, drank, and joked with his brothers and the men, and occasionally spied his mother directing the servant girls while she laughed and talked with everyone. He took a quick look for his wife, but didn't see her anywhere. He wondered where she was and sought to catch his mother's glance in order to ask her, but she didn't see him and turned away to disappear in a crowd of people.

Lachlan slapped his back and made a teasing comment that required an immediate response, and it soon had the three brothers battling wits and laughter.

It wasn't until Addie joined them an hour or more later that Cavan inquired about his wife.

"Do you keep my wife so busy that she is unable to join us?"

Addie looked at him with alarm. "I haven't seen Honora since she left the hall to see to your bath. Was she not waiting for you in your bedchamber?"

His father and brothers all showed signs of concern, and he was quick to ease their worries.

"I know where she is." He stood and left the hall, leaving his family wondering.

He didn't have to think twice about where she'd gone. She would seek the one who would console her the most—Champion.

He entered the stable quietly and stopped when he saw his wife asleep, curled up on a bed of hay, a wool cloak wrapped around her and Champion, who was tucked up against her chest, also sound asleep. But what tore at his heart was that he could see she'd been crying, possibly had fallen asleep with tears filling her eyes, and he knew it was his fault.

He need not have been so cruel to her. He had been angry with himself, not her, and she had suffered for his foolishness. Now she slept in the stable with the animals, and that irritated him even more.

Enough was enough. He gently scooped up Champion and placed him with the rest of the sleeping pups. Then seeing another pup curled at Honora's feet, he scooped the little fellow up and added him to the pile of pups.

Finally he leaned down and as gently as possible lifted his wife in his arms and stood. She stirred and her eyes fluttered open before she rested her head against his chest. As he turned, her eyes sprang open and she lifted her head to stare at him.

"You belong with me."

She shook her head.

He pressed his lips to her temple then whispered, "Yes, you do."

He strode from the stable with steady steps. She was no burden, not only in weight but as a wife. He had first considered her an encumbrance, but she proved to be far from it. And she was proving more of an asset every day. But perhaps he was finally seeing her true nature.

He avoided the great hall, instead taking the rarely used entrance which was employed mainly in case they were under attack and the keep had to be evacuated. He didn't want anyone to see them or know of their disagreement. There was enough gossip being spread about him, and he didn't need more, nor would he see his wife hurt because of his foolishness.

They made it to their bedchamber without passing a soul, and after a quiet click of the door, he eased Honora down on the bed and slipped her cloak off.

She lay rigid, staring at him as if uncertain or perhaps frightened of him, and that troubled Cavan. He did not want her fearful of him. She must have lived with enough fear of her stepfather. He would not have her feeling the same about him.

"I am so very sorry," he said, running the back of his hand along her soft cheek. "You did not deserve my anger and you were not the cause."

She sighed softly, as though releasing a long held breath. "I had thought I somehow offended you."

"No," he said, shaking his head. "You did nothing to offend me."

To his surprise, she took his hand and kissed it gently, then held their joined hands to her chest. "You did not find your brother."

He nodded, while a spark of passion ignited and began to flow through him. "The reason for my anger."

"You learned nothing of his whereabouts?"

"Nothing. Those who were left able to speak played ignorant or truly knew nothing of Ronan's whereabouts."

"We cannot give up hope."

His passion surged with the simple fact that she had said we. She was letting him know she supported his search for his brother and not only hoped along with him, but encouraged him to hope, and for that he was grateful. He didn't feel alone in his mission; she was right there beside him.

She released his hand, pushed herself to sit up, and stunned him when she pressed her cheek to his and whispered, "Thank you."

He near gasped from the shock of passion that surged through him, but contained himself and simply asked, "For what?"

"For sharing the truth with me," she murmured,

and brought her mouth to his and paused a moment before she tentatively kissed him.

She was waiting for a response without realizing his body had responded quickly, and he had all he could do not to grab hold of her and delve further into her innocent advance.

She grew bolder and enhanced the kiss while her hand ran over his chest and cautiously crept beneath his shirt.

Her warm hand sent a shot of heat racing through him and brought him to full alert. If he didn't separate from her soon, he doubted he would, and at the moment he wasn't feeling strong enough to deny himself any longer. Honora was his wife, and he had a duty, she had a duty, and damn if duty wasn't calling loud and clear.

He returned the kiss, he couldn't help it. She was so sweet, so innocent and willing. And what was the use of denying them both any longer? Sooner or later they would join together, why delay it?

She deserved more.

His own harsh voice intruded with a jolt, though not enough to separate them, just enough to keep him from going any further.

He pulled away from her and stood, and damn if he didn't feel her hurt of rejection. He paced by the side of the bed.

"I am not what you think."

She stared at him, perplexed. "You are my husband, a good man, a brave warrior—"

"No!" he shouted, then released a heavy breath and more quietly repeated, "No, I am not."

"But that is how I see you," she said softly.

"Then you are blind!" he snapped.

"No" she said firmly. "I am not blind. I know the nature of my husband."

"You know nothing of me."

She shook her head adamantly. "You may try to hide from me, but I have seen the truth."

"How can you claim to know me, see me when I do not know myself?"

"It isn't that you do not know yourself; it is that you refuse to see yourself."

He stopped pacing. "You speak in riddles."

"How can you show me kindness if you are not kind? How can you teach me to defend myself if you do not care? How can you continue to punish yourself over your brother when you risked your own life to try and save him?"

She spoke without an ounce of annoyance and with such sincerity that it made his heart ache, for her, or the truth of her words, or just because she made sense. He didn't know the reason. He did know that his wife, the woman he had first denied, understood him better than anyone, even himself.

The woman before him with the silky long black hair, enticing violet eyes, melodious voice, and gentle manner was not the little frightened mouse he once thought her to be, but perhaps she never was. Perhaps there had always been strength to her that he'd been too blind to have seen, and could only now detect and finally acknowledge.

He knew he should speak, say something, respond to her words, which were all too truthful, and yet speech failed him.

She smiled at him as if she understood his confusion and offered him even more. "Come share the bed tonight with me."

All he had to do was join her in a night of passion that would easily ease his tortured mind and free his troubled soul. It was that easy, that simple to forget.

But while he lost himself in making love with her, his brother could very well be suffering the tortures of hell. What right had he to know pleasure while his brother suffered pain?

Without a word to his wife, he turned and left the room.

Chapter 21

Honora woke with a stretch and a smile and wasn't surprised to find herself alone. She couldn't be certain if her husband had ever returned to their bedchamber last night, though it didn't matter. She didn't feel rejected by his absence as she once had; she now understood, and it would be up to her to set things right between them.

Cavan blamed himself for far too many things, and until he could see the truth and admit it, he would forever punish himself. She probably would have done the same in her own situation if it hadn't been for her mother's wise talks. Her mother had made her realize that Calum was not a good man, though he had tricked her into believing otherwise. However, once they wed, it had been too late, and the only thing to be done was to be wiser than he. Her mother had insisted until her dying breath that one day Honora would meet a man trustworthy and loving and that she would live a happy life.

Honora stretched herself out of bed, reaching up as far as she could, perhaps somehow wishing to reach out to her mother.

"I have found the man you spoke of, Mother. He requires some of your wisdom and I will generously share it with him."

She laughed softly and fell back on the bed. Life suddenly seemed good as she felt her own strength, her own self-worth. Not that she was completely courageous, but she had gained a modicum of confidence, and with its growth, courage was sure to follow.

She jumped off the bed and dressed quickly in a dark blue wool skirt and long sleeve gold tunic top that she belted at the waist with a strip of Sinclare plaid. She used a smaller plaid strip to tie her hair back after running the comb through it several times and slipped on her soft boots. She was ready to face the day and her husband.

She laughed walking out of the room. She doubted he was ready for her.

Her quick glance found him as soon as she entered the great hall. He sat with his father, mother, and Artair at the table before the hearth. Lachlan was absent, a sure indication that he had found a woman to spend the night with, since he would never rush from her bed the next morning. The rest of the tables were empty, since most warriors had gone home, recovering after a night of feasting or seeing to their duties.

Cavan caught her approach a few feet into the room and she held his gaze until she reached the table. She smiled and gave him a kiss on the cheek before slipping in next to him. "I'm starving."

Honora reached for a slice of honey bread, her favorite, and Cavan poured her a tankard of hot cider and slid his plate between them. She grinned and eagerly picked at his food, pleased that he wished to share it with her.

Talk was general until one after another was called away, leaving her alone with her husband.

"I have something to show you," she said, dusting crumbs from her fingers.

"What is it?" he asked, skeptical yet smiling.

She looked around the room, leaned in close to him and whispered, "It's a surprise."

"No one knows?"

"Me and one other." She pressed her finger to his lips before he could speak. "No questions, you will see for yourself."

She took his hand and tugged him off the bench, then grabbed one of the wool cloaks that Addie kept on the pegs near the door. Her husband wore no cloak, his wool shirt, plaid, and boots sufficient protection against the chilled air. He actually seemed impervious to the cold, and she assumed he had become accustomed to it during his capture, since the barbarians' lands were steeped in winter a good portion of the year.

Honora caught the surprised look on Cavan's face when they walked around the back of John the bow maker's place. He looked even more surprised when John, a man of bulk and with little patience for anyone but warriors, greeted her with a wide smile.

"You stand here," Honora said to her husband, and positioned him in view of the target range that John kept for the warriors to practice and try out their bows.

She took the bow John had fashioned especially for her and saw Cavan's brow furrow. He couldn't hide his surprise when she took an arrow, skillfully placed it in her bow, and with a quick aim released it, to hit a few inches from the middle of the target. She repeated the process twice more to show him it wasn't a fluke, that her aim was good and her skill natural.

Then Honora turned to him with a smile. "I begged John to teach me. I wanted to surprise you."

His face turned grim and his eyes narrowed, and for a moment she thought he was angry, but then he shook his head and smiled.

"My wife is a natural with the bow," he said proudly to John.

"That she is, sir, that she is," John agreed.

"Soon she'll be filling the coffers with food for the clan," Cavan boasted.

Honora gasped. "I could never kill an animal of the forest."

John's expression turned serious. "An arrow is for killing, keep that in mind."

Honora looked to her husband as John walked off, leaving them alone. "He's right," Cavan said to her. "A bow is used to hunt, whether it is man or beast. If you are not ready to kill, then do not shoot a bow. It is the same with a dirk or a sword."

"I have never killed anything," she admitted, the very idea making her stomach turn.

He took her arm, and Honora followed his lead. She was glad when he headed to the moors. Even though the day was crisp, the sun shone and the sky was blue with a plethora of white clouds; a good day for a walk on the moors, and a good place to talk.

"I have taught you to defend yourself without teaching you the sacrifice such an act would cost you," he said once they were at a distance from the village.

She took hold of his hand and walked to the outskirts of the small woods, plopping down to rest against a sizable rock and tugging him along with her. "Tell me what battle is like."

He sat close beside her, and she snuggled even closer, tossing her cloak across his legs, certain he must be feeling the chill and wanting to share the warmth. And if she were honest, she realized, she also wanted to be close to him, to feel his heat and tempt the flesh.

"You don't want to know that," Cavan answered.

She placed her hand over his, a hand she was sure had killed many men in battle but also had lovingly held her close and touched her gently. "I want to know more about you."

He hesitated.

She admitted aloud what of late she had been feeling. "I trust you. Won't you trust me?"

"Why do you trust me?" he asked, lacing his fingers with hers.

She liked the feel of his hand against hers. Though callused, it was strong and firm. "You've shown me no reason not to trust you."

"I called you a little mouse," he reminded.

"And I thought you a brute."

"The little mouse squeaks up."

Honora laughed and gave him a quick kiss, though it was no more then a brush of her lips across his. "Thanks to you."

She wasn't certain if it was the kiss or her appreciation that startled him, or perhaps it was both that turned him speechless.

"Will you tell me of battle?" she requested once again.

He hesitated as if weighing his decision, and then, resting their joined hands in his lap, he began. "Fear is friend and foe to a warrior in battle. It is fear surging through your blood that gives you strength, propels you forward without thought or consequence, and once in the throes of battle fear allows you to feel nothing. You simply defend and survive. It allows you to ignore the screams of the dying and the horrid smell of death, not once caring that this could be the day you meet your maker."

Honora remained silent. knowing he was lost in memories of battles fought. She placed her other hand over their clutched ones, giving it a comforting squeeze and reminding him that he was there with her and not in battle, and knowing she would never again be able to see him off to battle without being afraid that he would not return.

He pressed his forehead to hers, lingered for a moment as if needing to feel close, then turned away to look over the moors. "The worst is discovering the cost of the battle. Seeing family and friends who have fallen or hearing the cries of the wounded you know cannot be saved."

"But trying nonetheless?"

"You speak of my brother," he retorted quickly.

"You risked your life for him."

"And failed," he reminded.

"And suffered greatly for your attempt."

He turned away from her.

She refused to be ignored. "The barbarians must have treated you horribly. I have seen the scars on your back and watch you writhe with nightmares."

He turned his head sharply. "Why do you think I want so desperately to find my brother? He is being treated worse than an animal, and I cannot bear the thought."

"What happened, Cavan? What happened that day in battle?"

Cavan shook his head as if denying her, or perhaps denying himself. Did he wish to relive that day? Hadn't he relived it over and over since it first happened? What good would it do to repeat it all over again? And how could she truly understand?

He looked at her and saw determination in her violet eyes, and something else, compassion, empathy; she cared. It startled him that she could really care for him. Was it that he felt he didn't deserve it?

He sighed heavily, not sure how to answer, or if he should, and continued to shake his head.

"Why do you refuse to share your pain?"

"Why do you wish to share it?" he argued.

"You are my husband. I do not wish to see you suffer needlessly."

"Perhaps I deserve to suffer."

"Nonsense," she said sternly.

"You don't know," he quarreled.

"Then prove to me why you should suffer."

He almost laughed. She had wisely backed him into a corner without him even realizing it, and he admired her tactics. She truly was a warrior.

He reluctantly related the battle to her. "The barbarians overwhelmed us. They had more men than we believed, and it was obvious from the start that we were outnumbered. Every man fought bravely, but the onslaught continued and I called for the men to retreat."

He stilled and looked off in the distance, visualizing the scene that remained imprinted on his mind forever. "It was when I had ordered the last of the men to leave the battlefield that I heard my brother's cries for help. I didn't think twice, I charged forward, slicing down men as I went, until there were too many and I fell not far from Ronan. I reached out to him; he was covered with blood. I could see the fear in his eyes, and felt it as I did when he was but a young lad and needed rescuing. I never failed to rescue him then, but this time . . ."

He shook his head. "I reached out to him. If we were to die, at least it would be together. I would not let him die alone. Just as our fingers touched, we were ripped away from each other." He closed his eyes. "I still hear his screams."

"You did what you could."

"It wasn't enough," he said through gritted teeth.

"How could you ever believe that?"

He glared at her. "Because Ronan is not home."

"But you are?"

"Right."

"And you have no right to be here, because Ronan isn't."

"Now you understand," he said.

"You were willing to die to save him."

"Whatever it took."

"Are you willing to live?" she asked.

He stared at her and shook his head. "What nonsense do you speak?"

"Dying would not have helped your brother, living does."

He continued to glare at her.

"You warned me to not let the enemy know I care, for they will use that against me. You let the enemy know you would sacrifice for your brother, and so they used it against you. Tell me, did they taunt you with tales of your brother's suffering?"

Cavan wrinkled his brow. "The barbarians forever reminded me that my brother suffered because of me. They never let me forget it."

"So the only true way to help your brother was to survive, eventually escape and find him. And while the barbarians didn't believe you capable of it, your brother did, or he would have never reached out to you for help. Hope will never die in Ronan, knowing you remain alive."

"How do I know he believes me alive?"

"If someone told you that your brother lives, then your brother must also know that you live," she said confidently. "Which means Ronan knows you will come for him, and he will do whatever is necessary to survive, just like you did."

Cavan cringed. "It is no way to live."

"And yet you did."

Cavan turned silent, recalling his capture, then found his voice again. "They made me live like an animal. I can still smell my stench."

Honora kissed his cheek. "You smell good to me."

He grabbed her chin. "I have become like them—a beast."

She yanked her face from his grasp and pressed her cheek to his. "You are not a beast. You are a good, loving man, and I am proud to call you my husband."

He rested his cheek firmly against hers. "You do not know what you say."

She moved to brush her lips over his. "I know you are a man worth loving."

"Don't," he objected, turning his face away from hers.

She grasped his chin and forced him to look at her. "Make love to me," she told him. "Be my husband."

Chapter 22

C avan sat in the great hall with a full tankard of ale in front of him, without having downed a bit of the brew in the couple of hours he'd been sitting there. He couldn't get his response to his wife's blatant query for him to make love to her out of his mind. But then, he supposed he'd been out of his mind for answering her as he had.

"In time."

What time? What was he waiting for? And what of her response? She had smiled. Did that mean she was relieved? He had expected her, perhaps wanted her, to be upset. At least that would have proven that she hadn't offered herself out of duty to fulfill their vows and seal their marriage. She'd continued the conversation as if his rejection meant nothing, had not bothered her in the least.

Where he thought she'd be the one brooding, he was the one now brooding. While Honora? He didn't even know where she was. She had taken her leave of him as soon as they returned to the keep, and while he was curious, he also was perturbed, though he told himself it made no sense for him to be annoyed. The whole thing had been his own doing. Right now, at this very moment, he could be in his bedchamber making love with her.

"Had a disagreement with your wife?" Lachlan asked, joining him.

"It's none of your business and I'm not in the mood for company," Cavan snapped.

"Neither am I." Lachlan poured himself a tankard of ale.

"You look like shit," Cavan said, glancing over his disheveled brother.

"I spent the night with an insatiable woman." Lachlan downed a good portion of ale.

"Drink or sex?" Cavan grinned.

Lachlan raised his glass. "Both, and I pleased her over and over and over and over . . ."

Cavan laughed. "All night long?"

"She didn't even take a breather, except to down another ale," Lachlan said with a weary shake of his head. "I'm telling you, I'm thinking more and more of finding a good woman and settling down. At least then I'll have a woman to warm my bed and me every night, like you have with your wife."

Like he should have, Cavan thought. "You always bragged about not settling with just one woman," he reminded his brother.

"That's when I was young."

Cavan laughed. "I forget you are an old man of twenty and three years."

"Laugh if you like but I am *feeling* older of late."

"By this evening you will be eyeing the lasses once again," Cavan assured him.

Lachlan shook his head, though stilled it fast enough and rested it carefully in his hands, his elbows braced on the table for added support. "If I live that long."

"Another night of debauchery?" Artair asked, climbing over the bench to sit beside Cavan.

"His last, or so he claims," Cavan said, his grin huge.

"How many times has it been his last?" Artair asked with a jab of his elbow at Cavan.

Cavan chortled. "Not his first and definitely not his last time."

"The hell with you both," Lachlan chimed.

"You tell them, Lachlan."

The three men were startled to see Honora sweep past them with a wide smile.

"I must be in a bad way. I never heard her approach," Lachlan said.

"Don't feel bad, neither did I," Artair admitted.

"Add me to that as well," Cavan said, and grew perturbed that she could approach him and his brothers without detection. Or was it that they hadn't been paying attention? Or perhaps he was agitated that Honora appeared happy, content, and set on a destination? She simply had glided into the hall and then slipped right out. She hadn't even acknowledged him.

"I hope I find a woman who looks at me the way Honora does at you," Lachlan said.

Cavan was about to ask his brother what he meant when Artair spoke.

"That's because Cavan knows how to satisfy a woman, and a satisfied wife is a happy wife."

Lachlan took offense. "What do you think I was doing last night?"

"If it took you all night, then you must not have been doing it right," Artair accused with a laugh.

Lachlan spat an oath at Artair, downed his ale, and refilled his tankard. "Like you know how to satisfy a woman?"

Cavan paid little heed to the stinging barbs his brothers flung at each other. He was too intent on what Lachlan had seen and what Artair had voiced. Did Honora truly appear happy and satisfied?

Lachlan cut into his reverie with a blunt query. "Honora glows. Is she with child?"

Cavan stared at his brother.

Artair slapped him on the back. "If you have to think about it, perhaps you should ask her."

Cavan nodded and left his brothers to continue their squabble. He knew his wife wasn't with child, but he wondered why she appeared so happy, especially when he was feeling so miserable. What did she have to be happy about? He intended to have an answer, and headed for the stables, sure that she would be with Champion.

He was surprised when he didn't find her there, though the pup was glad to see him and the little fellow joined him in the hunt. It took some doing but they finally found Honora with Addie. She had joined his mother in her weekly venture of making her rounds of the ailing in the village. His mother would offer whatever assistance she could, even if it was merely to sit and listen to what ailed not only the flesh, but the spirit.

When he discovered what Honora was doing, he decided not to disturb her. Besides, he was pleased that she was learning his mother's ways, for one day he would be laird and she would take over his mother's duties, and she appeared to anticipate the same and was busy preparing for it.

He watched her from a distance, the pup busy sniffing the air and following the distinct trail to a little boy who was eating a slice of freshly baked honey bread. She did look as if she glowed. Her cheeks were tinged red, her violet eyes sparkled, her lips rosy, and her smile stunning.

Suddenly her eyes widened, her smile grew, and she waved at him. He stared at her, his eyes narrowing, turned abruptly, scooped up the pup and walked away. He hurried to drop the pup at the stable, and without a word to his brothers—who were still at the table in the great hall—he rushed past them to take the staircase two at a time.

He shut the door behind him and leaned against it, closing his eyes tightly, trying hard to chase away the visions that tormented him. He had been enjoying the sight of his beautiful wife when a harsh memory intruded and refused to retreat to the far back of his mind where he kept it locked away.

It had jumped out at him when Honora noticed him, and then, instantly, he had no longer been staring at his wife but at the woman who had caused some of his torture. She was the daughter of Mordrac, leader of the barbarian tribe, and he'd been caught staring at her, though in truth it was she who was staring at him. He had been whipped mercilessly, and she stood by and watched without a flinch as the fierce lash was delivered to his back.

He had made himself a promise while captured, that not only would he find his brother and bring him home, but he would make those responsible pay, a promise that not only included Mordrac, but his daughter as well.

Cavan dragged himself to the chair by the fireplace and dropped into it. He would have preferred his mind to be filled with thoughts of his wife than with memories of his capture, but the memories were haunts that refused to leave him. And when they took hold, so did the pain. He relived them time and again, and wondered if they would ever go away. Would he ever forget? Would he ever not relive the suffering?

He dropped his head back against the chair and didn't bother to close his eyes. It would not shut out the visions. They would come whether his eyes were open or shut. They would assault him until he felt drained and once again conquered.

What good was being a warrior if he repeatedly allowed himself to be conquered? What good was his anger if it caused innocent people to suffer? What good was pride if he couldn't hold his head up?

He stared at the clear vision of the nameless woman he had grown to hate, and gave in to the memories so that they would finally pass . . .

Until next time.

* * *

Honora followed Addie to another cottage, but her thoughts centered on her husband. Something was wrong. She could feel it, and she'd seen it descend on his face in an instant, and it had frightened her . . .

Frightened her badly.

"Addie," she said before they reached the next cottage. "I must go. My husband needs me."

Addie nodded and shooed her away. "Take good care of him."

"Always," Honora promised, and hurried off, though she didn't know why, just that it was necessary. Her feet flew across the earth and the chilled air slapped at her face. His earlier rejection of her offer hadn't disturbed her, *in time*, as he had said, and she knew it to be the truth. It would happen; they would make love and she would be patient and wait, for she knew their joining was inevitable. But this?

The look that had registered on his face chilled her to the bone, and she knew that patience would not work in this matter. Her husband needed her whether he realized it or not. *He needed her.*

She ran through the hall, not noticing how Artair and Lachlan stared after her nor hearing them joke about how they wouldn't be seeing either her or Cavan tonight at supper.

Her thoughts were solely on her husband. She didn't even think of what she would say to him; she only knew she needed to be with him. He couldn't be alone; she wouldn't let him be alone in his torment, not any longer.

She burst into the room, and the look on his face was no longer anguish, but one of pure rage.

"Get out!" he screamed at her.

She slammed the door behind her. "No."

"Don't defy me," he growled angrily.

"Tell me what is wrong," she insisted, stepping farther into the room.

Cavan sprang out of the chair. "Leave now."

"Why?"

"Out!" he shouted.

"Answer me," she demanded with strength, while her legs trembled.

He grabbed hold of her shoulders. "You dare make demands?"

She softened her tone and placed a trembling hand to his cheek. "You don't need to suffer alone. You have a wife who cares for you."

The growl started low in his chest and rumbled to a full roar when it spewed from his mouth. With its release, he lifted her off the ground and headed toward the closed door.

He wouldn't get rid of her that easily. She wrapped her arms tightly around his neck and whispered in his ear, "I'm falling in love with you."

He stilled instantly, her feet dangling off the ground while her arms remained firm around his neck.

She caressed his cheek with hers.

"You can't love me. You barely know me," he accused.

She pressed her lips near his ear. "I know you better than you think."

"I don't want you to know me."

"Too late," she murmured, and kissed his cheek, then moved tentatively to his mouth to kiss him ever so lightly.

He groaned and whispered against her mouth. "I am—"

"My husband," she finished. "Let me help you forget the pain."

This time he moaned loudly. "I am not fit to—"

"Love me?"

He didn't answer.

"Love me," she repeated, not a question this time.

Still he remained silent.

"Love me." She brushed his lips with hers.

He shook his head, though barely.

"Love me," she whispered against his lips. "It's time."

Chapter 23

Cavan felt the familiar heat of passion consume him, only this time her words had ignited his desire. He wondered if he had ever wanted a woman as much as he now wanted his wife. There had been times when any woman would have satisfied him. Not so now. He knew that he'd find no pleasure, no relief, with anyone but Honora.

Why?

He had no answer, or perhaps, like Honora, he was falling in love, but was too stubborn to admit it.

With a groan of resignation, he scooped his wife up in his arms, marched to the bed and placed her down gently. He eased her arms from around his neck, and they slipped away reluctantly.

He tenderly caressed her cheek with the back of his fingers and asked, "Are you certain about this?"

She nodded vigorously and smiled softly.

His own smile spread slowly. "It will be a night you never forget."

He kissed her while his hand inched slowly

beneath her blouse, tracing his fingers along her midriff until he gently cupped her full breast in his hand. She didn't startle but, rather, sighed with pleasure he anticipated that would soon see turned to a writhing passion, and he grew hard with the thought.

"We will do well together, wife," he whispered between kisses.

"That we will, husband," she agreed.

The rapid pounding at the door tore them apart.

"Cavan, news. Hurry!" Artair called out.

Cavan instantly left Honora's side, but stopped and turned before he reached the door. "We will finish this tonight, or upon my return if I must leave. Be waiting for me here in bed."

Honora near screamed in disappointment. Just when she finally had him where she wanted him and was quite enjoying it, her husband was ripped away from her. It wasn't fair. And if he thought she would remain in bed, not knowing what was going on, then he was a fool.

She scurried out of bed, righted her garments, ran her fingers through her hair and hurried after him. The only one in the hall when she entered was Addie, who stood looking at the closed door as if left in the wake of a stiff wind.

"Where did they go and why?" Honora asked as she approached the stunned woman.

"I am not certain. A warrior arrived with news that sent my husband and his sons off together. That is rare; one usually remains behind to protect the keep."

"They cannot have gone far," Honora assured her. "They would never leave the keep vulnerable."

Neither woman voiced the thought that the news stirring such instant reaction could have something to do with Ronan. Far too often news concerning the youngest Sinclare son had proven false, and their hearts suffered.

Honora kept herself busy with mundane chores, every now and again glancing in the distance to see if the warriors' approached. Finally, not far from sundown, she headed to the stable to spend some time with Champion in hopes of easing her mind. She was worried about her husband and feared for his safe return.

Calum appeared suddenly out of the shadows, startling her and causing her to stumble. Honora quickly righted herself before her father's rough grasp could reach her, and she stepped away from him, remembering what her husband had taught her.

Keep a distance between you and your foe.

She waited for him to speak, but then, she had learned to keep silent when in Calum's presence.

"You may be wife to Cavan," he said, "but you are still my daughter and will obey me."

She wanted to remind him that she was never his daughter, but her defiance would only serve to ignite his temper. Let him think what he would, she would protect herself, and no doubt her husband would too.

She stood defiantly silent.

"You best remember that."

Instead of responding to his remark, she questioned him. "Where have you been, Father?" She almost choked when she called him by that endearment. He wasn't her father, could never be her father, but he had insisted she respect him, and part of that respect was for her to call him Father.

"My whereabouts don't concern you," he said.

Neither does mine, she wished she could say, but held her tongue. She didn't want to infuriate him, for she would only suffer for her courage.

He pointed a finger at her. "You do as I say."

Suddenly, Champion came charging out of the stable and went directly for Calum's feet, yapping and biting and displaying his anger at the man.

Calum made the mistake of kicking the little pup and sending him flying with a horrific cry.

Honora hurried to the pup, scooping him up in her arms. Seeing that he was all right, she placed him on the ground, patted his rump, and ordered him to stay put. She would have turned with a fury on her stepfather but recalled her husband teaching her to never let an enemy know who you cared for. It would then be too easy to use against you, and her heart would break if anything happened to the pup. She would not give Calum that advantage.

She chose silence, which probably appeared to him as if she acquiesced; far from the truth, but Calum didn't need to know that.

"Remember, always remember," Calum warned. "You obey me."

Honora nodded, scooped up Champion and hurried off before he could stop her. It worried her that he continued to believe he had control over her. She felt as if she'd never be free of him, and Lord how she wanted to be free of her stepfather for good. She wanted to know that she would never set eyes on him, never hear him command her, and never suffer his harsh tongue or strong hand again.

When she was young she had wished him dead, and she'd never stopped wishing it.

She spent the next few hours playing with Champion, and when she left, the pup followed. He was ready to leave his family, she realized, for he had a new one, just like her. Cavan was her family now. Calum was no more, though he truly never had been.

She hurried to the keep, Champion bouncing happily alongside her. In the distance she saw no sign of the warriors. There was only one thing left for her to do—follow her husband's wishes and return to their bedchamber to wait for him.

Addie was sitting at the table in the great hall, and while Honora wished only to retreat to her bedchamber, she couldn't leave her alone. She walked over to the table, Champion dutifully following at her heels.

"I never stop worrying," Addie said after Honora joined her at the table.

Honora reached out to her and they linked hands, while Champion contentedly curled up at her feet.

"Every battle Tavish has ever fought, I have worried that he would not return, and then when my sons were old enough to join him, my worries doubled, tripled. It is a woman's lot to forever worry."

The door swung open, slamming against the wall, and in strode the Sinclare men, Tavish in the lead. He was a formidable figure, as were his sons, who followed him, though none looked happy, which could only mean they hadn't found what they looked for.

Addie immediately went to her husband, and he gripped her in a tight embrace. It was easy to see that the news was not good, for husband and wife clung to each other and tears shone in Addie's eyes.

Honora hurried to her husband's side, Champion joining her. She went directly into his arms and he dropped his head next to hers and squeezed her tight. She could feel his defeat and thought it best not to ask, not to speak, just offer him comfort and love.

Without a word they left the great hall, Champion quietly following them, his whimpers growing louder as he struggled to climb the stairs. Cavan stopped, turned, scooped him up and tucked him in the crook of his left arm, Honora in his right arm, and all three continued up the steps.

Champion was set before the fireplace to sleep, and Cavan kept his wife tucked in his arm until they reached the bed.

"We have something to finish," he said softly. "Unless you've changed your mind?"

"Have you?" she asked.

"No. I want you more than ever."

"Truly?" she asked.

He took her hand and slipped it beneath his kilt. He was hot, hard, yet silky soft and throbbed like a steady heartbeat.

That life-reassuring rhythm ignited not only her passion, but her feelings, and she spoke from her heart. "I belong only to you, and I want to feel no other but you inside me."

In response, he swung her up in his arms and had her down on the bed in no time, though then he hesitated, sat beside her on the bed and simply stared at her.

"What troubles you?" she asked thoughtfully, a comforting hand resting at his leg.

"Your beauty."

She was taken back and didn't know how to respond.

He smiled and kissed her gently. "Your beauty goes far deeper than simply your features. I've often heard talk of beautiful hearts, but never truly had the honor of meeting such a person. Imagine my surprise when I realized I married one."

Her heart soared along with her smile.

"Right now I ache for you, as you felt for yourself. It is an ache not only born of need, however, but of something much deeper. I have grown to appreciate you in the strangest of ways, one simply being that I feel *safe* knowing you sleep close by."

"Tonight we will sleep much closer, and I for one will be grateful."

"Want me in your bed, do you?" he teased.

She grew serious. "I very much want you in my bed—now and always."

"Don't intend to let me go?" he asked.

She took tight hold of his hand. "You are mine and I will never let you go. I will always protect and keep you safe."

Cavan laughed. "It is I who should be reassuring you about that."

"But I know you will always protect me and keep me safe. I want you to know I will do the same for you. I would give—"

He pressed his fingers to her lips. "Do not say what I think you intend. You will never, ever give your life for me."

She took hold of his hand and kissed it gently. "You would give your life for me."

"Of course, but that is different."

"Why?"

"I am a man, a warrior, it is my duty."

"And I," she said, sitting up to press her cheek against his, "love you and would give my life for you."

She felt his body grow tense and knew his reaction would be to take firm hold of her and command her never to do such a thing. How to stop his predictable response?

Could she be so bold? And before she could lose her courage, she slipped her hand beneath his kilt to first tentatively then gently run her fingers over the length of his hardness. Then finally she gripped him firmly in her hand.

"You do not play fair," he whispered in her ear.

"A good teacher taught me the art of warfare."

In seconds his hand slipped beneath her skirt

and his fingers quickly entered her while his thumb caressed her nub, which in no time throbbed madly.

"So we battle?" he teased, nibbling along her ear.

She moaned, laughed softly and murmured, "I surrender."

He laughed. "No, sweetheart, not yet you haven't."

He had them both undressed in minutes, and where Honora once worried about being naked and vulnerable in front of him, she felt no such qualms now that she was unclothed. She wanted him to touch her, kiss her, caress her. She wanted to make love with him.

"You are so very beautiful," he said between lavishing kisses over her breasts.

She raised her chest up for her breast to meet his lips, and when he took her nipple in his mouth, she moaned with the pleasure he brought her. He played with it, nipped at it, and suckled it until she thought she would go mad, and when he finished he moved to her other breast and did the same.

He continued to lavish kisses all over her body, and the more he did, the more sensitive her flesh became, until he could not touch a part of her without her moaning, arching, twisting, or writhing.

She couldn't think; she could only respond.

While he rained kisses over her stomach, his fingers worked their magic between her legs, and Lord did she respond. She didn't want him to stop; she never wanted him to stop. Never had she imagined that making love could feel so miraculous.

"You taste so sweet, so delectable," he said, slowly making his way down her stomach with kisses.

She almost jolted off the bed when his mouth replaced his fingers, and she thought she'd burst from the pleasurable torment. He tasted her with a mixture of tenderness and firmness until she believed she could bear no more. Then he slipped over her, and she took hold of him once more.

He stopped abruptly and growled deep and low. "Don't," he warned. "My need for you is too great."

She understood, and guided the full throbbing length of him into her as he braced his hands on either side of her and hovered above her.

"You feel so good," she couldn't help but say.

He pressed his forehead to hers and groaned.

Honora moved her hand off him as she felt him take command, and he slipped into her, slowly at first, and then as she writhed beneath him, he entered her harder and she arched up. He pushed, and a rhythm was set just before he plunged deep and she gasped, not from the pain but from pure passion.

He pressed his cheek to hers, his breathing rapid, all movement stilled. "Are you all right?"

"No," she whimpered, then accused. "You stopped."

He chortled, then warned her, "Hold on."

She gripped his arms tightly and was soon moaning loudly from the pleasure coursing through her body. Her damp flesh tingled, her body throbbed unmercifully, and she knew that only he, her husband, could bring her the satisfaction she ached for.

He had been right when he warned her that she hadn't surrendered yet, though she wanted to and he refused to let her. He teased her, slowing the rhythm just as she thought she would burst, then starting again until she thought she'd go mad.

Until finally she felt his surrender draw near, his rhythm steady, firm, certain, and she knew he would not stop, could not stop, and together they held on, riding harder, stronger, until . . .

When the explosive release hit her, she thought she would die from the pleasure of it and tightened her grip on Cavan, her writhing far from over until she finally felt spent, but far from empty; she felt full, whole, complete.

Unexpectedly, tears filled her eyes. Tears were streaming down her cheeks when Cavan lifted his head, brushed his cheek to hers, and looked at her, startled.

"What's wrong? Did I hurt you?"

He would have jumped off her if she hadn't stilled him with a tight squeeze. "No, don't go, and no, you didn't hurt me."

"Then why the tears?" he demanded gently, kissing them away.

She smiled. "I've never felt anything so beautiful. I've never felt so whole."

He tried to respond, but she pressed her finger to his lips. "I know you have probably made love many times, but this is my first, and I am glad it was with you—my husband."

He moved his lips off her finger. "I have had *sex* many times. Tonight I made love for the first time, and I'm glad it was with my wife."

"Truly? You do not jest with me?"

He wiped away the last of her tears. "Know that I speak the truth when I tell you that before tonight I have never known such satisfying pleasure with a woman."

She placed a gentle hand to his cheek and smiled. "You can please me anytime you like."

He laughed softly. "Be careful what you offer. You may find yourself forever in this bed."

She looked startled. "You mean we can only make love in bed?"

He laughed again. "I should be the one warned of you."

She slipped her arms around his neck. "Then be forewarned, husband, for I fear I have an insatiable appetite for you."

Chapter 24

The sun would rise shortly, but Cavan had woken almost an hour ago. He cuddled around his wife, who slept on her side, her back embedded against him. She was naked and had insisted on remaining so. She had expressed her pleasure in feeling his naked flesh against hers and how wonderful it would be throughout the night to feel him there, skin to skin, next to each other.

Naturally, she had excited him, and they made love again. She was certainly not the frightened little mouse he once thought her to be, but then he realized mice could be cunning little creatures, scurrying and forging until they found what they wanted and then contentedly nesting.

Honora showed no signs of being fearful or meek when it came to making love. On the contrary, she appeared to enjoy every moment and it was obvious she wanted to learn more. When she wasn't sure, she asked him, and damn if her honest curiosity didn't enflame him even more.

He thought he'd climax instantly when she asked

him, while holding his engorged member in her hand, if it was acceptable for her to taste him intimately, as he had her.

Needless to say, he confirmed with a hasty nod that it was, and damn if she hadn't taken sincere, lengthy pleasure in doing it, as he had with her. He grinned, remembering. Honora was more than he ever hoped for in a wife. and he felt lucky and also guilty.

She had expressed her love for him, which touched his heart and warmed his soul. He had no idea how she could have fallen in love with him since he hadn't been even pleasant since his return home, but she had nonetheless.

He should be grateful, but instead guilt haunted him. Not that he wasn't certain he loved his wife. Somehow, somewhere along the way, he had lost his heart to her. He had no idea when it happened; he couldn't pinpoint it, and it didn't matter. What mattered was that he had finally realized how he felt about her. And yet . . .

He couldn't bring himself to tell her. No matter how many times last night she had uttered her love for him, he couldn't respond in kind. He couldn't allow himself or her that joy, release, or pleasure. He had no right to be happy.

His failure to see his brother safe forever haunted him, as did information he had learned while held captive, and while he wished to share it with someone, he couldn't. He didn't know whom to trust.

Cavan glanced down at his sleeping wife. How he would love to tell her, but then the information might also place her in jeopardy. He was certain that it would prove a link to whoever held his brother, and could possibly be the key to Ronan's safe return. But so far he'd had no success in discovering the link.

Sooner or later he would have to trust someone. He had intended to do that upon his return, but the more he thought about the situation on his journey home, the more he realized it would be better to keep the news to himself and allow the truth to be revealed in its own time.

Honora stirred beside him, rubbing her backside against him and sighing softly. Her eyes remained closed, and he smiled. Even in sleep passion nibbled at her. He ran a gentle hand over her breasts, teasing her nipples to life and stirring her desire even further.

When her sigh turned to a moan, he ran his hand down over her stomach and between her legs, to enter her gently and pleasure her even more.

Her eyes drifted open and he nibbled at her neck, probed her deeper and whispered, "I want you." He knew it should have been *I love you*, but not yet, not yet.

"Then take me," she said with a long stretch as she turned, arching her back.

His mouth assaulted one of her nipples and she cried out with pleasure.

Cavan didn't wait; he didn't want to. He wanted

her right then, and he took her fast and hard. And she responded in kind, as if they had been lovers long denied and this was their first coming together after a lengthy separation. Their need was all that mattered, nothing else, and, insatiable as it was, they fed it.

The bed shook from their fierce joining, and their climaxes were explosive, both of them crying out in pure, unbridled pleasure. Afterward, neither could speak. Cavan rolled off Honora, to collapse beside her. He locked hands with her, and there they lay recovering, their bodies damp, their breathing heavy, their hearts beating wildly.

They lay quietly for several minutes, their fingers wrapped strong around each other's.

Finally, Honora turned on her side to face him. "Do I demand too much of you?" she asked.

Cavan laughed heartily and turned to kiss the tip of her nose. "Demand all you want."

Honora grinned. "Good, for I truly enjoy coupling with you."

"We'll couple as much as you want," he assured her, thinking how lucky he was to have her for a wife.

"And not only in bed," she reminded.

"Wherever you like."

"Or whenever the mood strikes," she said.

"Be moody all you want," he said, trying hard to sound more agreeable than gleeful.

They heard a little whimper then, and a moment later Champion appeared by the side of the bed, his tail wagging.

Honora bounced up. "I forgot he was here with us. He must need to go outside and he's probably hungry. I'm starving myself." She threw the covers back, but before jumping out of bed turned and kissed her husband soundly on the lips.

Cavan cushioned his head with his arms and watched her race around the room naked, gathering her clothes and searching for fresh ones to wear. She was a sight to behold and he savored the view, from her firm buttocks to her generous hips and narrow waist, and Lord did he favor her full breasts. He could still taste her on his lips.

Before she could slip into her clothes, he sprinted out of bed, grabbed her around the waist and hugged her close. "The day is ours to do as we wish."

She giggled, rubbed her body temptingly against his, and in a singsong voice warned, "Be careful what you wish for."

He nuzzled at her neck. "I'll be very careful, but I have a distinct feeling that all my wishes will come true today."

Champion whimpered louder, and Honora pulled away from him. "He really needs to go outside," she said and hurriedly dressed, slipping on a brown skirt and blue blouse. Then, with boots in hand, she rushed out the door.

Cavan intended to make certain that Champion didn't spend another night in their room. He didn't rush to join his wife, knowing she would be busy fussing over the pup, and besides, he could use time alone, time to think.

He was dressing in his plaid and his tan shirt when a thought hit him.

Hadn't he spent enough time alone? Hadn't he longed to return to family and friends? Hadn't he ached for his isolation and torment to end?

He enjoyed his wife's company, had enjoyed it even before they became intimate. Of late he also realized how much he enjoyed his brothers' company and how much he'd missed talking with his father. His father was a wise man and leader and had taught him much and could teach him much more.

He realized that for the first time since his return, he felt deeply grateful to be home.

He hurried to join his wife and family for the morning meal, feeling as if it truly would be his first meal since he returned.

Laughter continued to surface at the breakfast table, the Sinclare men telling Honora of a childhood beset by an older brother who tried to lead before his time, and Cavan defending himself by citing their youthful foolishness, which he said forced him to protect them at every turn.

The conversation turned serious when Addie addressed their hasty departure the day before.

"The false news yielded disappointment," she said, "but one day you will ride out and return with Ronan and our family will be whole once again."

The three sons nodded, and her husband confirmed her assessment. "Ronan will return home, I promise you that, Addie," Tavish said with determination. "Ronan will come home."

"With the stories you have told me, how could he not?" Honora said innocently.

"What do you mean?" Artair asked.

Honora smiled. "Ronan manipulated all of you and—"

The three brothers didn't let her finish; they voiced their disagreement loudly.

"Ronan wouldn't know how," Lachlan said.

"He never paid attention," Artair added.

"He forever needed help," Cavan finished.

Honora laughed. "Can't you see that he did that all on purpose?"

The three brothers shook their heads and mumbled denials.

She looked to Addie and Tavish for help. "You know your sons. You must have seen how Ronan controlled the three of them."

The three brothers stared at their parents sitting side by side, their hands clasped.

"Ronan could connive," Tavish admitted.

Addie nodded. "Ronan had his way of getting around people and getting what he wanted."

"The hell he did," Lachlan protested.

"Think about it, son," Tavish said. "Remember that mare that my stallion birthed and how it was intended for you?"

Lachlan nodded. "Yes, but she was not what I wanted so I let Ronan have her."

Tavish laughed. "Ronan talked you out of wanting her."

"He did not—" Lachlan stopped abruptly. "Damn it, he did." He pointed to Artair. "He talked you out of that sword you had specially made—"

"He did not," Artair objected.

Lachlan nodded firmly. "He did, claimed it was too light for a man of your strength."

Artair glared at his brother. "Damn, you're right. He convinced me that it didn't suit me at all. What of you, Cavan? What did Ronan get from you?"

"Nothing," Honora said. "Ronan respected his position as leader and knew that as such it wouldn't be wise to play tricks on him."

"You're very perceptive, Honora," Tavish said.

"It is easy to see when you look from the outside in," she said.

Tavish reached out, placed his hand over hers on the table and smiled. "You're on the inside now, so be careful."

"I have no worries," she admittedly freely. "I trust you all."

Cavan couldn't get over how freely she admitted her trust for them. She spoke confidently without an ounce of doubt, and he envied her.

Conversation turned light again, and then it was time to tend to daily chores and matters and she and Cavan left the hall. They walked toward the stable, a yapping Champion trailing along behind.

Cavan took her hand, needing to ask her a question that disturbed him. "You left something out about

Ronan and me. Something else you observed from the tales my brothers and I told."

"Did I?" she asked with an innocence he doubted.

He stopped and glared at her, his stern expression making it clear that they would not move until she answered him.

"You know me too well," she protested half-heartedly.

"You would do well to remember that," he said, and kissed her quick. "Tell me."

"I feared it would upset you."

"That makes little difference. I want to know that you will always be honest with me, that you will never fear confiding anything in me. I will always be there to help you, and I will never betray you."

She smiled softly. "Trust. You're asking for my trust, which I have already given you. That is what your brother knew. That he could always count on you, trust that you would never betray him."

"How do you know that?"

"From the story you told about how you and Ronan had accidentally fallen in the loch while catching fish. That wasn't how it happened. I would say it was you who had caught all the fish and Ronan was angry that he'd caught none, and you offered to split the catch with him, which angered him even more. He shoved you or scuffled with you and probably stumbled and fell in the loch and you jumped in after him."

"What makes you believe that?"

"Because you admitted to me that you always protected Ronan, and besides, he was so young. What? Barely six?"

"Two days from his sixth birthday," Cavan said.

"And Artair mentioned you're seven years older than Ronan, which would have made you thirteen at the time." She shook her head. "The story you concocted makes no sense."

"That is what my father said."

She laughed. "But not your brothers."

"And I suppose you know why?"

She grinned. "They were pleased to see the mighty leader not only take a foolish fall, but not catch a single fish. You let Ronan take the credit because he was probably upset and regretted his actions with a plethora of tears. While in truth that day you proved to your little brother that he could forever trust you."

Cavan nodded, released her hand and walked away.

She quickly followed, reclaiming his hand. "You did not fail your brother."

He wished he could believe that, but he couldn't, and no one understood that, nor did he think they ever would.

"We'll go riding on the moors today," he told her.

"Cavan," she said with a tug to his hand.

He stopped. "No more about Ronan. It is done."

She looked ready to disagree.

"Not another word, Honora," he said sternly.

She sighed and looked away. "I have little experience riding."

"You did well last night," he teased.

She turned with a smile and puffed out her chest. "I certainly did, but then you're an easy one to tame." She laughed and ran off toward the stable.

He chased after her, grinning.

Chapter 25

Honora couldn't believe how happy she was. In the two weeks since she and Cavan had become intimate, life was simply wonderful. They laughed, they kissed, they loved, while her husband gave her lessons in all sorts of things, including making love. She felt her cheeks redden from the cherished memories, but more so with the love for him that was growing stronger in her heart each day. And she let him know of her love often, even though he had yet to tell her the same. She knew without a doubt that he did and in time would speak the words to her. She'd be patient, and why not? Every day with him was amazing.

She shivered, a sudden chill descending over her, and her bright smile faded to a frown. Her joy actually frightened her. She feared somehow it would disappear, or worse, that she would be robbed of it. She pressed her hand to her chest, imagining the dreadful pain she would feel if Cavan were ever taken away from her. She could not bear it.

"What's wrong?" he asked claiming the bench opposite her, where she sat in front of the hearth.

Her smile returned when he gently peeled her hand away from her chest and kissed her palm. He was so very handsome, and grew more handsome by the day, but then, of course, she had heard that love did that to you, sharpened your sight for the one you loved. And while she could certainly extol his striking features, they weren't, in her opinion, what made him handsome. It was his loving, giving, caring heart that made her love him so very much, and while he refused to acknowledge that part of himself, she had no trouble doing so.

"Are you feeling ill?" he asked.

She shook her head. "No. I feel fine."

"Something troubles you. I watched your brilliant smile fade and your hand press your chest as if in pain."

She had no trouble confessing the truth to him. "I am so very happy with you—"

"Then what brought the frown?"

"Fear of losing you, being robbed of you." She shrugged helplessly. "I cannot bear to think of life without you."

He kissed her palm again, then firmly squeezed her hand. "Then don't. We have a whole life together to share. I would go to the ends of the earth and fight the devil himself to get you back. I will let nothing separate us."

"Cavan!"

Honora and Cavan turned at Artair's shout.

"Barbarians attack farms to the east. Father remains here. You, Lachlan, and I ride."

Honora stood and followed her husband to see him off. Before he mounted his horse, she grabbed hold of his arm. "You come back to me safe and sound, husband, and I promise you a welcome you will never forget."

Cavan scooped her up against him, kissed her soundly and whispered in her ear, "That promise will have me home in no time."

"I will have the fire burning and food aplenty so we don't have to leave the bedchamber for a whole day."

He grinned, planted a sloppy, wet kiss on her lips, released her and mounted his horse.

"I love you," she said, her hand at his ankle, holding onto him as long as possible. "Stay well." She backed away and stood watching him ride off. She had thought for a moment he would respond in kind. He looked ready to, but then stopped.

She wasn't sure what prevented him from admitting his love for her, but knew deep down in her soul that he did. She could see it in his dark eyes. They glistened whenever she professed her love, softened, then turned turbulent. She knew that's when he fought himself and refused to utter a word of love. Instead he would show her with a kiss, a touch, or if the turbulence turned heavy, he would make love to her.

She hugged her waist and smiled. It was then that he showed her how much he truly loved her.

Honora waved until he was out of sight, as was her way each time he rode off to battle. She wanted him to know that she would always be there waiting for him to return.

"You two do well together."

Honora turned and greeted Tavish Sinclare with a warm smile. "Yes, we do, and glad I am to have him as a husband."

"That is good to hear," Tavish said, and held his arm out to her. "Walk with me, I wish to talk with you."

Honora hooked her arm around his, knowing she could not refuse the laird, though he intimidated her a bit. She couldn't say why since he was a fair and pleasant man and spoke kindly to everyone. Perhaps it was the commanding quality about him, which demanded attention and respect. She waited for him to speak.

They walked a distance without saying a word, and Honora realized he was moving them away from prying eyes and ears. Not that many villagers lurked about, the cold, blustery day keeping many inside, while the warriors who remained behind were busy guarding the village and the keep.

When no one was near, Tavish finally spoke. "Has Cavan spoken to you of his capture?"

Honora hesitated, unsure how to answer. Did she keep her husband's confidence and refuse to answer, or did she obey her laird and betray her husband?

She shook her head, her answer easy. "My husband talks with me in confidence."

"I respect that," Tavish said. "But something disturbs me. Like you, I listen when people talk. It is a good rule to follow for you learn much that way. I have listened to my son Cavan, and I believe there is something about his capture that he purposely does not share, and I don't believe it has anything to do with Ronan."

"He speaks mostly of Ronan to me," she admitted freely.

"Then he keeps this from you as well."

"You believe he keeps a secret from everyone?"

Tavish nodded.

"Why would he do that?" she asked, curious.

"I've asked the same myself. What would make him keep a secret from everyone in his family?"

They both stopped walking, and Honora gave thought to his question when the answer suddenly hit her like a slap in the face. She turned wide-eyes on Tavish.

"Cavan does what he has always done. He protects."

Tavish nodded, his smile growing. "At first I thought perhaps his captivity had made him mistrustful of everyone. But then, as you knew immediately, I realized that Cavan was who he always was, a warrior who protected his family and clan at all cost. He protects. Whatever he knows, I believe that he fears sharing it could prove dangerous."

"He will realize soon enough that family will help, and then he will confide in someone," Honora said reassuringly.

"You have unerring belief in your husband, and that will serve him well when he is laird. It is good that you wed him instead of Artair."

"Why?"

"You and Cavan fit as if you were made for each other."

"But Cavan rejected Calum's first offer of a union between us, and I assumed you agreed," she said, perplexed.

Tavish nodded. "I did. You weren't ready yet, but in time I knew you would be. I watched you grow and knew you were a courageous one, and sharp-witted. You had to be since your lot in life was not easy."

Honora was shocked. "I never thought you noticed me."

"I know all in my clan; I must. When I am asked to settle disputes I must be familiar with those who lie and those who speak the truth. I must be aware of the weak so they are protected, and I must understand the misunderstood for they often prove great warriors, like you."

"I am honored—"

"Nonsense. You earned respect, and it is I who am honored to have you as my daughter."

She threw her arms around the large man without thinking and hugged him tightly. "Thank you, *Father.*" He was the closest she had to a real father, she thought. If her father had lived, surely he would have been as wonderful and kind as Tavish Sinclare.

He returned her hug, though had to pry her away

gently. "I believe if we work together, we may be able to find out the secret my son keeps and help him."

"I agree," she said, nodding vigorously.

"Good. I feel better knowing someone shares this burden with me. My son is a good man, a great warrior, and will make a better laird than me. I am proud of him and would do anything to see that he no longer suffered." Tavish wrapped Honora's arm around his. "We have a secret, daughter; we share with no one until the time is right."

"Agreed," she said with a final nod.

A few hours later Honora was in the stables feeding the pups. Champion would return with her to the keep, but she would see him settled by the hearth in the great hall, his usual spot in the evening. Cavan had made it known that he didn't want the pup in their bedchamber, and she understood why and agreed. Besides, the pup did not mind at all since Addie spoiled him at night with snacks and a walk.

Honora had made it her chore to make certain that the pups, weaned from their mother, were fed scraps from the kitchen until they were capable of foraging on their own. While lost in her chore, she thought of Cavan and hoped he was safe and that he would return soon, but she doubted an early return. He could be gone days, though she hoped not weeks.

She just finished with the pups when a large shadow fell over her and she turned with a start ready to defend herself. She was shocked to see her husband in the doorway, blocking out what little daylight was available, the skies having darkened with storm clouds. Terror gripped her when she spotted heavy splatters of blood on his hands, face, shirt, and legs.

Her legs trembled but she moved quickly and was at his side in seconds. "Are you all right?" She didn't let him answer, grabbing hold of his arm. "Come let me get you to the keep and see to your wounds."

He wouldn't budge; he remained solid where he stood.

"Cavan," she said softly. "Let me help you." She noticed that his sword still dripped with blood, and she couldn't fathom the carnage that must have taken place. "Cavan . . . " she repeated.

Still he did not respond.

She placed a tender hand to his blood-covered cheek and almost sighed with relief when she realized the blood wasn't his, for there was no wound. His dark eyes were glazed and hard and unrecognizable. It was as if she touched a stranger, so cold was his glare.

He grabbed her around the waist so quickly and unexpectedly that she gave a shout, and when he lifted her up against him and ground his lips against hers, she became frightened. That fright grew as he rushed with her in his arms to the back of the stable and shoved her against the wall, his hand hoisting up her skirt and reaching roughly between her legs.

He smelled of sweat and blood, and her fear escalated.

She wasn't sure what to do, and when his fingers dug intimately into her, she grabbed his face and stared into his dark eyes. "I love you, Cavan. I love you so much."

It was as if she had thrown a bucket of cold water on him. His eyes lost their glare, his hand slipped from under her skirt, and his forehead fell to rest against hers.

"I'm sorry," he said, "so very sorry."

"It's all right. I'm all right. We're all right."

He moved to release her but she refused to let him go. She clung tightly to him.

"I'm no better than a bar—"

"You are a man seeking redemption from the carnage of battle."

"How could you say that after what I was about to do to you?" he asked incredulously.

"Because the only redemption is love, and you sought out the one person who could give you that unconditionally—your wife who loves you beyond measure."

He shook his head. "I don't deserve you."

"I deserve you," she confirmed. "And I want you. I want to love you." She slipped her hand beneath his plaid and felt the familiar swell of him. He was so thick and hard that she thought he was probably hurting for release.

"*Honora*," he said on a harsh breath.

"Take me here and now," she demanded, her breath heavy at his ear.

He shook his head. "I fear I will hurt you."

"I fear *you* already hurt."

He growled deep in his chest. "For the want of you. I left the men after I felled the last barbarian with my sword and rode directly back here to you, knowing you'd be here waiting for me, wanting me, loving me."

"Then love me here and now. Slip into me and let me ride you strong and hard so we both may release the hurt and pain that consumes us."

He protested with a groan and a shake of his head.

She responded by hoisting herself up just enough for the tip of him to snuggle between her legs. "Take me," she urged, and tried to slip him inside her.

It was enough to force a response, and he lifted her and settled himself with one deep thrust inside her. She cried out in pleasure, tossing her head back against the wall while holding onto his shoulders. He continued to plunge in and out, in and out, until her cries turned to pleas as she built toward a climax she was certain would kill her, though she didn't care.

The wall behind her creaked as he shoved into her hard and heavy, the odor of blood and sweat disappearing, swallowed by the distinct scent of their lovemaking. She was completely lost in unbridled passion, and dug her fingers into his flesh as her climax built to an uncontrollable force. It erupted with such fury that she screamed out like she never had before.

She thought she was spent, but her husband had yet to finish, and the driving force of his thrusts soon swept her up again, to her shock and pleasure.

When Cavan climaxed with a roar of his own, she did so as well and smiled with sheer joy.

It took a moment to regain their breathing, and they remained attached, Cavan's one arm firm around her while he braced the other against the wall beside her head.

"I didn't hurt you, did I?" he asked.

She heard his concern and a tinge of guilt as if he regretted his actions. She was quick to rectify that. "I came twice. I didn't know that was possible. I actually came twice, and it felt glorious. Do you think it will happen again? I want it to."

Relief flooded her entire body when the soft rumble of laughter spilled from him. Then he brushed his lips over hers. "I can make you come more than twice, if you like."

"Really?" she asked, bewildered, then poked his chest. "You're not teasing me, are you?'

"I'll prove it later tonight."

"Promise?"

"My word," he said softly.

She smiled, and he slipped out of her and slowly lowered her to the ground.

"I should never have come to you straight from such a vicious battle. I was heated with rage—"

"And looking for solace," she finished.

He raised his bloody hand to cup her face and stared at it briefly before turning away. "I am filthy. I had no right to—"

"Love me?"

He turned around, spreading his arms. "How

does a blood-drenched man make love to his wife? I wanted you, like an animal after a female in heat."

"Was that how it was? You admitted yourself that you knew I'd be waiting here wanting you, ready to love you. You returned to the one person you felt safe with, who you knew would accept you unconditionally."

"Still, I could have—"

She pressed her fingers to his mouth. "I refuse to hear any more nonsense. I need to get you cleaned and fed and rested, for you have a promise to keep tonight."

He shook his head, wrapped his arms around her and hugged her tight. "I don't know what I would do without you."

His words excited her heart for they were as close as he'd come to an admission of love. He would have to feel some modicum of love to feel he couldn't do without her.

She smiled and rested her head on his chest, knowing that he loved her.

Chapter 26

"**S**omething isn't right," Honora said, popping up in bed.

Cavan admired his wife's naked breasts, her nipples still hard from their recent lovemaking. He smiled and sat up, relaxing against two pillows he shoved behind his back. "You seemed satisfied enough." He held up his hand and began counting. "How many times did I make you come? One, two, three—"

Honora playfully slapped his hand down. "It has nothing to do with our lovemaking, and the answer is four." She shook her head.

"Can't believe it, can you? Don't worry, I guarantee you'll get used to multiple climaxes."

"It has nothing to do with that," she said, turning to sit crossed-legged beside him, the blanket covering her just below her navel. "And I'd prefer your word on the latter."

He laughed and reached out to tweak her nipple. "You have my word, and my curiosity. What isn't right?"

Honora ran her hand through her tousled dark hair and sighed. "Haven't you noticed it yourself?"

Cavan crossed his arms over his bare chest, enjoying the view. "The only thing I've noticed lately is my beautiful naked wife."

"Pay attention," she ordered with a smile. "Before your return there wasn't even the remotest news of Ronan, but since then, possible sightings of Ronan have arrived steadily."

Cavan almost shook his head, but then gave her suggestion thought and realized she was right. His curiosity aroused, he asked, "What are you thinking?"

"That something is afoot," she declared on a whisper.

He realized that her caution in lowering her voice even though they were alone meant she thought the problem could possibly come from within the keep. "You murmur. Who don't you trust?" he asked.

Her voice remained soft. "That's just it, I'm not sure. It just seems odd that your return brings sudden news of Ronan that has you giving chase but solves nothing."

He voiced his sudden thought. "A diversion."

"Which would mean that someone wants you looking elsewhere, but the question is, where are you looking in the first place?"

Cavan wasn't sure if he should confide in her. He had kept his secret for a reason, but perhaps his wife's keen perception could be of help.

Besides, he felt safe with her, and even more so since she had eased his burden without taking offense. She'd dealt with him purely out of love, and her unselfish actions had been his saving grace. Not to mention the times she had slept beside him and offered solace during his nightmare ravished nights.

He took her hand, and when he looked into her violet eyes, saw her love for him was so blatant, so strong, he knew he could trust her with anything. "There is something I haven't told anyone since my return."

She laced her fingers with his, and he knew it signaled solidarity between them.

He continued without hesitation. "During my capture I learned an alarming fact. It seems that the barbarian attack had one intention—to capture and kill me. Only once I was captured, it was determined that I might be of more help if kept alive. Worst of all, the plan had been devised with the help of someone from Clan Sinclare."

"How can you be sure?" Honora asked, stunned.

"The slaves had a way of spreading information among themselves. Anything learned by another was always shared. It was for protection and use if any should make a successful escape."

"What if the information had been intentionally planted to turn you against your own?"

"The thought crossed my mind, which was one of the reasons I kept it to myself, but more so to protect my family and clan. It was the one time I felt ignorance would shield everyone. If I announced to all that there was a traitor in the clan, I would unleash fear, doubt, and possibly panic; clansmen accusing clansmen and anger flaring out of control. And of course the culprit could very well be the one who instigated the panic. It was better if I searched for the guilty one myself."

"But you've had no luck?"

Cavan shook his head. "I haven't been able to find out anything, but with you pointing out the frequent and sudden sightings of Ronan since my return, it makes me think that the person responsible still lurks about and could be planning something."

"You could confide in your father and brothers and still continue to keep it a secret."

"Secrets never last when you tell even one person."

"I will not betray you," she said adamantly.

He raised their locked hands to kiss the back of hers. "We are one, you and I, and always will be."

"You trust me," she said, startled.

"I do," he admitted, wide-eyed, as if he had just grasped the depth of that trust and what it represented.

Love.

He had thought he loved her, but he truly hadn't realized the depths of his love. He only knew he didn't intend to fight it any longer. Voicing it was another matter. He knew there was no reason he couldn't blurt out his love here and now, and yet the words refused to spill forth.

"I am very pleased to know that you trust me."

Tell her, you fool. Tell her you love her.

"We will work together to find out who is responsible for this," she said confidently. "I am good at appearing invisible. It was a skill I acquired when young."

"To protect yourself from your stepfather?" he asked, suddenly needing to know everything about his wife. Or perhaps searching for a reason to divert his thought away from his inability to voice his love?

"Calum was less likely to anger if he didn't notice me."

"Did he anger often?"

"Daily. Neither I nor my mother could do anything to please him. He found fault in the smallest word or action. I realized that fast enough and learned the art of invisibility."

"How does it work?"

"You must remain silent in word and movement. Sometimes I would hold my breath when I passed by him or creep along in the shadows. It worked—he never noticed me. I became invisible."

"And the times you weren't invisible?"

She shrugged. "I would receive a slap across the face, or if he was very angry, a beating with his fists."

Cavan contained his anger, when what he wanted to do was find the man and beat him senseless. He couldn't fathom the life his wife had been forced to live, especially since he had grown up in such a loving family. How alone and frightening it must have been for her, an innocent child.

"I learned to duck and dart when he threw things, though he would get mad when he missed so I learned to judge which object would cause the least pain and allow it to hit me. Calum would be satisfied, and the bruises lessened considerably."

"I should have killed him that day he struck you," Cavan said with anger. He wanted only to protect his wife from a rotten beast of a man.

"Oh no," she said, alarmed. "You did much more for me by teaching me to protect myself. Just the other day Calum approached me and I kept my distance, as you taught me to do with a foe. And though I felt a moment of fear in his presence, it soon turned to confidence, knowing I would never allow him to raise his hand against me again."

Cavan sprang forward, his fingers squeezing an imaginary neck. "If he ever does, I will—"

Honora giggled.

"You laugh at my attempt to protect you?"

She placed a gentle hand over his gnarled fingers and chuckled as she said, "Calum's neck is too fat to strangle."

Cavan smirked. "You're right. My sword would work better and be more thorough."

Honora kissed his cheek. "Thank you for defending me. No one other than my mother ever defended me."

He slipped his hand around the back of her neck and drew her lips to his mouth. "I will always defend you. I—I—"

She whispered as she brushed his lips with hers, "Love you. I love you."

He claimed her mouth with a hungry kiss, as if he could not taste enough of her, as if he depended on her breath to feed him, and in no time he laid her on her back and slipped over her to hastily, with a burning need, bury himself deep inside her. And she welcomed him with a similar hungry need and together they lost themselves in making love.

Champion happily bounced alongside Honora as they took their usual morning stroll. Slowly and steadily she was becoming more familiar with everyone in the village. She had decided on beginning the daily ritual about a week ago, shortly after Tavish told her how necessary it was for him to know his clan. If she was to be a good and helpful wife to Cavan, the next laird, then she should know the clan members as well as possible. This way, if her husband asked an opinion on someone, she would be able to respond truthfully. It also gave her a chance to uncover the culprit she and Cavan searched for.

She had no way of expressing the depth of relief she felt when Cavan confided his secret to her. It proved to her, without a doubt, that he loved her. It took a deep trust and an even deeper bond to share such potentially dangerous information. Only love could have driven him to confide in her, a loving trust that left no room for doubt. Her heart filled with joy, her steps were light, and the sun shone more brightly than she had ever seen it.

Honora continued her walk, enjoying the friends

she was making. Never having been allowed friends, it felt good to talk with other women, hear tales of childbirth, raising babies, or admire an herb garden and listen to loving complaints about husbands.

"Wait until you birth one yourself," Sara said, resting her hand on her large extended belly. "You swear you'll never go through the pain again, and then—" She laughed and patted her stomach. "Before you know it, you're having another one."

Honora thanked Sara for the mix of dried herbs that she said would make a delicious hot brew and walked off with a wave. Champion followed a bit reluctantly since he had enjoyed playing with Sara's three-year-old son, as had the young lad, who was shedding mountainous tears over the pup's departure.

But Honora had to move on, her mind chaotic with the thought that she herself might very well be with child. It was too soon to tell, of course, but the prospect delighted her. Having been a lone child, she'd always hoped for a large brood of children. When she was to marry Artair, he had made it known to her that he wished children, but then she found herself wed to Cavan and wondered what he felt about it.

She chuckled, wondering no more. At the rate they couldn't keep their hands off each other, she would be with child more times than she wasn't. Life was suddenly very good.

Even with a culprit in their mix she was certain they would soon detect the man and that he would suffer his just reward. But for the moment she wished to merely bask in the thought of growing large with Cavan's child. He would make a good father and she would make a good mother, for her mother had taught her the qualities and virtues of being one.

"Daydreaming when you should be tending your husband," Calum accosted.

Honora stopped abruptly and realized Champion had been barking, attempting to alert her to Calum's approach. She silently chastised herself for not being attentive to her surroundings, since she stood much too close to her stepfather, making her more accessible to his quick hands.

"I tend my husband well enough," she informed him, and took a casual step away. He quickly bridged the distance and stood nearly face-to-face with her.

"Well enough isn't good enough. Cavan will be the next laird of the Clan Sinclare, and you would do well to remember that and treat him as such."

Honora stepped away from him again, needing to put distance between them, sensing his mounting anger and fearing his hand was sure to strike at any moment. She wished to tell him that none of this was his concern, but knew that would enflame him all the more, which could prove a serious problem for her.

He raised a pointed finger at her. "You better listen to me, daughter or—"

"Or what!"

Relief rippled through Honora, and she smiled, looking at her husband. He was so tall and broad and imposing, his arms crossed over his full chest, dark eyes narrowed and square chin raised defiantly. She walked over to him, Champion having already trotted over to stand beside Cavan, with a growling snarl directed at Calum. The pup's bravery, had grown considerably with Cavan's presence, she noted with amusement.

Calum fumbled his words and sputtered a few times before finally answering. "I only wish for her to serve you well."

"Honora concerns you no more," Cavan said curtly.

It pleased Honora when he took her hand and clasped it firmly. It seemed he was silently informed her that he was there now and there was nothing to fear. He would protect her.

"She is my daughter—"

"She is *my wife*."

Cavan announced it with such firm vigor that Honora wasn't surprised to see Calum shiver uncomfortably. She had even felt a rush of ripples wash over her, but for an entirely different reason. She wasn't intimidated by his forceful reproach; rather, she was excited that he felt so strongly about her being his wife.

"I meant no disrespect," Calum said apologetically.

"Then apologize to my wife for being so rude to her."

Calum's eyes near bulged from their sockets and red splotches stained his full cheeks. Her stepfather had never ever apologized to her. She had always been the one at fault, the one who deserved punishment, the one available for him to berate, and she could see in his raging eyes that it remained so; he blamed her for this.

Her body grew rigid, until it seemed she had turned to stone. But she was aware of Cavan's strong hand squeezing hers firmly, and she allowed herself to relax, knowing that with her husband beside her, Calum could do her no harm.

"Now!" Cavan shouted.

Calum jumped and uttered a barely audible reply.

"I didn't hear you, Calum. Do you hear him, Honora?" Cavan asked, never taking his heated glare off the man.

"No," she said, speaking up strongly. "No, I didn't hear what he had to say."

Calum pierced her with such an angry scowl that she almost felt as if he'd slapped her, but she remained standing firm and confident.

"Say it so we can hear it and know you mean it," Cavan demanded.

Calum took a couple of breaths and raised his head. "I am sorry if I was rude to you."

Cavan snorted a laugh and shook his head. "*If* you were rude?"

Calum blustered and his cheeks turned an even brighter red. "Forgive me for being rude."

"Is that an acceptable apology, Honora?" Cavan asked gently.

"I believe it will do," she answered with a smile to Calum.

"Good, then we'll be on our way."

Cavan turned, and Honora followed, as did the pup, but then Cavan stopped abruptly and turned back.

"Fair warning, Calum. If you ever disrespect my wife again, you will be banished from this clan."

Chapter 27

〰〰〰

"**K**eep your distance from Calum," Cavan said as they walked through the village and were surprised by the many who called out cheerful greetings to them.

"I always have, or at least I've tried." Honora smiled. "And though I can't say that he still doesn't put a bit of fear into me, I can claim quite proudly that I do not fear him as much as I once did, thanks to you. Besides, your last warning probably did the trick. Calum would never want to be banished from the clan."

He loved the way her violet eyes shone brightly when she was happy, and they had been shining constantly lately, which did his heart good. He leaned down and stole a kiss. "I'm glad I could give you some peace of mind, but I believe Calum is more devious than I first thought."

"I'll agree to that, but it's a beautiful day and I don't wish to spend it discussing my stepfather."

Champion agreed with a bark.

"I think you could use more practice with a

bow," Cavan said, and with an arm around her waist, directed her steps toward the bow maker's place.

"You only recently praised my skill with a bow and claimed I possessed a natural skill," she said, confused.

"I did, didn't I." Cavan nodded and grinned.

"What are you up to?" she asked.

Cavan laughed when she attempted to stop, digging her boots into the ground, but he just hoisted her up around the waist then set her feet down on the ground and proceeded with their walk each time she tried. "You know me too well, wife."

Honora gave a quick glance around and lowered her voice. "Does it have to do with the culprit we search for?"

Cavan whispered back. "No."

She sighed. "You're not going to tell me, are you?"

"You'll discover it for yourself soon enough."

Sure enough it didn't take her long to realize what he was up to, and he didn't mind since he was sure she'd approve.

He braced himself flat against her back as she picked up her bow and arrow. He loved being melded to her, feeling the whole length of her braced against him. He felt himself grow hard when she purposely rubbed her bottom against him, knowing that just as the bow responded in her hand, she would respond in his. He ran his hand slowly up the curve of her waist, recalling the small half-moon scar he so often kissed before moving farther down or up to taste her delicate flesh. This time his hand continued up along the side of her breast and he was tempted to squeeze a handful of her round tender flesh. Instead he slipped slowly along underneath her arm as she raised the bow. His other arm worked the same sensual rhythm along her right side until together their hands fit the arrow to the bow.

He breathed softly beside her ear. "Keep it taut, very taut."

"Now I know what you're up to," she whispered with a gentle gasp.

"Then know what I start here, I will finish in our bedchamber."

"You will stay taut?" she teased softly, and grinned as he nuzzled her neck with playful nips and laughter.

"Watch how you challenge, wife."

"Ah, but I am proficient with *my* bow and arrow," she quipped, and with a quick glance at the target— a large bale of hay with a circle painted on a white cloth attached to it—she let her arrow fly.

Cavan cringed as it hit dead center. "An adept opponent, but still I'm confident with my prowess."

"Then I should continue to practice."

"I agree," he said, and resumed his stance behind her as she took up another arrow.

By the time they finished, they were both running back to the keep, Champion having difficulty keeping up with them. They ignored Addie's call once they were in the great hall, since each was trying to beat the other to the stairs. Champion, however, caught scent of the food and headed straight toward Addie.

No sooner had the door slammed shut than they tugged and pulled off each other's clothes and fell on the bed in a tangle of arms and legs wrapping around each other and lips meeting and parting only for air.

Cavan couldn't get close enough to her, taste enough of her, and even though she protested when he began to take his time kissing every inch of her body, she soon capitulated and writhed in the pure pleasure.

Her skin was so soft and tasty, sweet, fruitful, with a tinge of tartness here and there. He didn't want to stop tasting her delicious flavor, and when he settled between her legs, she was soon so drunk with pleasure that she cried out in sheer delight.

He slid over her, and was surprised and enthralled when she pushed him on his back and settled over him.

"I need practice riding as well," she claimed, and mounted him skillfully.

He grabbed Honora around the waist when she seemed to tire but refused to relinquish her ride and assisted her in keeping a steady motion. But when she drew near to another climax, he switched positions, keeping himself buried firmly inside her, and she gasped with a grin and laughed.

"How talented."

"Wait, you've seen nothing yet."

They laughed and giggled and hugged each other until Cavan could stand it no longer and she cried out her need. They followed one another, bursting with pleasure and clinging in the aftermath, letting the last ripples of lovemaking wash over them.

Cavan fell off her onto his back, his breath still heavy and his thoughts of love. He loved this woman beside him. She was everything and more that he had wanted in a wife, and how lucky for him that he'd been wed to her without knowing it. Otherwise he would have never chosen her for a wife and had the chance to learn just how truly remarkable she was.

He wanted to blurt out *I love you.*

But it didn't seem the right time, since it would appear as if he only remarked on it because they had just finished making love. It had to be a special time, a time she would never expect him to declare his love. A time that she would know without a doubt that he meant every word he spoke, that it was from deep within his heart, down to the very core of his soul.

"That was exquisite," she sighed, and rolled on her side to rest her head on his chest.

Cavan wrapped his arm around her and caressed her damp skin. "I agree."

"Then I please you?"

He lifted her chin with one finger to glare at her incredulously. "You are joking, aren't you?"

Her violet eyes so brilliant with passion just

moments before now ached in need of an answer. His heart still thudding from his explosive climax, he suffered a quick stab and hastily sought to ease both their pain.

"You please me more than I ever thought I possibly could be pleased. It is as if I have never known the pleasures of true passion, true lovemaking, until now, with you." He took her hand and pressed it to his chest. "Feel my heart and how it beats madly because of you and for you. You are part of me, Honora, and I would have it no other way."

She took his hand and pressed it to her chest. "Our hearts beat the same."

He could feel her heart pounding madly beneath her damp flesh, and it was as if the wild tempo reached up and out to tingle his fingers. "As I have said before, we are one, you and I, and always will be."

She rested her head on his chest with a satisfied sigh. "I will keep your words close to my heart and tucked in the corner of my mind so that I may recall them whenever I feel the need."

"I will not let you forget how much you mean to me."

"That is good for I like to hear it from time to time," she said with a yawn.

"You will," he said, knowing what she wanted was to hear that he loved her, though she would not ask that of him.

He felt her body ease into a peaceful slumber, and laid there hugging her against him, not wanting to let her go. As their bodies chilled, he drew the blanket up over them and wrapped his legs around hers to warm her. Then he settled down, resting his cheek upon the top of her head and ever so softly whispered, "I love you."

Chapter 28

Cavan and Honora were startled out of sleep by a drawn-out, piercing scream of agony. They dressed quickly and ran out of their bedchamber, catching a glimpse of dusk settling over the land and realizing they had slept for a few hours.

Cavan preceded his wife down the flight of stone stairs, his heart pounding, for he felt that something dreadful had happened. He stopped abruptly, Honora near colliding with him when he spotted his father's body stretched out on the table where he and his family gathered for meals, to laugh, debate, sing, and sometimes cry together. His mother had thrown herself across her husband's body and was howling in agony.

He rushed to his father's side, Artair and Lachlan already there, shaking their heads as he approached.

Addie's eyes bulged from her color-drained face when she saw her son, and she turned frantic until her sight settled on Honora. She reached a blood-stained hand out to her. "Help him, please help my husband."

Honora hurried to her side and froze, her face turning pure white as she looked to her husband.

Cavan could see that his father had died, and it had clearly not been an accident. A dagger handle protruded form his chest; he'd been stabbed in the heart.

"Please," Addie pleaded, grabbing hold of Honora's arm. "Help him."

Honora slipped her arm around Addie and attempted to walk her away from the body. Addie would have no part of it. She yanked away from her and returned to her husband, throwing herself over him again, wailing uncontrollably.

Cavan looked to Artair and Lachlan, and Artair motioned them away from their mother while Honora went to the woman's side and placed a consoling hand on her shoulder.

"Father staggered from behind the stable and died in my arms before he could tell me anything," Artair said, tears filling his eyes but not spilling down his face.

"It's my fault," Cavan claimed.

"What nonsense do you speak?" Lachlan demanded.

Cavan confessed the secret he had harbored since his return, and told them that he'd been worried the culprit might attempt something else.

Both brothers were startled and upset, but defended him.

"You chose to protect us all. I for one cannot fault you for that," Artair said.

"Artair is right," Lachlan agreed. "If such information circulated amongst the clan, the culprit could have done more damage."

"He's done the worst damage of all," Cavan said, glancing to his father's body and his heartbroken mother. "He has taken our father from us."

"He will pay," Lachlan swore with a shake of his fist.

"First, we need to attend to mother and prepare Father for the burial he deserves, and then . . . " Artair placed a firm hand on Cavan's shoulder. "You must assume leadership. You are the new laird of Clan Sinclare."

Cavan hadn't even thought of what his father's death meant. He didn't want nor was he ready for such a powerful position. He had always gone to his father with his problems and often wondered who his father had gone to with his.

His eyes fell on his mother and he knew, as he always had, that she had been the one his father sought out when needing consoling. Cavan looked to his wife. She stood beside his mother, her hand on Addie's shoulder, her tears flowing as steadily as his mother's, yet strong and ready to help.

His father had been right about Honora making him a good wife, and he ached to be able to speak to him one last time. Their last time together had been a good one, laughter and talk and . . .

Never again would he hear his father's voice, his hardy laughter, or be able to go to him for advice. He was gone. His father was truly gone.

Cavan walked over to his mother and intended to ease her off her husband's body, but when he stopped beside her, he wanted to do as she had done, throw himself across his father's body and weep.

Artair and Lachlan joined them, and both men placed a hand on their father's body. Cavan rested his hand on his shoulder and the other on his mother, and the family mourned together.

The whole clan wept. There wasn't a dry eye to be found. Tavish Sinclare, their laird, was dead, and nothing could console the people for he had been a good, fair-minded man and loved by all.

Cavan was proud and grateful to his wife for tending his mother. She remained by Addie's side throughout the whole ordeal, helping her dress, seeing to the preparation of the meals, keeping vigil with her beside her husband's body throughout the night while Tavish lay in the great hall for all to pay their last respects.

Honora had even helped his mother prepare his father for burial, and he had watched as she cried along with Addie and mourned Tavish's loss as if he were her own father.

Cavan and his brothers spoke quietly in their father's solar—now Cavan's. He wondered if he could ever truly feel it his. The room belonged to his father and bore his achievements with dignity. His battle shield hung on the wall, riddled with dents and a hole that almost proved to be his death. Various weapons he had confiscated from enemies were displayed, and gifts from leaders far and near joined them. His father was a well-respected clan leader, and he wondered if he could ever really fill the void Tavish had left behind.

"Have you found out anything?" Cavan asked Lachlan.

"No one saw anything, and believe me when I tell you everyone is upset that they didn't. The clan wants the murderer found and punished."

"That information tells us something," Cavan said.

"I agree," Artair said. "It means the person who murdered father is known to us all."

Lachlan shook his head. "I didn't want to believe it, but all the facts point to that conclusion. Father would have never allowed anyone he didn't know to get too near to him. He had to have known his assailant and the attack had to be quick—"

"And unexpected," Artair finished.

"The dagger?" Cavan asked.

"It's not familiar to anyone," Lachlan said.

"The murderer must be found," Cavan said firmly. "No one will feel safe until then, and I will not rest until I see him quartered and hung for the coward he is."

A rap at the door turned them silent.

"Enter," Cavan ordered.

Honora peeked her head in. "Your mother asks for all of you."

They all froze for a moment, for this was it—the day they bid their father farewell. It would be an all day affair, concluding with a feast of great proportion in honor of their beloved laird.

* * *

The great hall was empty, the feast honoring a great leader finished. The immediate family sat at their usual table. It was very late but none of them wished to leave their mother alone, to face her first night without her husband in over thirty years.

Cavan wasn't surprised at how well his mother had handled the funeral. After all, she was the wife of a brave laird, and would not disrespect his memory by showing weakness. She had stood tall and regal as Tavish was laid to rest, and accepted condolences with grace and strength.

However, he couldn't help but worry what life would be for her without her beloved husband, though he would not say so aloud. "We will do well," he said instead, sharing in the vast loss that was apparent on everyone's sorrowful faces.

"Of course we will," Honora confirmed with a knowing nod. "Your father was certain of it."

They looked at her strangely, but it was Lachlan who asked, "What makes you believe that?"

"Your father told me."

They stared at her and she smiled.

"Your father and I shared many a walk together where he extolled his sons'"—Honora turned a gentle smile on Addie—"and his wife's virtues."

"What did he say?" Lachlan asked anxiously.

She smiled. "I can hear your father's laughter now, so bold and strong, which was how I knew he would speak about you. He loved your passion for life and was pleased to see you live it so vigorously, but"—she shook her finger—"he knew without a doubt that when the time came, you would do whatever duty demanded of you. He had no doubt of your strength and honor. You did him proud."

Lachlan nodded slowly. "Thank you, that was good to hear."

Honora turned to Artair. "Your father always turned serious when he spoke of you. He felt safe with you for he knew you dependable. He never worried or gave it a second thought when he asked you to settle an issue or see to a problem. He told me proudly that you once informed him there were no problems, only solutions. He had no doubt that you would bring order when there was chaos. He greatly admired your wisdom."

Artair could only nod, his throat choked with emotion.

Honora beamed when her glance settled on her husband. "Your father always shook his head and sighed when he spoke of you."

Cavan felt his heart catch. Had his father been disappointed in him?

"He felt that you were a leader from the day you were born, and he felt guilty that you never had a chance to be a child."

"Oh my, did he ever feel that way," Addie chimed in.

Honora nodded. "He'd go on and on about all the responsibility Cavan took on as a child."

"Mostly with us," Artair said.

"He was right," Lachlan agreed. "Cavan was always there, helping us, teaching us, covering our mistakes when he felt it appropriate and letting us suffer our punishment when necessary."

"Your father wanted you to enjoy life while you had the chance," Honora continued, "for he knew the burden of being a clan leader. And though he knew you more than capable of being a great laird—better than himself, he claimed—he wanted you to taste the joy of freedom until it came time to surrender to your duty. He knew the clan would be safe and protected when in your hands. He loved you very much." She glanced around at all three brothers. "He loved you all very much."

"What of Ronan?" Lachlan asked. "Did he speak of Ronan?"

Honora nodded. "He told me that he had no doubt Ronan would survive and return home. He believed Ronan was a strong warrior, and that once he claimed that powerful warrior within himself, he'd find his way home."

There was silence for a moment, then Artair asked, "What of Mother?"

Addie smiled weakly, and Honora placed a hand over hers. "His words are for her alone."

The three brothers stood. Cavan kissed his wife on the cheek, told her he would see her in their bedchamber, and to take as long as she needed.

Each son hugged, kissed, and told their mother they loved her, then left the two women alone in the great hall.

Honora prepared them each a special herbal brew, and added a potion to Addie's, to help her rest. They sat side by side in silence until Addie spoke.

"I loved my husband very much."

"He loved you very much," Honora said.

"I know. Tell me what I don't know."

Honora grinned. "He told me you could infuriate him, but he so enjoyed making up afterward that he decided it was one of your qualities and not a hindrance."

Addie laughed. "I knew it. He would never admit it, but I knew it."

"That was another thing. He admitted that you knew him too well, that there was nothing, absolutely nothing, he could keep from you. But he also admitted that it was another quality that served him well for he did not have to explain everything to you, and you would comfort him without him saying a word."

"I could see in his eyes, know in his walk, tell by his voice, and know what he needed."

Honora squeezed her hand. "Most of all he knew without a doubt that he could trust you and count on you to always be there for him. Right or wrong, you would defend him, though voice your opinion in private. And he never once in all the years doubted your love for him. It was solid and steadfast. He felt himself a lucky man to have found you."

"Found me?" She laughed, wiping tears off her cheeks. "Why, I had my eyes on the man from when I was young. There wasn't another woman who had a chance with him."

Honora laughed hard. "He told me the same himself. He claimed that when he first saw you—I believe he said he was twelve at the time—he knew you were the woman for him."

"He was almost thirteen, and I had just turned ten. It was love at first sight."

The two women talked for over an hour, then Addie began to yawn, and told Honora that she believed she just might be able to sleep that night. She asked if it was all right if she took Champion along for company, since the pup, who had grown considerably in the past few weeks, had not left her side since Tavish's passing.

Honora agreed, knowing that Champion had just acquired a new master, which was fine with her. She saw Addie to her bedchamber and then went to join her husband.

He was in bed, sitting up, his back braced against several pillows. He stretched his hand out to her when she entered, and she went to him, sensing she knew what he was about to say to her.

Chapter 29

Cavan had waited with a minimum of patience for his wife. He had known when she'd spoken about him that there was more to what his father had said about him. How did he know? He could not say for sure; he only knew he could see in his wife's face that she was holding something back.

When she entered their bedchamber, he was relieved to see her. He needed her, needed her beside him in bed to hold onto, to feel her heat, her heartbeat, and to lose himself in her and forget the sorrow that filled his soul. But first he had to know what else his father had confided in her.

She shed her garments as she approached the bed and he was content to know that she felt confident and safe to stand naked in front of him. They had truly become one.

He grasped hold of her hand and tugged her to land in his lap, tossing the blanket over them both. He hugged her close, nuzzled her neck, and tucked her comfortably in his lap.

"There was something you didn't tell me abou Father and me," he whispered before kissing he gently, needing a quick taste of her. "Tell me."

She did so without hesitation. "He knew you kep a secret."

"How?" he asked unbelievingly.

"Your father knew you well. He knew something disturbed you other than your year of capture, and knowing you, he could only surmise that you did what you always had done—protected."

"He wasn't angry with me?"

"Oh my, no," she assured him. "He was very proud of you. If anything, your actions proved to him wha a worthy leader you would make. You would rathe have taken the burden on yourself than worry th clan. To him you were a true leader."

He felt a great sense of relief and remorse. He wa relieved to hear how his father felt but wished tha he had confided in him. Was it right or wrong t have kept what he knew to himself? With his father' death, he worried that he had terribly misjudged hi foe and brought upon his father's demise.

"Your father was a wise man and understood much, and he believed the same of you."

"Then I should easily be able to discover—" Abruptly, he sprung forward, taking his wife along with him. "My father discovered the identity of th culprit!"

Honora was startled, her violet eyes turning wid and brilliant.

"Don't you see? He no doubt had fit the pieces o the puzzle together."

"But why not confide in anyone?"

Cavan smiled sadly. "My father was the laird of he clan, and knew it was his duty to protect, just as e said of me. He believed himself capable of dealing with the culprit on his own."

"Or," Honora said excitedly, "he didn't think the ulprit was a threat."

Cavan nodded. "You're right. He might have een secure in the knowledge that he could efeat the man no matter what. But then, what appened?"

"Perhaps the culprit surprised him?"

"Or perhaps there was more than one person involved?" Cavan said.

"It is hard to believe that anyone in the Sinclare lan would mean your father harm."

"I thought the same myself."

"It is a mystery we must solve," she insisted.

"I will not see you in harm's way," he demanded.

"You think to leave me out of this?"

He nodded. "For your safety."

"Not likely."

"You disobey me, wife?" He attempted a commanding demeanor, though he was proud of her ourage. She had developed much strength in the ew months since they had wed.

"We"—she said, poking him in the chest—"work ogether."

"Do we, now?"

"I won't have it any other way. We keep nothing rom each other. We confide everything—"

"We trust each other," he finished.

"That we do," she said, planting a fat kiss on hi
lips.

"I want more of that," he whispered, and nuzzle
her neck. She giggled, and he kissed some more
and then he stilled and buried his face against he
breast.

He felt her arms go around him and then he
hands caress his back.

"I love you," she whispered.

He needed to hear that, needed to know that sh
loved him. He needed her.

He eased her onto her back and kissed her gentl
"I'm going to make love to you now, slow an
easy."

She nodded, her smile soft, and wrapped he
arms around him.

They loved and talked on and off throughout th
night, and near morning finally fell asleep wrappe
snugly around each other.

Once again when Honora was sound aslee
Cavan whispered, "I love you."

The rumors began shortly after the funeral. A
first, Honora dismissed them as nonsense, mer
speculation produced by fear. After all, who i
their right mind would even think that Cava
could murder his father? But that was the gossi
spreading like bugs devouring the harvest. I
was only mumbles at first, perhaps begun with
conjecture that marinated in people's minds unti
many were convinced of its truth.

Regardless, it had gained momentum and angered Honora beyond reason. Artair and Lachlan felt the same, but no matter how hard all three of them tried to circumvent the gossip, it continued.

Honora held firm to her husband's hand as they walked through the village. The glares and mumbles had irritated her, but she remained smiling, supportive of the man she loved.

"They will realize soon enough," she said as they finally reached the moors and left the village behind them.

"I have only myself to blame."

"Nonsense," she insisted. "You did nothing wrong."

"I argued much too often with my father after my return."

"You made amends."

"Not in front of the clan, and that's what they needed to see. That I show my father, the clan leader, the respect he deserved. I failed to do that and now I pay the price. My clan judges me."

"When we find the person who killed your father, those who judged you will be sorry," she said emphatically, protective of her husband, though looking at his imposing form, it seemed unnecessary. He wore the clan plaid with distinction and carried himself with confidence. Though people threw silent barbs, he had deflected them with dignity and humility.

"In time the clan will see that I only wish to serve them as my father did, fairly and wisely."

Honora stopped, the winter wind strong, stinging her cheeks and causing a shiver. Or was it her own worries that caused that? "But they hurt you."

"I think more that someone hurts them. The rumors started immediately after my father's passing. It was as almost as if dissention was planted amongst the clan."

"You're right," Honora said. "That would mean that—"

"The murderer remains amongst us," Cavan finished. "He never left, which leads me to believe that he's not finished. He has other plans."

Honora visibly shuddered, and was glad for the comfort of her husband's arms. He wrapped them slowly around her and eased her against him until she was snugly tucked in the crook of his arm, where no one could harm her and he could lovingly reassure her. He had the courageous strength of a born leader, and she was proud to be his wife, though worried over his safety.

"We must find him before he inflicts more damage," Cavan said.

"How do we find him when he pretends to be one of us?"

"That's just it, he pretends. He truly isn't one of us. His allegiance isn't to the clan."

"Who is it to?" she asked.

Cavan took her hand so they could continue to walk. "That's only one of the many questions that need answers, but we leave that for later. Time now for you and me."

"There's no time for you and me," she blurted out.

He swung her around and grabbed her around the waist. "The last few weeks have been an ordeal for everyone. Routines were disturbed, sorrow filled every hour of the day. It is time things return to normal for the well-being of the clan, and that starts with you and me."

"You are right," she agreed, albeit reluctantly. It had been a difficult time for all, and the clan would naturally be looking to their new leader for direction. If he took firm hold and demonstrated his confidence, then the clan members would follow suit. A thought struck her. "If we show unity and strength, the clan will follow, and the culprit—"

"Will reveal himself without even realizing it," Cavan finished with a smile.

Honora smiled along with him. "He will not be able to sway the clan as he does now, for they will once again be content and confident in their new laird."

Cavan gave her a peck on the cheek. "Your intelligence excites me."

"You would never tell it from that—" She scratched her head. "Kiss? Was that a kiss? Because if it was, then I must protest—"

Her mouth was suddenly plastered against his, with his tongue diving deep inside to tease and mate with her own. She slipped her arms around his neck and fed off him with the same frenzy he did her.

Squeals and giggles parted them slowly, and with frowns and annoyance at being disturbed, they turned to stare at a group of little girls standing at the edge of the village, pointing at them from a few feet away.

"We have an audience," Honora whispered.

"Good. They will take the news back to their parents and new gossip will soon replace the old, and I wouldn't be surprised if bets were placed as to when an heir will be born."

Honora had considered the possibility, knew it her duty, but duty aside, she would love to give her husband an heir, a babe made from their love, raised and cherished with love. A tense well of emotions suddenly rushed up to choke her and bring tears to her eyes.

She broke free of her husband to turn away not wanting him to see her expressive reaction. He however didn't allow her the distance, he stepped up behind and she couldn't help but melt against him as his arms wrapped around her waist and drew her close.

She dropped her head back against his chest, and when his hands rested over her stomach, she placed her own hands over his strong yet tender ones.

"You would tell me if you were with child?"

She laughed softly. "I would shout it from the battlements, I would be so proud and happy."

He nuzzled her neck. "I am glad to hear that."

"You doubted I would?" she asked, surprised.

"I haven't exactly been the best husband."

She turned around in his arms, her smile broad. "I'll agree, but only partly. And in honesty I can understand your first reaction, for I felt the same myself."

"You didn't want me as a husband."

"No, I didn't. I was relieved when you rejected me the first time my stepfather approached your father with the idea. When you returned and were forced on me, I liked it even less. But—"

"You fell in love with me," Cavan boasted.

Honora laughed. "Completely and forever."

"Because I'm irresistible," he teased.

She shook her head and her smile softened. "Because you are a good man. I always wanted to wed a good man. You are honest and fair and I can trust you—a good man."

He stared at her, speechless, and she giggled.

"Of course, being handsome and a great lover help as well."

He shook his head and grinned. "I got more than I bargained for when I accepted you as my wife."

"You got a good woman."

"No," he said. "I got a *remarkable* wife, and proud I am to have her."

Chapter 30

⌒◯◯⌒

Cavan kissed his wife. Actually, he didn't want to stop kissing his wife. She was more than a remarkable woman. There were truly no words to describe how he felt about her, and he didn't intend to try. It was easier and oh so much more enjoyable to show her.

She tasted sweet, but then she usually did, and he could have lingered in their kiss for hours if duty didn't call. However, since his father's death, there was much to be dealt with and his time was not what it once had been.

He rested cheek-to-cheek with his wife. "I must meet with my brothers."

Honora sighed contentedly. "Then I will spend time with your mother."

Cavan took her arm and reluctantly began their return walk to the keep. "I appreciate the time you spend with her. I fear her grieving will not end for some time."

"She loved your father too much to simply forget him. Her heart will forever mourn him, but I'm sure having her sons helps greatly."

"And eventually Artair and Lachlan will marry." Cavan snickered. "Artair will choose a sensible wife, but Lachlan . . . " He shook his head and laughed. "I wonder over his choice."

"He may surprise everybody and choose a most fitting wife."

"Not likely."

"He can be wise when he chooses to be," Honora said in his defense.

"You mean you hope he is wise when the time comes."

Honora gave him a playful jab. "You're being unkind to your brother."

"I'm being truthful. Lachlan enjoys women but pledges allegiance to no one. He does what he wants when he wants."

"Perhaps you should search for a wife for him."

Cavan was still laughing when they entered the keep a few moments later. After hanging their cloaks on nearby pegs they joined Artair and Lachlan at the table.

"Do you know what my wife suggests?" Cavan said to Lachlan.

"That I'm a wonderful man and she wished she married me."

That brought a round of laughter from everyone.

Cavan corrected him. "She thinks I should find you a wife."

Lachlan grabbed his chest. "You wound me, sister. I need no help in finding a wife."

"I think that is a good idea," Addie said, stepping out of the shadows with a platter of bread and cheese,

Champion ever dutifully by her side, sniffing the delicious scent that drifted off the platter.

Lachlan slapped his chest again. "Twice wounded."

"Dramatics will get you nowhere," his mother warned, placing the platter in the center of the table.

Lachlan reached for a hunk of dark yellow cheese. "Then I'll be blunt. I will choose my own wife in my own good time."

"You don't choose love, it chooses you," Addie corrected him. "And when it does, it will snag you firm and hard and you will be able to do nothing about it."

"I don't intend to let love control me," Lachlan said.

"I agree," Artair chimed in. "I intend to look for a suitable wife who will fit my needs and serve me well, as I will her."

Cavan laughed, for at one time he had felt the same. A wife was a means to an end. A woman who would serve his needs, provide him with heirs. and, of course, he would be good to her. Now, however, he didn't feel that way at all. Love mattered in a marriage. It bound two people together and helped them survive and thrive.

"I can't wait to watch you two eat your words," Cavan said, continuing to laugh.

Addie stood behind Artair and Lachlan, placed a hand on each of their shoulders and smiled. "I'm with Cavan. I look forward to the day."

Cavan kept his smile strong while his heart felt a surge of relief. It was the first time since his father's death near a month ago that his mother had smiled. He hoped it was the beginning of her lovely smile returning permanently.

She had always been a beautiful, vibrant woman, but her vibrancy had seemingly passed away with the death of her husband and, selfishly, he wanted his mother back. The mother who greeted every day with a smile, who always had a good word to speak, who managed to bring reason to chaos, and who had been there for her sons through many a difficult time.

He saw a hint of that woman when she smiled now, and hoped that she was ready to emerge once again into life.

"Honora," Addie said, her smile still intact. "I thought perhaps you might like to help me gather some pine to scent the rooms."

"I would love to," Honora said.

"I thought we'd go to the small cropping of woods on the moors."

"Wait just a minute," Lachlan chirped.

"That's not a good place to go," Artair added.

"The spot of woods near the stable is perfect for what you need," Cavan said, sounding as if he commanded it.

Addie took hold of Honora's arm and turned a broad smile on all three sons. "You wouldn't be thinking of telling me what I can do and can't do, now would you?"

Lachlan and Artair looked directly at Cavan.

"Cowards," he muttered beneath his breath while glaring at them.

"Did you say something, Cavan?" Addie asked.

Cavan shook his head, though it wasn't at his mother. He was shaking it at himself, for he knew he was just as much a coward as his brothers. He couldn't forbid his mother from doing what she wished; besides, it wouldn't work. She'd do what she wanted anyway.

"Honora knows the woods well. I'm sure you both will be fine," he said with a sense of surrender.

He was glad when his wife kissed his cheek, for he took the moment to whisper in her ear, "A couple of hours, no more, or then I search for you."

She smiled and pressed her cheek to his to whisper in his ear, "I wouldn't do that. The magic of the woods may swallow you whole."

He stared after her and his mother as they chattered while grabbing cloaks off the pegs near the door and rushing out.

"Mother always gets her way," Artair said with a respectful smile.

"It seems that Honora does as well," Lachlan teased with a wide grin.

"Wait. Just both of you wait," Cavan said confidently. "Wait until your wives do the same to you."

"Not likely," Lachlan boasted.

"I agree," Artair said. "My wife will not challenge my commands, though I will be reasonable."

"There's something you two should have learned by now," Cavan said tersely. "There's no reasoning with women, ever, never. Not a single solitary woman can you reason with. It's impossible."

"You just don't know how," Lachlan said.

Cavan shook his head.

"Lachlan's right," Artair said. "You just don't know how. Women can be reasonable creatures."

"Pliable, is more like it," Lachlan beamed. "You just have to know how to get them to bend, be flexible, and eventually surrender."

Cavan broke out into a fit of laughter. "Are you two in for a surprise. No, a shock is more like it."

"We'll see," Artair said confidently.

"We certainly will," Cavan said, and raised his tankard of ale, silently toasting his brothers' foolishness.

Honora realized her stepfather was following her and Addie as soon as they left the keep. Many wouldn't have noticed, but think he was strolling about, waving to those he knew. But Honora knew better. He was up to something, and she didn't like the disturbing feeling that gnawed at the pit of her stomach.

It wasn't until they reached the edge of the village that Calum made himself known. Honora was shocked to see that he held a bouquet of flowers. It looked as if he'd made an effort in seeing to his appearance, his garments fitting him well, with only a few stains here and there and a button missing from his vest.

"For you," Calum said, handing the flowers to Addie with a slight bow. "These beautiful flowers pale next to your beauty."

Honora wanted to choke. Her stepfather couldn't be serious. Did he intend to woo her mother-in-law? The idea was outrageous, and Addie was simply too intelligent a woman to be swayed by Calum.

"Thank you," Addie said. "It is very thoughtful of you."

Honora was struck silent. Addie actually smiled softly and sniffed the few wildflowers smothered by green foliage, only the most hardy having survived the start of winter. Honora was horrified that Addie would even consider the prospect of accepting the token gift. After all, it would announce to everyone that she was open to a courtship. And it was just like Calum to do it publicly, where all could see his respectful and honest intentions.

Addie inspected the flowers and gave them another sniff. "In all the years Tavish and I were married, he could still surprise me with flowers. I never knew when to expect them, and it made the flowers all the more precious to me."

Calum stuck out his chest proudly, and Honora grew annoyed seeing that several villagers were watching the exchange, knowing that gossiping tongues would soon be busy.

Addie sighed and shoved the bouquet back at Calum. "I can't accept these, nor do I want to. The only man who will ever give me flowers is my beloved husband, Tavish. I will accept none from any other man. Do I make myself clear, Calum?"

Honora wanted to hug Addie tightly and whoop with delight. Instead she remained by Addie's side with a beaming smile.

She wasn't surprised to see her stepfather's cheeks flush red with embarrassment. He deserved the discomfort for even considering that Addie would be interested in a man so soon after her husband's passing. But true to her stepfather's selfish nature, he continued to try.

"Perhaps in time," Calum said.

"No!" Addie said curtly. "No time will heal my broken heart. Tavish was the love of my life and there will be no other. Do not dishonor me or disgrace yourself by attempting another overture, for next time I will not be polite."

Addie turned, and Honora did the same though her steps were abruptly halted when her arm was grabbed.

She knew whose hand was on her, and turned on Calum with a fury. "Take your hand off me."

"How dare—"

"No," she shouted. "How *dare* you touch me."

"Quiet," he warned harshly. "Or you will pay for your insolence."

Addie had stopped and turned to stare at them, though she did not attempt to intervene. She obviously felt Honora could handle Calum herself, and that made Honora feel proud.

"Get your hand off me, Calum, and I won't warn you again," she said firmly.

"I am your father—"

She yanked her arm free, though it hurt since his

fingers had a firm bite on her flesh. But it also felt good, as if she were freeing more than her arm, but freeing herself of him, something she had wanted to do for so very long. "You are not my father and never have been."

"You will obey me—"

"I will not," she said. "Not now, not ever."

Calum rushed toward her, and she braced her hand on the dirk in the sheath at her waist. He halted so fast that he almost toppled over.

"You wouldn't dare," he choked.

"Are you so sure?" she asked calmly.

He turned a startling red. "You'll be sorry."

"I am sorry."

He sneered confidently.

"Sorry that I didn't stand up to you sooner. Don't ever cross my path again—"

"Only your husband can banish me from the clan," he said furiously.

"Is that what you wish me to do, wife? Have him banished?"

Honora smiled at her husband, having watched him approach slowly, allowing her to have her say while letting her know that he was there to protect her. Calum, however, turned with a start.

"It is your choice," Cavan said, walking past Calum and taking a stance beside his wife.

"Banishment is not necessary, but I don't care if I ever lay eyes on him again," Honora said, glaring at Calum.

"You speak bravely with your husband by your

side," Calum accused, then looked as if he bit his tongue, but too late.

Cavan rubbed his chin. "I think you should earn your keep here, Calum." He turned to Honora. "Use him as target practice for your bow lessons."

Honora contained her chuckle. "That would not be fair. He is so large that I would not miss hitting him."

Calum looked ready to burst, he grew so red, and she suddenly grew cautious. He was not one to be taken lightly. He always found a way to retaliate against those he felt deserved his wrath, which she knew, having been on the receiving end most of her life. Had she truly expected him not to make her pay for her defiance?

"Let him be," Honora said abruptly, old memories disturbing her.

Cavan nodded. "Your choice." He looked to Calum. "Stay away from my wife and my mother."

"As you wish," Calum said, and bowed respectfully, though his angry eyes settled on Honora as he did.

She felt them bore slowly into her like dagger points finding the flesh, digging deeper and little by little. Calum would make her pay, she had no doubt, and she would have to make her final stand and once and for all be free of him.

Chapter 31

Cavan wrapped himself around his sleeping wife; though a fire roared in the hearth, the room still held the chill of winter. He smiled, recalling how only a couple of hours ago they had heated the bedchamber considerably with their fierce lovemaking. After a heated debate, they tore at each other's clothes, to tangle amidst the bedding until they finally succumbed to their passion with a series of crazed climaxes.

His body would have sprung to life at the recalled memory if he hadn't been so satisfied by their joining. Now, however, he preferred to snuggle against her and simply enjoy their closeness.

The last few weeks had proved trying, with everyone adjusting to his new role, including him. He would enter his father's solar, his mind filled with pending issues, and for a moment expect his father to be there with the answers, or at least guidance. Once again he'd be overwhelmed with the loss and he'd sit, not in his father's chair behind his desk, but in the chair he used to take when talking with Tavish in confidence.

He was still trying to accept that his father was no longer there, that he, Cavan Sinclare, was now laird of the clan. And while plagued with that daily thought, he was also determined to solve his father's murder. He owed it to his father and the clan so that all rumors could finally be laid to rest and a sense of safety and peace might once again return to the clan.

Honora continued to be a great help to him in his search for the killer. She had gotten to know many of the villagers and quickly discarded most as the potential foe. Her stepfather had even been considered a possible suspect, but was discarded since he had gotten what he wanted with his stepdaughter's marriage to Cavan. The more digging they did, the shorter the list of suspects became. By now they'd begun to wonder if it could have been someone passing by, a merchant who stopped to sell his wares, a weary traveler looking for shelter, or a man purposely sent to kill his father. But for what reason?

He and Honora discussed the possibilities endlessly, as did he and his brothers. None of them would rest until the man was found and punished for his crime. But as the weeks passed, it seemed less likely that they would ever find the culprit.

The one constant that continued to plague him and Honora was that in all likelihood it appeared that Tavish either had known his killer or not felt threatened by the person. His father had been too wise a warrior not to be able to defend himself, even in a surprise attack, which meant that Tavish hadn't felt himself in danger. Two conflicting thoughts that they couldn't seem to join, but no doubt would prove the link in solving the murder.

Honora stirred, disturbed. Cavan soothed her with a caressing hand over her naked flesh, and she settled soon enough. They had grown even closer since his father's death, and perhaps that was due to his need for her and her unconditional love. It amazed him that she placed no boundaries on her love for him.

She loved him plain and simple. It didn't matter if he brooded or smiled, complained or rejoiced, her love was constant. She understood him, and oddly enough, he understood her. He knew there were times she preferred to walk the moors alone or venture in the woods. He knew she rarely had a bad word to say about anyone, and listened to complaints without complaining. She made time for Addie whenever she needed it, and continued to practice with her bow even though he had less time to teach her how to defend herself. And she always, always, responded to him when he touched her intimately.

He was completely and madly in love with his wife, and yet still found it difficult to tell her.

Why?

He wished he knew. It made no sense to him. The words should spill easily from his lips because she was so easy to love. But every time he tried to tell her, the words stuck in his throat. They came easily while she slept and could not hear him, but otherwise they remained locked away, and he hadn't been able to find the key to unlock them.

She stirred again and turned to wrap herself around him, snuggling against him, her full breasts pressed hard against his chest. She had fast gotten used to and comfortable with being naked in front of him, and they slept that way every night.

Naked and wrapped around each other.

He had been lucky, so very lucky, to have found himself wed to her. When Honora confided that his father had thought them a good match from the very first time Calum approached Tavish, he was surprised. But then, his father had been a wise leader and knew his son well. His father had seen in Honora what he hadn't been able to see. He'd seen the shining gem among the stones. And he blessed his father every day for being the one who had brought them together.

Cavan yawned and settled himself against her, ready for sleep—ready to be a good husband, ready to lead the clan, ready to finally love.

Honora had the next couple of hours to herself. Her husband was busy meeting with his brothers in the solar. Addie was busy in the kitchen with the cook, baking a special treat for her sons, and though she'd asked Honora if she wished to help, Honora understood that Addie was better left alone to do for her sons. This was a mother's treat, something she did, had been doing, for years for them, and Honora had no intention of interfering. Which actually worked out well since Champion was handed over to her for safe keeping. If he had remained in the kitchen, he would have only gotten into trouble and eaten whatever he could have reached.

Instead, she took Champion, intending to walk around the village and visit with people, to see if there was any gossip she could pick up. The dog, however, had other plans, and headed for the stable and his brothers and sisters.

Honora followed, knowing there were only two out of the five in the litter left, a few villagers staking claim to the others. She felt that Artair and Lachlan should claim the last two, both females and both beautiful animals. Where Champion was all black, the one female was black except for her paws, which were brown and gave her a regal appearance, and while she appeared docile, she could hold her own. She was a perfect companion for Artair. The other female was a mixture of brown and black and had a distinct personality. She followed no commands, doing exactly as she pleased, a fitting partner for Lachlan.

Honora followed Champion behind the stable, where the two females were tossing a bone between them. Champion joined in. She stood watching, realizing this was the place where Tavish had died.

She had been here before, with Cavan and his brothers, and all of them agreed that anyone could have easily hid in the woods that bordered the area and ambushed Tavish. But that wouldn't have explained what Tavish was doing behind the stable. What had brought him there? Had he been looking for something? Or had someone called to him?

She had asked herself over and over who would want to hurt the laird of Clan Sinclare. There were none in the village who had a bad word to say about him. The clan members were content, well looked after, well provided for, well protected. There wasn't one reason for anyone among them to harm the laird.

It would stand to reason, then, that it had been someone outside the clan. Of course, like any clan leader, Tavish had enemies, though none close enough to do him harm, unless someone was sent to purposely eliminate him.

But there were guards posted around the land, not only along the borders but throughout, for that specific reason—to spot any intruder—which was why the village always knew that a stranger approached before he even reached the outskirts of the village.

How, then, could Tavish have been killed by a stranger? He had to have known his assailant.

Champion bounded over to Honora, and she noticed that he was chewing on something. Spying the discarded bone and the other two dogs stretched out in a sunny patch, she worried that he'd found something that could hurt him or make him ill.

"Drop it," she ordered sternly, her hand under his mouth.

He looked reluctant.

"Now!" she commanded, and he obeyed.

She grimaced at the small object covered with slime and took a closer look. It was a bit chewed but she could see that it was a button, or at least had been. There was something familiar about it. She washed it off in the rain barrel by the side of the stable and took a better look.

It was familiar but she couldn't recall where she'd seen it. Then she realized what she held. The button could very well belong to the man who killed Tavish, ripped off in the scuffle, possibly as Tavish attempted to defend himself before he dropped to his death from the knife wound.

"Good boy," she said, praising Champion and patting his head. "You found a clue, possibly the only clue."

She hurried to the keep, Champion fast on her heels, and when she'd almost reached the steps, stopped dead. She realized where she had seen the button.

It belonged to Calum.

Her skin turned to ice and all color drained from her face.

Her stepfather?

She couldn't move, couldn't shake her head at the ridiculous thought, couldn't believe that he was capable of such a horrendous act. And why? What possible reason could he have to do Tavish harm? He had gotten what he wanted, his daughter married to the next laird of Clan Sinclare.

Why?

Why had he insisted that she wed the next laird, heir to Clan Sinclare? He had insisted that the marriage documents be drawn up specifying as much, and he'd argued vehemently when Cavan returned on her wedding day that she had not wed Artair, but Cavan, since he was the head of the clan.

Had there been a plan behind it?

If so, that would make her responsible for Tavish's death.

She placed a hand to her chest, and though she still could not move, it felt as if she were about to collapse. This couldn't be possible. Her stepfather couldn't have killed Tavish.

But why then had she found his button in the very spot where the murder had taken place?

She was so consumed by her thoughts that she didn't notice that people had approached her. She could think of nothing but the shame of it. Her father had murdered Tavish Sinclare.

Good Lord, how would she ever tell her husband?

"Honora?"

She blinked a few times, thinking herself dreaming. That was it, she was dreaming. This was nothing more than a bad dream and she would wake up and everything would be all right.

"Honora!"

Her husband's strong voice startled her. She jumped and stared at him, standing in front of her, and saw that Artair, Lachlan, Addie, and several villagers were there as well.

"She's just been standing here like this for a while, drained of color," she heard someone say, and saw Cavan nod.

"What's wrong?" he asked, reaching out to take hold of her hand.

She jumped back, not wanting him to see what

she held, not wanting him to know just yet, not wanting to have to tell him that her stepfather had murdered his father.

He would hate her.

The thought flashed strong in her mind, and she wanted to cry out in pain. It wasn't fair. She had finally found love, a good love with a good man. This couldn't be happening.

"Honora," Cavan said softly. "It's all right. Everything is all right."

She looked at his dark eyes, filled with concern, heard the tenderness in his voice, and recalled how just last night he had loved her so fiercely and then so tenderly.

He loved her.

He might not say it, but she knew that he loved her. She didn't doubt it for a moment. He showed her every day how much he loved her when he touched her, protected her, laughed with her, talked with her, shared every bit of his life with her.

"Honora," he said, taking a step closer. "Trust me. It's all right."

She felt the chill that had frozen her dissipate, felt the color rush back to her cheeks and a rush of warmth run up her legs and spread throughout her body. She stepped into her husband's outstretched arms and he quickly wrapped them around her.

She pressed her face against his shirt, taking in his familiar scent, cherishing it, thankful for it. No matter what Calum had done, her husband would not blame her for it. She had been foolish to think so, but then, Calum had enjoyed making her think that she could never be loved and that no man would want her.

The good match had to benefit him, but in his selfishness he'd actually made her a very good match.

"Tell me that you are all right," Cavan begged softly.

She sighed, and didn't want to move from his strong, protective embrace. She tilted her head back to look up at him, wanting first to ease his concern over her. "I am fine."

"Then what is wrong?"

Sorrow filled her heart as she said, "I know who killed your father."

Chapter 32

Cavan sensed that the news was better kept between them for the moment, for if it had upset his wife this much, it could very well upset others even more. He ushered her into the great hall, telling his brothers and mother that Honora wasn't feeling well and he would see her to their bedchamber.

Artair and Lachlan expressed their concern and urged him to take all the time he needed, saying they could talk later. Addie, as he suspected, insisted on helping, but he managed to convince her he'd do fine on his own and pointed out that Champion might be hungry. The animal obliged him by barking and trotting toward the kitchen.

"You'll call me if you need me?" Addie asked, hurrying after the dog.

"Without a doubt," Cavan confirmed, and with his arm snug around his wife, climbed the stairs to their bedchamber.

He secured the door behind them while his wife walked to the fireplace and warmed her hands in front of the flames.

"You're chilled," he said, standing behind her, rubbing her arms, his first concern her well-being.

Honora turned and held out her hand. "I found this where your father was killed."

Cavan studied the bit of scrap she placed in his hand. It appeared unidentifiable, and he shook his head. "What is it?"

"A button, before Champion finished chewing on it."

Cavan's eyes turned wide and he took a closer look at the object. "There aren't many who wear buttons in the clan. Ties and fastenings, yes, but buttons?" He shook his head. "I see them occasionally on travelers who pass by and particularly on merchants." He held it up. "You know who it belongs to, don't you?"

She nodded.

Cavan could see her reluctance to tell him in the way she bowed her head and tried to avoid his eyes. She seemed ashamed, and that troubled him. What connection could she have to the button?

The thought hit him like a blow to the chest, and he blinked away the vivid image as he whispered harshly, "This button belongs to your stepfather."

"Yes it does," she admitted. "I noticed he was missing one when he approached your mother the other day." She sighed, then reluctantly continued. "He is also good at inciting doubt in people. A few chosen words and suggestions perfectly placed and he'd have people believing the worst."

"Why?" Cavan asked, shaking his head. "Why would he want to kill my father?"

"I asked the same of myself. I believed him satisfied once I was wed, but I recalled how adamant he had been about the marriage documents stating that I was to wed the next laird of the clan."

"Which you did, thanks to his persistence," Cavan said, bending over to steal a kiss and press his cheek to hers. "I am grateful to have you as my wife and I do not want you to think that any of this is your fault. This is all Calum's doing. He used you as a means to an end, but what that end is, we must find out."

"I thought, for a brief moment, that you might think me responsible."

"Is that why you froze not far from the door of the keep?"

She nodded. "With a bit of reasoning, I realized it a foolish thought, though the disgrace of my stepfather's actions lingers."

"Do not attach yourself to his shame. It belongs to him and him alone. You are an innocent in all of this, a pawn in his game; a game we must learn how to play if we are to win."

"How do we make sense of it?" she asked, befuddled.

"I believe the wisest way is to keep an eye on him for a while."

"You don't plan to confront him?"

"Eventually, but right now this button," he said, holding it up, "is the only thing we have that may connect him to the murder. Calum has also disappeared for days at a time and no one knows where he goes, except for his word that he was busy buying and selling wares to other clans."

"But we don't know for sure that he does."

"No, we don't. We have no knowledge of where Calum truly goes when he leaves here or who he has befriended."

"You will have him followed?" Honora asked.

"Yes, I plan on putting my two best warriors on his trail, and I will discuss this matter with Artair and Lachlan so we have as many eyes on him as possible."

"What of your mother?" she asked.

"I think it best that she not know of this right now. She mourns my father's passing every day, and I have no doubt that if she knew the identity of his killer, she would gut the man herself."

"I agree. Your mother is hurting very badly, and I believe she would love to make the culprit suffer even worse."

Cavan ran the back of his hand along his wife's warm cheek. He loved to touch her; she was so soft. Sometimes he loved just holding her hand, the warmth of her skin, the feel of her slim fingers locked with his, and seeing the love that sparkled in her lovely violet eyes filled him with immense pleasure. His heart hurt just thinking of life without her.

"I do not want you going off alone until this matter with Calum is settled. I do not trust him, and while I believe you have learned to adequately defend yourself, your stepfather does not play fair. If he did, he would have never been able to kill my father. I will not see the same fate for you. So give me your word that you will not go off alone."

"I give you my word."

He was relieved that she had not hesitated or argued with him. She respected his wishes and would do as he asked. Her willingness to oblige him, trust him, made him love her all the more.

"That means more to me than you will ever know."

"Then know that I will always honor my word to you. I will not lie or play you for a fool, for I love you too much to disrespect you."

"You can count on the same from me."

"Of course I can," she said with a slight smile. "I know you well, and know what you will say or do before you do it, and I am aware of what you don't say but will eventually."

"You know too much about me," he accused playfully, for her words had moved him more than he wanted to admit. She had all but told him that she knew he loved her. She didn't even question why or how he would *eventually* declare his love for her. She simply knew, accepted it, and was satisfied for the moment.

He did not know if he would have felt the same way if the situation were reversed, but he doubted he'd be as generous. He'd probably demand that she confess her love for him, and do it often.

She pressed her cheek to his. "I know all I need to know."

He kissed her then, a subtle taste that tempted them both, skimming the edges of passion and suggesting a more savoring flavor. They did not wrap their arms around each other and their hands remained at their sides, yet the kiss continued, deepening and intoxicating.

Cavan relished the taste of her, and while he ached to touch her, knew it would be a mistake. They would then wind up in bed for the next couple of hours, and he had duties to attend to, his brothers to speak with, warriors to command.

He reluctantly moved his mouth away from hers, resting his forehead to hers. "I have matters to attend to."

"You certainly do," she said breathlessly.

"We can't do this now."

"Are you sure?" she asked with a disappointed sigh.

He wanted to growl, grab her and . . .

"I want you," she whispered, and nipped playfully at his ear.

"Honora," he warned with a low growl.

She moaned. "I love when you say my name with such passion."

"I must see to my duties."

"Bedding me is your duty," she said with a breathless sigh. "We can be quick." And she took his hand and tugged him to the bed.

She was right. It would be quick because he felt as if he were ready to explode from the want of her. And when she fell on the bed and slowly spread her legs, inviting him, he lost all reason.

He claimed her quick and hard, like a man in dire need. Or was it more like a man in love? They finished as fast as they started, though with the most unexpected, breathtaking climax he'd ever had, and he grinned, realizing that love would always be like that with Honora—unexpected and satisfying.

They both descended the stairs a while later, to find Artair and Lachlan in the great hall.

"We need to talk," Cavan said when he and Honora reached them.

"You're feeling better?" Artair asked Honora.

"Shouldn't you rest?" Lachlan chimed in.

"I feel fine," she said. "Cavan will explain it all to you while I go see if Addie would like to share a soothing brew with me."

"It is good you spend time with her," Lachlan said. "You have been a balm to her since father's passing."

"So has Champion," Artair said. "The dog refuses to leave her side."

"Which reminds me," Honora said, her smile growing. "Champion has two sisters who would be perfect for each of you. I'll bring them to the keep later."

"No," both of them shouted, but Honora waved them off as she hurried to the kitchen.

Both men eyed their brother. Artair was the first to speak up. "We don't need—"

"Or want—" Lachlan tried to finish.

Cavan held up his hand. "That's between you and Honora. I have nothing to do with it."

"But—" Lachlan said, attempting to protest again.

"I will not listen."

"You won't because you know it's a losing battle," Lachlan complained. "Honora will force those dogs on us."

Cavan laughed. "She won't force, you'll simply surrender."

"Like you?" Artair teased.

Cavan thought about their quick tryst only moments ago. "I gladly surrender to my wife."

The three men laughed, then retired to the solar after Cavan told them that they must talk.

Silence soon followed when his brothers learned that Calum was responsible for their father's death. Plans were laid out, two loyal warriors decided upon to follow Calum's every move, and a promise made between the three brothers.

"We do not rest until father's killer is punished and Ronan is returned home," Cavan declared.

Artair and Lachlan joined hands with him and the pledge was sealed; even if it took years, even if one of them should die, or two of them, whoever was left would see that the promise was fulfilled.

The three brothers left the solar solemn but satisfied with their agreed upon plans, for they knew that none of them would rest until the promise saw fruition.

Honora entered the great hall as the brothers did, and Artair and Lachlan attempted to hurry off while Cavan stood grinning, knowing his wife would not let them escape unscathed.

"Good, you're finished. One of you can accompany me to the stable to get the pups," she said skirting the tables to hurry to her husband's side and give him a peck on the cheek. When she reached him, she whispered, "They know?"

He returned her peck to answer, "They know, and no one blames you."

Honora smiled at both anxious men. "I can see that you both are eager to have a pup of your own."

Lachlan made the first protest. "I have enough females to contend with. I don't need one who will never leave my side."

Cavan grabbed his wife around her waist and held her close. "I like the one that never leaves my side."

"Then you take the pup," Lachlan complained.

"I think Lachlan should accompany you to the stable," Cavan said with grin.

"I agree," Artair said. "Let him choose first."

"I've already chosen for you both," Honora informed them. "Unless, of course, the pups themselves have a preference."

"Let Artair go first," Lachlan said

"No," Artair protested.

"Enough!" Cavan laughed. "Lachlan, you go and see that my wife is kept safe, while Artair and I go talk with the men."

Lachlan didn't hesitate; he walked off with a chatting Honora. Cavan knew that once he'd presented it to him as a duty to protect his wife, Lachlan would gladly do as instructed.

He would have felt safe with either of his brothers

protecting Honora. It might have taken him some time upon his return to trust and confide in them once again, but once he had, it was as if they'd never spent time apart. They had even begun to ask him about his capture, and little by little he told them about it, and had begun to heal. Of course, his wife had played the biggest part in his healing, and continued to do so. She was always there for him, always willing to listen, always willing to love him, no matter what.

The winter wind whipped at his face when he and Artair left the keep.

"A storm brews; we will see snow by nightfall," Artair said. "It is good we place trackers on Calum now, for if he should leave before we had the chance, the snow would make tracking him difficult."

"Agreed," Cavan said, though the promise of snow also had a bright side, for it meant more time spent indoors, and he intended to spend that time making love with his wife as often as possible.

And finally doing what he should have already done—tell Honora how very much he loved her.

Chapter 33

"**S**he wasn't the one I chose for you," Honora said as she watched the black one with the brown paws licking and adoring Lachlan until the man simply lost his heart to the vivacious pup.

"She's beautiful and so loving," he said, patting the pup, which had crawled in his lap to settle with her head on his knee.

Honora looked over at the contented pair across from her while the other pup, the one she had thought perfect for Lachlan, ignored him and pranced around her, tugging at the hem of her skirt playfully.

"She's quiet and docile," Lachlan said, surprised. "Not like that one."

The pup dropped her hem and barked forcefully at Lachlan, while the pup in his lap raised her head and retaliated with a sharp bark.

"She protects me already, that's my kind of woman." Lachlan smiled and scratched under his pup's neck. "We make a good pair."

She sprung up and licked his nose as if agreeing, and once again stole Lachlan's heart.

"She's yours, there's no denying it," Honora said happily.

"I think Artair deserves that one," Lachlan said with a nod to the pup that did as she pleased. "We should take her to him right now."

"You don't think he'll mind?" Honora asked.

Lachlan stood with his pup in his arms. "No, believe me when I tell you he needs a female like her. She'll do him some good."

Honora had her doubts as to Lachlan's motive, but did want the last pup to find a home, and if Artair wasn't pleased with her, Addie would probably keep her along with Champion. The pup would not go homeless or have to fend for herself. One way or another she would be looked after.

They left the stable, Lachlan placing the pup on the ground so she could run and play with her sister up ahead of them.

The bitter wind whistled around them, and Honora realized she had forgotten her cloak.

"I'll get it," Lachlan said.

"No, I know where I left it. I'll only be a moment," Honora said, and hurried back into the stable. She retrieved her cloak from the barrel she'd draped it across and stopped at the open door, securing the warm cloak around her shoulders and watching with delight as Lachlan ran in play with the two pups.

She went to join him, and that was the last thing she remembered before everything turned dark.

* * *

Lachlan burst into the great hall with two yapping dogs at his heels.

Cavan was about to tease him when he saw the distraught look on his face and realized his wife was nowhere in sight.

"I can't find Honora," Lachlan said. "She was there one moment and gone the next. She went to retrieve her cloak from the stable. I was outside only a few feet away with the pups. I saw her standing in the doorway, putting on her cloak. I was distracted by the pups only a moment, and when I looked back, she was gone. I ran to the stable but she was nowhere to be seen."

"Did you search elsewhere?" Artair asked.

"Behind the stable, the edge of the woods, but there was nothing, not even foot marks to follow. I can't believe she could disappear so fast. It was only a moment. I was right there, a few feet away."

Cavan, his brothers, and Addie, who refused to be left behind, went in search of Honora. After a short time the whole village was searching for her. The villagers had grown to love Honora and were concerned for her safety.

Cavan was beside himself with his wife's disappearance, but sensed what the villagers must be thinking. If the laird's wife could so easily be snatched away, how safe was the clan? He knew that his wife's abduction had nothing to do with the clan's safety. It had to do with her stepfather's ambitions, and more than likely plans that had been fermenting long before he himself returned home.

So far he could make no sense of it, but perhaps if the clan knew of Calum's deceit, they could be of some help, and so the truth was circulated and Cavan waited.

He retreated to his solar; he had to or else it seemed he would explode. His anger was so great, he wanted to rage and rant and pound on someone. He wanted his wife back safe and sound, in his arms, in his bed. He wanted to tell her he loved her, cherished her.

Lord, why hadn't he told her that he loved her?

He would move heaven and hell to get her back. No matter what it took, even if it meant his own life, he would see her safe.

Cavan plopped down in his father's chair behind the desk which was now his and planting his elbows at the edge, dropped his head into his hands. He felt completely lost. He wanted to ride out and find his wife yet, knew that wasn't the way to go about it. He had to send out men, hunt down tracks, and make plans, and all the while his wife could be suffering.

He pounded his desk with his fist and wanted to roar, but instead walked out of the solar.

"Has Calum been found?" he asked, joining his brothers outside, where snow was falling, dusting the land.

"No one has seen him," Artair said solemnly. "And now with this damn snow—"

"Tracks will be covered fast enough," Lachlan finished. "Though we had men out before the first flake fell so hopefully we will have news soon."

"It had to be Calum," Cavan said, pacing in front of the steps of the keep.

"I know you're anxious to ride out—"

Cavan interrupted Artair abruptly. "That would be foolish."

Artair and Lachlan exchanged glances, though they remained silent.

"I could go in one direction while he takes my wife in another. And tell me why our border guards did not see them?" Cavan snapped as he paced.

"A question we're trying to answer," Artair said.

"Why did he take her?" Cavan asked, stopping abruptly. "I can't make sense of it. What does he want with her? Was it a sudden decision or planned?"

He turned to stare off in the distance, the snow falling heavier and the sky turning dark. He looked to the fading heavens and raised an angry fist.

"Hear me, Honora, I will come for you. Stay strong. I will come for you."

Honora woke, her head aching and spinning simultaneously. She blinked several times to clear her vision and stared at the starless, night sky. At first she thought the clouds rushed past the partial moon but then realized she was the one moving.

A sudden bump in the road jolted her and the cart she lay in, and she winced from the pain that resonated in her head. She raised a trembling hand to the back of her head, felt a sizable bump and shivered. Not from the tender spot, but from the snow that fell, covering the light blanket that looked to have been carelessly tossed over her.

She imagined she had traveled a distance from the keep, and hoped they had yet to leave Sinclare land, for that would mean there was still a chance of a rescue tonight.

She knew her husband would come; she had no doubt of it, and it would be up to her to survive until he did.

"Good, you've woken just in time."

She titled her head back to stare up at her stepfather, not at the reins, but seated beside the driver. She chose to remain silent in hopes that he would explain.

"Finally, you know your place, silent until I dictate otherwise," Calum said sternly. "I have raised you well."

Honora wisely held her tongue, though she would have much preferred to ask why, then, had he abducted her from Cavan? Hadn't their marriage already furthered his ambitions?

"You served as the perfect pawn." He grinned. "And now you will serve your true lord and master— the man you shall wed once Cavan is dead."

His remark startled her heart, and she quickly had to remind herself that Cavan was far too intelligent and a brave warrior to let the likes of Calum lead to his demise. Her stepfather was simply attempting to frighten her and bring her under control once again. She had to remain strong in the knowledge that she knew her husband far better than Calum.

"Good obedience," Calum said confidently. "Your new husband will expect that from you at all times."

She couldn't imagine who he spoke of, and she was curious. Who was this fool who would join forces with her father and believe they could defeat Clan Sinclare?

A bone-chilling cold crept over her body that had nothing to do with the snow that continued to fall. There was only one tribe, one person, who would dare try to defeat Cavan, and perhaps that was because he had already done so once.

Mordrac.

Honora trembled. It couldn't be possible. Her father could not have been insane enough to join forces with the barbarian leader Mordrac. And why first wed her to the leader of the Sinclare clan if all the while his intention had been for her to wed Mordrac?

Answers would be forthcoming, for she would not rest until she uncovered the whole of her stepfather's evil doings.

"I can see by that fixed glare in your eyes that you're thinking, searching for answers as you did so often when you were a child, though you were, as you are now, too stupid to understand anything. In time, daughter, you'll get only the answers I deem necessary. Presently, it is time for strict obedience not curiosity."

Calum turned away from her as the cart began to ascend a steep incline and she began to worry. The steepest mountains weren't on Sinclare land, and that meant more time had passed than she had hoped. In all likelihood, this climb and then the descent would place them in barbarian territory.

The blanket was suddenly snatched off.

"I've had my fill of keeping the snow off of you so that I don't present a corpse to your future husband. See to your care yourself now or you will feel the back of my hand."

Honora complied. It would have been foolish of her not to. Her situation called for a clear head and planned action. She had to let Calum think that she was once again his docile daughter. And while the thought made her sick, it also brought a small smile to her face.

She wasn't afraid. She had spent so many years being afraid of Calum, and never thought there would ever be a day when she wasn't. However, little by little, with the help of Cavan and his endless lessons, she had not only learned how to protect herself, but gained confidence in doing so.

Of course, she was no match for a tribe of barbarians, or against her stepfather while weaponless. What she needed to do was prepare for Cavan's rescue and aid him in any way she could.

It certainly would be a challenge, but if she succeeded, she would be forever free of Calum. When she was young, she had wished and prayed that her mother would one night sneak away from him, but it was more a dream than anything. There was no place for them to go. They would have been homeless if they hadn't remained with Calum.

So she watched her mother suffer year after year, all so that they could have a roof over their head and food in their stomachs. And when her mother took ill and knew she would die, she had told her to obey Calum until she finally wed a good man, and then would be free. She would be free for them both.

A few tears fell from her eyes before Honora realized she was crying. Though few, the tears were painful. They always were when she thought of her mother. She wiped them away quick enough, not wanting Calum to see them.

She would free herself, and then she would do what her mother had advised. She would live her life with a good husband who loved her.

She blinked back tears and silently prayed.

I promise I will be ready to help you when you rescue me, Cavan. I promise, and know how very much I love you. I love you. I love you. I love you . . .

She closed her eyes and allowed her litany to flow out into the night and drift along so her words would reach her husband and he would know that she waited for him.

Cavan stood on the battlement, snow covering his hair and his fur cloak. It was very late, and so far there had been no word about his wife. Two more warriors had yet to return, and if they brought no news . . .

He shook his head, looking up at the night sky. Nothing would stop him from finding her. Nothing. He had been giving thought to all that had happened since his return, and recalled something he and his wife had discussed. It seemed that since his return, barbarians raids on surrounding clans had increased. It had even been the topic of gossip, with some implying that perhaps he'd had something to do with it.

Someone had, but not him. That left just one likely candidate. Calum. And that left only one likely scenario. Calum had befriended the barbarians, and more than likely had taken Honora to the barbarian stronghold over the mountains, to disappear into their territory.

Cavan was caught off guard by a sudden splash of warm wind that all but kissed his cheek yet sent a decisive chill through him, and he thought he heard a whisper. It had been faint but he could have sworn he had heard it.

He braced his hands on the edge of the stones that forged the battlements and sent the same message on the strong cold wind to his wife.

"I love you, Honora. I love you. I love you. I love you."

Chapter 34

Honora stood defiant when presented to Mordrac, leader of the barbarian tribe. This was the man who had made her husband suffer brutally. It had been his cruel hand that inflicted the numerous scars not only on Cavan's back, but on his soul. She could not with good conscience play the submissive, frightened female.

"Bow your head," Calum whispered harshly with a yank to her wrist.

She snatched free of him and held her head high, though wisely kept silent. What she wished to say would only damage her chances of escape. While she wouldn't appear docile, she also wouldn't appear completely insolent.

Besides, Mordrac wasn't a man to offend. His cruelty was obvious in his dark eyes and in the folds of his frowning brow. His square jaw jutted out and his thin pinched lips warned of a man who forever brooded. His brown hair was long and streaked with considerable gray. He towered over all the men and was broad and firm in body, muscles bulging around a gold cuff that hugged his arm.

He shocked Honora when he first spoke to her.

"Tell me you carry the laird of Clan Sinclare's child. I want him to know that I will be the one to raise his child as a barbarian before I kill him."

Honora smirked, though his remark dug at her heart. "Sorry to disappoint."

Mordrac turned on Calum. "I gave you plenty of time for her to get with child."

While Calum tried to appease the raging barbarian, Honora watched, seemingly indifferent, though her worries mounted. She had only recently realized that there was a good chance she was carrying Cavan's child. A week or two more . . . She almost shook her head, but caught herself. She didn't need any more time. She knew without a doubt she was with child. She didn't know what had kept her from telling Cavan about it.

Again she almost shook her head. She knew why she hadn't told him. She wanted to hear him say that he loved her. She wanted to know for certain that their child had been conceived from love, not duty.

Now she had not only herself to protect, but her unborn babe. She would never allow the barbarian to raise her child. Her child was a Sinclare and would grow and flourish on Sinclare land with his family, alongside a father who would love him dearly.

Calum leaned in close to her. "You fool. I told you to do your duty."

"Did I foil your plans, *Father*?" she asked sarcastically.

She should have been prepared, should have known he would retaliate. The blow was severe and sent her tumbling to the ground, her jaw throbbing madly.

Mordrac laughed along with the young woman beside him. Honora managed to look at her as she struggled to stand, and was taken by her beauty. though she was obviously as cruel as Mordrac. She wasn't very tall, rather slim to the point of being petite. Her blond hair fell in waves around her face and down over her shoulders to rest upon her full breasts, and her eyes were a brilliant blue like a bright summer's sky. She was dressed in bright silks and sparkling gems, her slim fingers weighted down with several large rings.

On her feet now, Honora braced herself as Mordrac advanced, reaching out to grab hold of her throat. "Perhaps I shall give you and Cavan one last moment together before I kill him."

She gasped for breath, his grasp growing tighter as he spoke, and at that moment knew she would have to escape. She could not allow her husband to be captured and face death for the sake of protecting her. She and Cavan would either live a good life together or die together, but she would not lose him, especially to this evil man.

The beautiful blonde had walked to Mordrac's side and placed a gentle hand on his arm. "Easy, Father. You do not want her too damaged before her husband arrives."

Mordrac released her instantly and grabbed a tight hold of his daughter's chin. Honora was surprised that the young woman didn't flinch, cry out, or even narrow her brow in pain. She simply stood there unaffected by his forceful grasp.

"Keep your place, daughter," he warned, then shoved her away.

She bowed respectfully while backing away, and resumed her place next to Mordrac's oversized chair.

Mordrac turned back to Honora. "You will not be held prisoner while here," he informed her. "There is no escape from this place, and besides, your husband will arrive soon enough and then the games will begin." She would have corrected him, but didn't wish to anger Mordrac any further. Besides, she couldn't be certain this was where Cavan had been held captive. And she needed the promised freedom so she could roam the area and plan the impossible.

After all, who would have ever thought that she would be the wife of the laird Sinclare, or that she would be happy about her status and even happier that she loved her husband and he her? That had been impossible, barely a dream, and yet here it was a reality, and her escape would be, too.

Mordrac circled her while his dark eyes took pleasure in examining her from head to toe then back again. She was repulsed by his thorough inspection, the fiery look in his eyes much too intimate. He had no right; only her husband had that right.

Mordrac addressed his daughter sternly while tugging at Honora's blouse and skirt with disgust.

"Carissa, my future wife resembles a slave in these rags; see that she is dressed appropriately."

His daughter bowed to his demand and directed Honora to follow her.

Calum grabbed her arm tightly, holding her back momentarily. "Behave or you will feel my wrath."

She winced when he released her and knew from past experience that his fingers had dug hard enough to bruise her skin. She hurried away from him, to follow Carissa. She wanted to keep a good distance between her and her stepfather, for there was no one there who would protect her.

Mordrac had grinned when Calum took a hand to her. He actually had followed with his own, near choking the breath from her. She would have no champions here. She only had herself to count on, and the fact that she was with child made her all the more determined to escape.

Carissa was indifferent to her. She simply carried out her father's orders, which Honora assumed was a common enough task for the woman. She let Honora know immediately that she was prepared to deal harshly with any attempts to fight her father's edict.

"You will be sorry if you do not follow his rule," Carissa warned sternly.

Honora had no such intention, though she nodded. She was more interested in fresh clothes and food for her growling stomach, and voiced her appreciation when Carissa provided a bounty of flavors for her. She intended to keep herself strong and well clothed so she would be ready to make her escape when the time came.

In the morning she would tour the landscape and see what she was up against, and learn more about her enemy, especially her stepfather. She wanted to know one thing.

Why?

Why had he done this to her and Cavan?

Cavan issued orders as soon as he received the news confirming his suspicions. The barbarians had his wife, but worse, she had been taken to Mordrac's stronghold, a place he knew well.

"A sizable troop is probably already on their way here," Cavan advised his brothers while going down on his haunches to trace his finger in the snow.

His brothers flanked him as they hunched down as well.

"Surprise will be your best approach," Cavan explained. "The barbarians will hit hard and quick and in great force. Post the neighboring clans where they cannot be seen and use them for a surprise attack. While the barbarians believe the sheer number of them will decide the battle, it is the warrior who fights wisely who will know victory."

"What of you?" Lachlan asked.

Cavan stood and his brothers followed. "You, Lachlan, will come with me. Artair will lead the battle here. Once Mordrac's capture is known, his tribe will surrender."

"You are sure you can capture him?" Artair asked. "We have never been able to penetrate his territory. It is as if his surroundings protect him. And—"

Cavan placed his hand on Artair's shoulder, knowing why he hadn't finished. "And he has Honora, who he will use against me."

"How then will you conquer him?" Artair asked.

"With whatever it takes," Cavan said, and walked away.

The morning brought a clear sky and gave Honora a chance to explore. She slipped out of the stronghold that served as their keep. It was well guarded and no one could leave or enter without being seen. She hadn't been stopped, so she assumed orders had been given that she was not to be held a prisoner.

The village consisted of small cottages that were better maintained than she had expected, though the people were not friendly, nor did she wish to make friends with anyone. How could she when she could trust no one and no one would trust her?

She almost recoiled when she saw how captives were treated. They were forced to live in well-guarded pens like animals. A trough held their food, though it looked more like slop, and they had to scoop it out with their hands. Their only shelter from the weather was a small lean-to that clearly could not hold them all at one time.

If Cavan had been held here, this had been his lot. While that hurt her heart, it also made her angry. She grew angrier as she walked around and realized that it had been her father who had brought such suffering to Cavan's family.

The only sensible reason was wealth and power. While he would have been held in some regard in the Sinclare clan because of her marriage to the clan chieftain, his life would not change all that much.

"Don't think you can escape."

She recognized Calum's sneering laugh and she turned, taking a few chosen steps to put a safe distance between her and her stepfather.

"Why?" she found herself shouting, unable to contain the anger that had built inside her.

He raised his hand, ready to strike her, but her fierce glare stopped him dead in his tracks.

"Don't dare touch me," she warned through gritted teeth.

He lowered his hand and his sneer spread confidently. "You're right. Why waste my time? You're Mordrac's problem now. You served my purpose. I have what I want."

"Wealth and power," she confirmed for herself.

"See, you even know I deserve it," he boasted.

"I know you will most certainly get what you deserve."

He laughed. "You foolishly think that your husband will save you. Cavan will do his duty and save his wife, and at what cost?" Calum's sneer faded to one of disgust. "He will trade his life for his wife's, foolishly believing that his clan will be saved. Then Mordrac will attack and conquer all the Sinclare lands and continue into Scotland, conquering clan after clan."

Her stepfather was a madman to believe such foolishness. The Scots were a proud people who would defend their land fearlessly and never surrender to the likes of Mordrac. And while she didn't believe Cavan unwise enough to trade his life for hers, her being here, a captive of his enemy, placed his life in jeopardy. And it limited his options to attack. She had only one choice, and that was to escape and reach him before he reached the stronghold.

"And you needed me for this?" she asked, wanting to clarify her part in his plan.

"You were nothing more than a pawn so the pieces could be put in the right places at the right time. You were never meant to wed Cavan. He was meant to die once he was captured, but Mordrac got it into his head to torment the mighty warrior and make him suffer before he took his life. No one expected him to escape from here, since no one ever had. I had little time to make certain the wedding documents stipulated that you wed the next heir of Clan Sinclare, for I knew Cavan would return home. And lucky I was that he made it home just in time to claim his bride."

"What difference did I make in the plan?"

"As the wife of the chieftain of the clan, your husband would be honor bound to rescue you. While he brought his warriors here, Mordrac would send his hordes to devastate the Sinclare clan, using you as a ruse to delay your husband from returning home too soon, guaranteeing him victory."

"You think Cavan that foolish to leave his clan and land unprotected?"

"What choice does he have? His own memories remind him what Mordrac will do to prisoners, and so he will ride as soon as possible to rescue you while leaving a minimum of warriors behind. Of course, he will leave an order for other clans to be called to duty, but it will be too late, for Mordrac already has his hordes there. As soon as Cavan leaves Sinclare land, they will attack and kill everyone in sight."

Honora's blood ran cold and she shivered. She would be the cause of all their deaths. She could not have that. She had to escape. If her husband could, then so could she.

Calum laughed. "You served me well, daughter. And you will serve Mordrac well until he tires of you, though if you wish to survive, I'd advise that you give him many sons. He has none, and he will spare the woman who gives him what he so desperately wants."

"What of Tavish Sinclare?" she asked, knowing he would enjoy the boasting.

"Tavish had to go. His son had to rule. I distracted him. The barbarians were quick. It was over and done before he or I even realized it. After all, we wanted it to look like one man was responsible."

"Cavan."

"Nothing like turning the clan against their laird, for then warriors are less likely to enter battle with him. I've done a good job. The pieces are all in place. Soon the game will be over and I will be victorious."

Honora stared at Calum's back as he walked away, a bitter taste filling her mouth. She hated him.

He had been the cause of so much misery and loss in her life. He was a man who cared for no one but himself. It didn't matter who he hurt, who suffered, as long as he got his way.

She glanced around the village and knew there had to be a way out. Cavan had found it, and so would she. She refused to be a pawn in an evil game, and refused to allow evil to win.

Chapter 35

I t had been three days since she entered Mordrac's stronghold, and she knew she had little time left. There was word that Cavan's warriors were not far off, and all was set for battle. But she'd had no luck in finding an escape route.

While Mordrac paid her little heed, whenever he saw her he boasted about how much he would enjoy killing her husband. Intent on power and domination, he would let nothing stand in his way.

A woman was of little consequence to Mordrac, which was obvious from the way he treated his daughter. She, like a dutiful child, did his bidding without challenge. Honora supposed it had been no different for her with Calum, but at least she'd learned to be courageous, and in a sense had gained her freedom. She didn't fear Calum anymore, and that meant he couldn't hurt her ever again, even if he struck.

With her chance of finding an escape route diminishing by the hour, Honora sat in the small bedchamber provided for her and lightly touched the bruises on her face. Her father had taken his hand to her more than once, and each time in front of Mordrac, so she'd little chance to defend herself without suffering severe consequences. Besides, she didn't want to take the chance of offending anyone and lose the privilege of roaming the village at will.

A young slave girl entered her room with food and a hot brew. A sprig of winter pine graced the tray, as always, and Honora picked it up, sniffed its potent scent, and thought of the small woods on the moors at home where it grew.

She gasped. Winter pines lived in the thick of the woods. How had this sprig gotten here? Someone had to have gathered it, which meant going into the thick of the woods, beyond the stronghold.

"Where did you get this?" Honora demanded.

The girl bowed her head and crunched her body in fright, as if waiting for a hand to strike her.

Familiar with the reaction, Honora went to her, placed a comforting arm around the girl and spoke in a soothing tone. "I mean you no harm. Please, I just need to know."

"My master's daughter gathers it from the woods," the young girl answered. "She likes the forest and goes there often."

Honora hugged the girl, grateful to her and feeling terribly sorry for her lot as a slave. "Thank you, and please tell no one I asked of this."

The girl nodded and smiled briefly before leaving.

Honora waited, her cloak secure around her, until she was certain the girl was gone and would not see her leave. She then slipped out and cautiously made her way through the village. She feared that with the news of Cavan being so close, someone might stop her and order her confined to the stronghold. But no one paid her heed and she walked and watched until she saw the person she sought.

Carissa rode a beautiful black mare, and while Honora hoped she would not notice her watching, their eyes met. Carissa, however, looked away, uninterested, her horse taking a slow trot.

Honora followed without appearing to do so. She was grateful that she had learned how to be invisible to people, blending, not drawing attention to herself, and continued to follow Carissa without notice. Mordrac's daughter rode a short way before directing her horse behind a tree. Honora waited patiently for her to round the large trunk, but Carissa didn't. It was as if she'd magically disappeared from sight.

No one seemed to notice, not the villagers nor the guards. This had to be the way into the woods and away from the stronghold. A secret spot that no one knew of, or at least only a chosen few knew about.

The alarm sounded then, blaring through the village, and Honora cringed as people rushed around her. There was no time left; she had to leave and now or it would be too late.

Among the shouts and chaos of everyone preparing for battle, she slipped behind the tree and found the entrance to the woods bared by thickets that could tear the clothes and sting the skin. But once past the prickly branches, there lay an open path, and she broke into a run.

Cavan sat mounted on his stallion, a line of his warriors stretched out along the ridge, looking down at the barbarian stronghold. Attack would not be easy. The barbarians had the protection of a stone wall that extended from one end of the woods to the other and a clear line of fire from the top of that wall. The dense woods at the rear of the stronghold also served to protect. The place appeared impenetrable.

That, however, was the least of his worries, for Cavan knew that Mordrac would use Honora to force his surrender. And he knew that he couldn't only think of her; he had to consider his clan. He thanked God for the wisdom his father had taught him, for without it, he doubted that he could face this situation with confidence.

Lachlan approached at a gallop. "We are ready and await your word."

"Mordrac will make the first move," Cavan said, and as he spoke, the wooden doors centered in the stone wall opened.

Mordrac emerged, dressed in fur and leather, another rider alongside him. From the shape and size of the man, it was easy to recognize Calum.

Cavan and Lachlan rode down the ridge to meet with the enemy. Meanwhile, Cavan prayed that his wife was safe and unharmed, for if she wasn't, he intended to make Mordrac suffer before he killed him.

He had tried to keep thoughts of Honora's possible suffering from his mind, to keep it clear so he could devise a plan that would succeed. He couldn't allow her to be the only goal in this battle, had to think of more than just his wife, no matter how difficult. It was the only way he could save her and his people.

Cavan sat tall in his saddle and wore his clan colors with pride. He kept his face stern, and a firm grasp on his reins as well as his anger. If not, he feared he would lunge at Mordrac and kill him with his bare hands.

He wasn't surprised that Calum rode with Mordrac. Calum would want to flaunt his supposed victory, and Cavan could hardly wait for the chance to punch the smug smile from the man's face.

"Welcome back," Mordrac said with a boastful grin. "Your pen awaits you."

"I won't need it," Cavan said with a bold conviction that startled the two men.

"You forget I have your wife," Mordrac reminded him.

"You better pray you haven't harmed her," Cavan warned with the same boldness.

Mordrac gripped the horn of his saddle. "I'm going to take great pleasure in taking your wife in front of you before I kill you, and then I'll raise your child a barbarian."

Cavan sprang up in his saddle but quickly regained control of himself. Honora was with child? His child.

Good Lord, he wished he had her in his arms right now. He'd never let her go, never ever let her go.

Now more than ever, he needed to keep Honora and his child safe, no matter the cost.

"You will surrender and I will let your wife and your clan live under my leadership," Mordrac ordered sharply. "If not, I will see that every Sinclare dies, and not an easy death, starting with your wife, and of course your unborn child along with her." He looked up at the clear sky. "It is a good day for torture and execution."

"How can I trust you?" Cavan asked, though he would have preferred to be choking the life out of the man.

"I give you my word," Mordrac said.

"How do I accept the word of a liar?"

Mordrac grinned. "What other choice do you have? You're beaten, Sinclare, accept it and save those you can."

Cavan knew Mordrac's word meant nothing. As soon as he surrendered, the barbarian he would kill the entire Sinclare clan. He was known for making certain that any enemy who challenged him would die, and those he took prisoners were always enslaved.

Lachlan rose in his saddle then and looked past Cavan. The other men did the same, surprised by the lone rider who appeared on the rise just past the end of the stone wall at the edge of the forest.

The rider's identity was obscured by the dark hooded cloak wrapped around him, which blended him with the black horse. The image was more that of a demon emerging from the depths of hell and bearing down on them.

"What is this?" Mordrac demanded.

"He is not one of mine," Cavan retorted sharply.

"You lie," Mordrac yelled.

The rider rode with skill and approached at a rapid pace. He looked as if he would collide with the four men if it not for the swift and skillful handling of the animal. The horse pranced the last few feet to the men, and with a quick yank of the hood, the rider was revealed.

"Honora!" Cavan cried out. Directing his horse to her side, he reached over, grabbed her around the waist, and swooped her up, to plop her in front of him in his saddle. He wanted her safe in his arms, where he intended to keep her. He would not take the chance of losing her again. He did not want to ever again feel that abject fear and intense emptiness that her absence had caused him.

"I escaped," she said with glee, and kissed him quick.

There was so much to say to her, but all he could do was stare. He was so very happy to gaze into her lovely violet eyes again, to feel her body snuggled against his, to hear her voice, see her smile, and feel her warmth, her love.

His dark eyes turned murderous when he saw her bruised cheek and jaw. He wanted to roar with fury and reach out and kill the man responsible for harming his wife, but Honora's soft smile tamed his warring heart.

"I'm all right now. I'm in your arms."

Cavan gathered his senses and did what he had to do, though he promised himself that later he would say the words he felt in his heart deep down to his soul. Words he should have told her long before this.

He turned to Mordrac. "You've lost what little bargaining power you had."

"It doesn't matter. As we speak my hordes are attacking your clan and claiming your land."

Cavan laughed. "Do you really think me that much of a fool?"

Mordrac eyed him guardedly.

"My clan and several neighboring ones have been prepared for your attack. By now my brother and the other clan leaders are in the process of capturing your men, and easily I might add, since you are a predictable lot."

Mordrac grew furious. "You lie."

"Unlike you, I speak the truth, but then the choice is yours."

"You think me a coward that I would surrender?" Mordrac spat.

"You forget that I escaped from here without detection. Didn't it ever occur to you that I could enter without detection?"

Mordrac's face suddenly glowed with anger. He quickly turned in the saddle to see his men being overrun by Cavan's warriors along the stone wall.

Cavan gave the signal for his men on the ridge to advance, and the sight of them charging down greeted Mordrac when he turned around.

"I used this meeting time for my men to penetrate your stronghold and find my wife," Cavan explained, and gave his wife's waist a hug. "However, she saved me valuable time. But then, she is a courageous woman. I should have known she would escape."

Cavan's men soon circled them and more of his warriors spilled out of the stronghold and the woods.

Cavan's expression turned stern and his voice forceful. "You're surrounded. *Surrender*. This is now *Sinclare* land."

A cheer rang out from his men, and with little effort the stronghold was secured, prisoners released, and new prisoners confined. A tent was erected for Honora and him since neither wished to spend any time within the walls of the stronghold. Cavan had already spent enough time there, and Honora wanted no more of the place.

It wasn't until later that night that they got to be alone. They lay naked on the makeshift bed, a soft woolen blanket covering the thick straw and another wool blanket covering them.

Cavan laid a gentle hand to her bruised face.

Honora laid her hand over his. "I am fine. I was proud of myself. I was brave, though not completely fearless."

He laughed and gently kissed the bruise on her cheek. "The sign of a true warrior. I am proud of you."

Her brow narrowed.

"What's wrong?" he asked, not wanting anything to mar their happiness.

"I wondered. If you knew a way into Mordrac's stronghold, why didn't you attack him before now?"

"We intended to," Cavan admitted. "My father, my brothers, and I were devising an attack. We laid the plans and were about to set the date when Father was killed. I thought it best we wait, sure that his murder would connect with the barbarians, and then the warriors would be even more eager to go to battle for their fallen leader."

"So this attack was your plan all along?" she asked.

He nodded. "Every step of it. We felt it was the one way of finally ridding the area of the barbarians and hopefully finding Ronan."

"He isn't here," Honora said sadly.

Cavan could barely repeat the upsetting news he had learned about Ronan. "No one knows where he is now. Mordrac sold him to mercenaries, and since they sell their services to whoever is willing to pay their price, it means they could be anywhere. They could have even left Scotland."

"While that is a disturbing thought, perhaps it is better for him. It will give Ronan more chance to escape," Honora said with hope.

"I pray you are right, though I fear he may suffer worse at their hands. But then neither can I trust Mordrac's word. He could be lying to me, as he did about you. He told me that you were with child, but then I heard a different tale later. I realized he lied to me hoping I would react out of anger, and I almost did." He splayed his hand on her stomach

"I would love to see you grow round with my child. You would be even more beautiful than you are now."

She smiled softly but did not reply. Cavan leaned closer and kissed her gently, letting their passion build slowly so their hands could explore, touch intimately, caress lovingly. It didn't take long for their passion to soar beyond reason. After all, they had been separated for three days and had never gone that long without making love.

Love.

The word buzzed in his ear, swirled in his mind, beat in his heart as he slipped over her and entered her gently. They soon became lost as their bodies worked as one and peaked as one in glorious climax that left them damp, breathless, and clinging to each other. Neither of them moved or wanted to. They simply wanted to relish the exquisite pleasure of their climax and enjoy every lingering ripple.

Cavan felt the last of his throbbing release dissipate and pressed his cheek to hers. He fought to steady his breath, fought to say the words that should have already been said, and finally, even though his breath remained labored, he whispered, "I love you, Honora. I love you."

Her body grew taut beneath him and she turned her head slowly to look at him, her eyes misted with fine tears.

"Truly, you do?" she said, her voice quivering.

"Truly, I love you. I love you. I love you. I love you. I will say it over and over until you know it is true."

She giggled. "Then say it again and again."

He did, though after only a few times she stopped him.

"You would say it forever, wouldn't you?"

"I will say it forever. I will tell you every morning, remind you every night, and whisper it throughout the day so you will always know how very much I love you."

"That's what I've been waiting to hear, needed to hear."

"I know," he confessed. "I should have told you sooner. I knew I loved you, but I couldn't say it. I don't know why but—"

"It doesn't matter," she said softly. "Now I can tell you—"

He laughed softly. "You've told me many times that you love me."

"But I never told you that I carry your child."

He stared at her, stunned, and hurriedly slipped off her and gathered her against him in his arms. "Truly?"

She smiled. "Truly."

His hand went to rest at her stomach. "You have known?"

She nodded. "Not for very long, and I would have told you. It was just that I wanted to know that our child was conceived out of love and not duty."

"Believe me, Honora, it was not duty that brought me to make love to you. It was purely love."

She pressed her hand over his. "Strange, isn't it, that we *did not choose* each other as husband and wife, but now we *do choose* to be husband and wife."

"Forever . . . and ever . . . and ever," he said, kissing her after each *ever.*

"If I were to take my vows today with you, they would be recited willingly and with much love," she said.

"I don't regret not exchanging vows with you, for if I had, they would have been recited out of necessity, not love."

"It doesn't matter now," she assured him. "All that matters is that we love each other."

Cavan grinned and kissed her. "And I'm going to spend the rest of the night showing you just how much I love you."

Chapter 36

~~~~~✦✦~~~~~

Honora walked the moors alone. Winter had allowed a warm day to slip through, and though she still required a wool cloak, there was no bitter chill in the brisk air. She took several deep breaths and whispered numerous prayers. She was so very grateful for all the good in life.

Cavan treated her wonderfully. She couldn't believe she had such a good man or that she now had such a generous and loving family. They were all excited about the babe who would be born sometime in the fall. The whole village had grown joyous over the news. After all, a future laird of Clan Sinclare was about to be born.

Yes, life was very good, and it would only get better.

She didn't mourn the loss of Calum. He deserved his fate and she had not intervened. She wasn't surprised when Cavan had spoken to her before he announced Calum's punishment. He had already determined what it would be but wanted her to understand why he'd reached the decision he had. He didn't have to discuss it with her, and as the laird, his decision was final. She was grateful he'd nevertheless thoughtfully taken her into consideration.

She understood Tavish's death could not go unpunished and that those who were responsible would suffer the ultimate punishment.

Cavan hadn't discussed Mordrac's destiny, but everyone expected him to face death for there was no other way to secure the safety of Sinclare lands. He was a man who conquered and could live no other way, and Cavan decided that his people could either join the Sinclare clan or face the same destiny as their leader.

Lachlan had been left at the stronghold with a myriad of men. They would keep the area secure until Cavan decided who he would appoint laird of the land answerable to him. It would be an important decision, and she knew that he and Artair spent much time discussing various candidates.

Right now peace prevailed, which was fine with her. There had been enough suffering and loss, and Ronan was still missed. Every day, when Cavan gazed into the distance, Honora knew he wondered if that was the day his brother would return.

Addie, Artair, and Cavan, and she as well, believed Ronan would find his way home, and then Addie would have her sons together once again.

Honora strolled along, wishing spring were here and the flowers in bloom. She could pick a handful for Addie. While her mother-in-law still mourned the loss of her husband, her old self was returning slowly but surely. Honora doubted that a day would go by that Addie wouldn't think of Tavish, but it eventually would be with a lighter heart and fond memories.

The sun suddenly shone down bright on her, and she spread her arms out to her sides and whirled around as she had when she was young. She had dreamed then, and believed them to be only dreams, but her dreams had come true and she felt like the luckiest person in the world.

She felt the tremble before she heard what sounded like thunder, and turned without worry for she knew instinctively she was safe. The black stallion approached at a fast gallop, and on it rode her husband.

His dark brown hair blew wildly around his handsome face. Some might have thought his scar marred his fine features, but she had always believed it added to his appeal, even when the chilled wind would sting the slim blemish red.

He wore no cloak, only his shirt and plaid, though he did wear a broad smile. When he got close, he leaned over and she reached up.

His arm wrapped tight around her waist and scooped her up without effort. She landed in front of him in the saddle and he slowed the horse to a gentle trot and tugged her closer against him.

"When I saw you walking, not paying attention, I thought of the very first time I had rescued you on this very spot," he said.

Honora smiled. "You frightened me that day."

He laughed. "You frightened me."

"I did?" she asked, surprised.

"Of course you did. You weren't paying attention

and you were drifting closer to the edge of the cliff. I thought for sure you would go over to your death before I reached you."

"I did not think you rode to rescue me."

"I did," he said, and kissed her.

She smiled and kissed him back. "You're my hero."

He turned the horse toward the keep. "And you are the love of my life."

They meandered back, talking, laughing, kissing, and when they reached the keep, the sun was low in the sky.

Laughter and talk continued that night with family over the evening meal, and Cavan sent her to bed with apologies. He had some matters to discuss with Artair that couldn't wait, but he promised to join her as soon as he could.

Addie accompanied Honora with a gift, a beautiful soft blue night shift with long flowing sleeves, gathered beneath her breasts to float down around her ankles, and the neckline scooped low and intertwined with yellow and white ribbons.

It was almost too pretty to sleep in, but it was also too pretty to take off. She thanked Addie profusely, and after her mother-in-law left, crawled into bed, intending to wait for her husband. But she grew sleepy fast and dozed off.

She didn't know whether it had been a few minutes or hours later when her husband woke her. He did so gently, urging her to get up and come with him. It was important.

She rubbed the sleep from her eyes and told her to put her sandals on, which she did. He slipped a fur-lined cloak over her shoulders before he ushered her out the door of the keep.

The sky was bright, with a full moon and thousands of twinkling stars. The air had chilled considerably, and as he rushed her through the village and out on the moors, she grew worried.

"What's wrong?" she asked, tugging at his hand.

"Nothing, nothing at all."

A lantern waited at the edge of the moors, and he scooped it up and proceeded to walk her to the small cropping of woods that most claimed were magical and refused to enter.

They entered without hesitation and he seemed to know the terrain and his destination, for his pace was sure and steady. When they arrived at the clearing where she had hid often as a child and she and Cavan had once talked, she stood silent, too shocked to speak.

Numerous lanterns lit the area, and the cleric stood beneath a pine garland arch. Artair stood to one side and Addie the other.

Honora glanced at her husband, speechless.

Cavan took her hand and placed a gentle kiss on it. "We have never gotten the chance to exchange our vows and I want that for us. Our choice. Will you marry me, Honora, here before our family, God, and the Heavens?"

She threw her arms around him. "Yes. Yes, I'll marry you. My choice."

They stood as one in the magical forest; though perhaps the magic came from their love, for fireflies not known to winter danced around them and birds chirped a melody while they recited their vows willingly and agreed to be husband and wife and share a long loving life together.

And when they kissed they both could have sworn they heard his father's familiar laughter ripple along the air.

New York Times
bestselling author

Julia Quinn

The Bridgerton Novels

On the Way to the Wedding
978-0-06-053125-6

Gregory Bridgerton must thwart Lucy Abernathy's upcoming wedding and convince her to marry him instead.

It's In His Kiss
978-0-06-053124-9

To Hyacinth Bridgerton, Gareth St. Clair's every word seems a dare.

When He Was Wicked
978-0-06-053123-2

To Sir Phillip, With Love
978-0-380-82085-6

Romancing Mister Bridgerton
978-0-380-82084-9

An Offer From a Gentleman
978-0-380-81558-6

The Viscount Who Loved Me
978-0-380-81557-9

The Duke and I
978-0-380-80082-7

JQ 0609

At Avon Books, we know your passion for romance—once you finish one of our novels, you find yourself wanting more.

May we tempt you with . . .

- **Excerpts** from our upcoming releases.

- Entertaining **extras**, including authors' personal photo albums and book lists.

- Behind-the-scenes **scoop** on your favorite characters and series.

- **Sweepstakes** for the chance to win free books, romantic getaways, and other fun prizes.

- Writing **tips** from our authors and editors.

- **Blog** with our authors and find out why they love to write romance.

- **Exclusive content** that's not contained within the pages of our novels.

Join us at
www.avonbooks.com

An Imprint of HarperCollinsPublishers
www.avonromance.com

Available wherever books are sold or please call 1-800-331-3761 to order.

FTH 0708